CRYPTIC CRIMES

*A Chilling Catalogue of
Mysterious Murders*

John Dunning

ARROW

First published by Arrow Books in 1990

5 7 9 10 8 6 4

© John Dunning 1990

John Dunning has asserted his
right under the Copyright, Designs and Patents Act, 1988
to be identified as the author of this work

Random House, 20 Vauxhall Bridge Road, London SW1V 2SA

Random House Australia (Pty) Limited
20 Alfred Street, Milsons Point, Sydney,
New South Wales 2061, Australia

Random House New Zealand Limited
18 Poland Road, Glenfield
Auckland 10, New Zealand

Random House South Africa (Pty) Limited
PO Box 337, Bergvlei, South Africa

Random House UK Limited Reg. No. 954009

A CIP catalogue record for this book
is available from the British Library

ISBN 0 09 972680 7

Printed and bound in Germany by
Elsnerdruck, Berlin

CONTENTS

INTRODUCTION

Murder without mystery is uninteresting, a sordid, violent business little different from the butchering of pigs. As a result, not much is written about such murders. Indeed, there is not much to write.

Otto or Pierre comes home unexpectedly, finds Oscar or Paul in bed with Emma or Marie-Claire, puts an end to one or both and runs to the police station, smoking gun or dripping knife in hand, to confess in an agony of repentance. The entire process can be described in a page.

A great many killings fall into this category, and the perpetrator is frequently tried not for murder, but for manslaughter. Otto and Pierre did not sit down and plot the death of Emma and Marie-Claire. They were merely presented with a situation which exceeded their emotional tolerance and they reacted with typically human violence.

Some murders are, however, more complicated. They are committed not in the heat of rage or passion, but calculatingly and with malice aforethought. The murderer has no intention of confessing to the crime and has time to prepare the means to conceal his or her guilt. Such murders are mysteries and they are not all solved. Jack the Ripper is a particularly famous example. His case has retained its interest for over a hundred years.

With Jack the Ripper, the principal mystery lies in the identity of the murderer, and this is often the case.

No one knows who he or she is for a very long time or, perhaps, ever.

Speculation concerning the murderer's identity provides a vicarious sensation of danger pleasing to those who do not feel themselves personally at risk. The murderer could be the next-door neighbour, Aunt Nellie, the vicar, the police officer investigating the case. Murderers cannot be identified by profession, appearance or personality. Anyone can be a murderer.

Concurrent with the mystery of identity, there is often the mystery of motive. Why was the person murdered? The answer to this question often provides the answer to the murderer's identity. The motive is, therefore, usually the starting point for the investigation and, because those closest to the victim are the most likely to have reason to murder him or her, the spouse or lover automatically becomes the leading initial suspect.

In some cases, however, the motive is so obscure that it is never learned, even though the identity of the murderer is established; and in other cases the motive, although known, is so strange that no one can understand it. This, again, is the case with Jack the Ripper. It can be assumed that he disliked prostitutes, but so do many who do not disembowel them.

Mystery also arises on some occasions as to how the murder was committed and what has become of the body. Many people, including not a few murderers, believe that there can be no conviction for murder if there is no corpus delicti, and some very ingenious methods for disposing of the corpse have been devised. The corpus delicti is, of course, more than the body of the victim and consists of the total circumstances and facts surrounding the crime. Murder convictions have often been handed down when there was no trace whatsoever of the body of the victim. What the prosecution must prove is that death has taken place, that it was the result of wilful violence and that the victim was the person believed to have been murdered. There is a surprising number of murderers sitting in jail at this moment who failed to grasp this.

With the exception of identity, and even that is dubious in some instances, all the forms of mystery are represented in this book. None of the cases was easily or quickly solved, and in several the motive remains unclear to this day.

The cases end with comparatively recent convictions, but most of the murders, because of the length of the investigation, actually took place many years ago.

They are scattered over Europe for, although there is some difference in the manner and motive of murder from country to country, murder is one thing that humans everywhere share in common. We all have a great penchant for killing each other.

LOVE AMONG THE JEWELLERS

It was approaching midnight of Thursday 1 October 1987, when Moritz Schwarz, rolling southeastwards along the E5 Autobahn from Frankfurt to Wuerzburg, succumbed to his wife's pleading and pulled in to the filling station and rest stop at the Weiskirchen turn-off. Gerda had been complaining for over an hour that she had to go to the toilet.

While Mrs Schwarz sprinted for the ladies' room, Moritz stretched, rubbed his eyes, leaned back and lit a cigarette. He had been driving steadily for over six hours and his arms and shoulders were beginning to feel the strain.

Standing a hundred feet in front of him on the tarmac of the forecourt was a magnificent white hard-top Mercedes 500 SEC convertible and, as his gaze roved appreciatively over it, he was startled to see that one of the rear lights appeared to be on fire. A thin trail of smoke was rising from it and he could even see a wisp of flame.

Schwarz's reaction was immediate. The very thought of such a fine car being damaged was enough to make his blood run cold and he seized the fire extinguisher under the seat, jumped out of his own car and ran to the Mercedes.

However, before he could make use of the extinguisher, he saw to his astonishment that what was burning was a rolled-up piece of cloth which had been thrust through the broken rear light and, as he stood staring at it, it was wagged vigorously back and forth.

Recovering from his confusion, he realized that there could be only one explanation for this strange phenomenon. Someone inside the boot of the car was trying to attract attention.

Stepping forward, he tapped on the metal with his fingers and called out, 'Is anybody in there?'

A muffled voice responded. He could not make out what it was saying, but it was clear that there was somebody in the boot and there was little doubt that he or she wanted to get out.

The boot was locked, so Schwarz ran to the filling station. He explained the situation to the attendant, who, rather sceptically, accompanied him back to the car.

The attendant brought a large screwdriver with him to pry open the boot, but it turned out not to be necessary as the keys were sticking in the ignition.

The boot was unlocked and a slender, dishevelled man with a large moustache emerged from it.

'My wife!' he cried. 'My son! They've been taken hostage! Call the police!'

It was the special services section of the Aschaffenburg police who were called away. Weiskirchen is actually nearer to Frankfurt, but Manfred Graf, a wealthy jeweller, lived in the village of Hoesbach, which is less than a mile to the north of Aschaffenburg, and the hostage-taking had, it seemed, taken place there.

The luxury villa at Am Sportplatz 16 was, very shortly thereafter, surrounded by officers in bullet-proof vests, armed with sniper rifles, machine pistols and riot guns, but no attempt was made to enter it until Graf had arrived from Weiskirchen. It was important to know as much as possible of what might be encountered inside the house.

Graf arrived shortly after midnight in his own Mercedes, but was unable to tell the officer in charge of the detail very much.

Two armed men, two foreigners, he said, had burst into the house the preceding evening at around ten o'clock and taken him, his wife Ursula and their son Marco prisoner.

While one of the men remained at the villa, the other forced him to drive to his parents' home for the key to his jewellery shop in Goldbach, half a mile away. The key was kept there to forestall just such robberies, but his parents were absent and, in any case, with Ursula and Marco being held hostage, there was nothing he could do.

After robbing the shop, the robber locked him in the boot and left the car parked at the Weiskirchen rest area. He had been able to break the rear light from inside, set his pullover on fire and shove it through the hole to attract attention.

The robbery did not surprise the police in the least. There had been many cases involving the abduction of wealthy businessmen or their families in West Germany in recent years, and a jeweller was a natural target.

So far, it had gone off better than most such affairs. Graf had escaped without injury. If his wife and son could be recovered unharmed, the problem would be mainly one for the insurance company.

The robbery of the jeweller's had been some considerable time earlier, so there was no reason for the robbers still to be in the house, but there had been no call to the police, as might have been expected if Ursula had been released, and, ominously, the lights were on in nearly every room. The most optimistic interpretation was that the robbers had tied Ursula and her son hand and foot before leaving.

On the other hand, the robbers might still be hunting through the villa for more booty, and the possibility left the inspector in charge faced with a difficult decision. Either he had to storm the villa or he had to call upon the robbers to come out and surrender.

Either course was fraught with danger for the hostages, but hailing the robbers would deprive the police of the element of surprise. The encirclement of the house had been so silent and discreet that the robbers were, presumably, not aware that the police were present.

The most favourable development would be if the robbers came out alone; but by one-thirty they had not, and the inspector gave the order for the assault. It was to be sudden, swift and violent. If all went well, the robbers would be caught off guard and overpowered before they had time to harm the hostages.

At the signal of a whistle, doors and windows were kicked in and the special services officers charged into the house, weapons at the ready.

Only to withdraw immediately. There was no sign of robbers in the building and two-year-old Marco was peacefully sleeping in his bed, undisturbed even by the noise of the attack, but twenty-seven-year-old Ursula Graf lay dead in the living room, her skull shattered by a chunk of beech firewood from the box beside the fireplace a yard away.

Graf, naturally, had not taken part in the assault and he was not allowed to enter the house now. Instead, he was taken away to police headquarters in Aschaffenburg while a detachment of the special services group took up guard positions around the villa and the dispatcher sent his patrol cars to pull the members of the homicide squad out of their beds and bring them to the scene.

As Aschaffenburg is a town of under sixty thousand, there is only one homicide squad and it is not on duty round the clock, there being too few homicides to justify it.

None the less, during a career spanning more than twenty years, the squad's chief, Inspector Holgar Frank, a neatly built man with dark grey hair and moustache, had accumulated a vast amount of experience, and he took over the direction of the investigation promptly and decisively.

The special services men were relieved. The police medical expert was summoned. The photographer, the fingerprint expert and the technicians from the police laboratory were called out and the squad's second-in-charge, Sergeant of Detectives Kai Borchert, was sent to obtain descriptions of the robbers from Manfred Graf. If they were sufficiently detailed, road blocks were to be set up and all police units in the area placed on alert.

The descriptions were not adequate. There had been two men, said Graf, olive-skinned, black-haired, black-eyed. They had spoken German with an accent, and he thought they might be Italians. He had not yet been told that his wife was dead and, presumably, thought she was still in the hands of the robbers.

Two typical Italians was not enough of a description as central West Germany was full of Italians, Turks, Yugoslavs and others of a similar appearance, left-overs from the Economic Miracle when Germany's industrialists were short of cheap labour.

In any case, it was by now past three o'clock in the morning and the robbers had a minimum of four hours' head start.

'Assuming that they left immediately after the murder,' said Dr Walter Schleicher, the tall, thin medical expert, raising his long face to look at the inspector, 'she didn't die later than eleven o'clock yesterday evening and, possibly, as early as ten.'

'She was raped?' asked the inspector, looking at the corpse, which was clothed only in a dressing gown that had fallen open.

'No indications of it,' said the doctor. 'As far as I can see, she was simply hit such a violent blow over the head with the piece of firewood that she was killed instantly. There are no bruises on the hands or forearms, no traces of skin or hair under the nails. I doubt that she even realized she was in danger.'

'Must have, if she was being held hostage,' commented Sergeant Borchert, who had just returned from taking Graf's statement in Aschaffenburg. 'Even if she wasn't concerned for herself, she would have been for the child.'

'And for the one not yet born,' said the doctor sadly.

'She was in her eighth or ninth month of pregnancy. The child died with her, of course.'

'About as vicious a crime as I can recall,' said the inspector indignantly. 'Anyone could see she was pregnant.'

'And a pointless one,' added the sergeant. 'Why kill the hostage? They weren't being threatened.'

'I can only think of two possibilities,' said the inspector. 'Either she knew them and could identify them, or they're psychopaths who killed purely for the pleasure of it.'

The sergeant shook his head in distaste and went off to supervise the efforts of the technicians who were going over the villa in search of clues. He was a dark, stocky man in his forties with a broad, high-cheekboned face, and he had been a sergeant for a long time. Promotion would come only when the inspector retired, but Sergeant Borchert was patient.

The inspector remained only a little longer at the scene before returning to his office at Aschaffenburg police headquarters. Graf had to be told that his wife was dead and the responsibility for that devolved upon the officer-in-charge.

Graf, whose nerves had presumably been badly tested already that evening, had a sort of a breakdown and bounded around the office, yelling hysterically and beating his fists on the walls.

When he had calmed a little, the inspector asked him if he had anywhere to go other than home, or would he like to spend the night in the police station.

Graf said that he could stay at his parents' house, and the inspector arranged for him and Marco, who had been brought to the police clinic and was still sleeping soundly, to be driven there in a police car. He was in no condition to drive himself and, in any case, the Mercedes was in the police garage, where it would remain until the specialists had had a chance to look at it. It was possible that the kidnapper had left fingerprints on the steering wheel or elsewhere.

If he had, Graf had obliterated them in driving the car from Weiskirchen to Hoesbach. No prints other than his own were found, or anything else of significance except the broken rear light and the burned pullover.

The information on the car was only handed in the following afternoon, and by that time the inspector already had the autopsy and laboratory reports.

Dr Schleicher's report was short. The estimate of the time of death made at the scene had been narrowed to between eleven and eleven-fifteen. There were no indications of sexual activity of any kind. The victim had not been involved in a struggle nor had she been aware that she was in danger. The level of adrenalin in the bloodstream was normal.

The laboratory report was shorter. Nothing had been found at the villa to indicate the presence of a third party or parties. None of the doors or windows had been forced or tampered with. Jewels and other valuables to the value of over half a million marks – two hundred thousand pounds – had been left untouched.

'This is a very strange robbery, an even stranger hostage-taking and a totally incomprehensible murder,' said the inspector. 'It cannot be what we originally thought.'

'Meaning?' said the sergeant.

'To begin with, that the motive could not have been robbery,' explained the inspector. 'Somebody hated Graf or his wife and tried to conceal murder with a fake hostage-taking and robbery.'

'But wouldn't Graf have recognized them?' said the sergeant.

'A couple of hired thugs, perhaps,' suggested the inspector. 'Frankfurt is full of Sicilian professionals and they're neither hard to contact nor very expensive.'

'Well, yes,' said the sergeant in bewilderment, 'but would they have left half a million marks' worth of jewellery in the villa and, besides, if Graf has such a bitter enemy, he must know it, so why doesn't he say something?'

'Precisely,' agreed the inspector. 'They went to a lot

of trouble to steal the jewellery from the shop and let the jewellery in the house lie. Graf becomes hysterical when he learns that his wife is dead, but he doesn't make a squeak about who might have killed her. Did he mention to you how much they took?'

'No,' said the sergeant, 'but he must know. He was present because he had to open the safe for them.'

'That's explainable,' the inspector told him. 'He's probably rich and there could have been a good deal in that safe that he'd rather lose than have the tax people learn about. Unless I'm mistaken, it'll turn out to be insured.'

The sergeant gave him a quick, sidelong look.

'You sound as though you thought Graf was the murderer,' he said. 'How do you explain his being locked in the trunk of his car?'

'The spouse is always the first suspect,' said the inspector. 'As for the business with the car, he could have locked himself in. When you pull down the lid of the boot, it locks automatically.'

'If Graf is behind this, it's going to be hard to prove,' commented the sergeant. 'It will have been planned in advance and he'll have made certain that he's covered. The man's not stupid.'

'He's not so bright either,' said the inspector. 'If they'd cleaned everything out of the house, we might have bought his story, but he was too greedy or, maybe, he was afraid that, if his thugs got their hands on his property, they'd keep it.'

'If we could identify them, maybe they'd talk,' mused the sergeant.

'Not a chance,' said the inspector. 'In the first place, we can't connect them to the murder. No fingerprints. A weapon of convenience. Probably no prior contact to the victim. Even if Graf swore they did it, his unsupported statement wouldn't stand up in court.'

'And his description of them would be as phony as the rest,' added the sergeant. 'Anyway, they're probably out of the country by now. The man murders his wife and unborn child and we can't even charge him! He'll get away with it!'

'He'll get away with it,' said the inspector, 'as long as nobody lost any money. If it was a personal motive, he'll be tried for manslaughter, get ten or fifteen years and be released in five. If he skinned the insurance company or a bank, he's liable to spend the rest of his life in jail.'

'You seem to think he'll be tried,' remarked the sergeant. 'I thought we just agreed. . . .'

'You and Graf are both overlooking the fact that, if he did do it, he had a motive that can be traced,' said the inspector. 'He wanted to marry somebody else. His wife had a lover. Or she was suing for divorce and wanted a property settlement. You can start by looking into that.'

Determining that Ursula Graf had not been suing for divorce was a matter of a telephone call to the clerk of the divorce court. She had not been, nor had Graf been suing her for one.

There had, it seemed, been no reason for such an action on the part of either one. Ursula's relatives, Manfred's relatives and all their many friends and acquaintances described the marriage as happy.

And of mutual benefit financially. Twenty-eight-year-old Graf had taken over the jeweller's shop in Goldbach from his father-in-law, a now retired jeweller and watchmaker, and fifty per cent of it was in Ursula's name.

'There,' said the inspector, 'we have the motive. Graf could not divorce his wife because it would have ruined him.'

'There's no evidence that he wanted to,' argued the sergeant.

'Of course not,' said the inspector. 'Filing for divorce would have been cutting his own throat and he knew it. Dig hard enough and you'll find that either he or she was having an affair.'

'If it was her, there could be a question about the paternity of the child she was carrying,' mused the sergeant. 'I don't suppose that Schleicher . . . ?'

The doctor could not.

'I took blood and tissue samples from both mother and child,' he said, 'and both have the same blood group as Graf. That means he could have been the father, but not necessarily that he was.'

The medical opinion was discouraging, but it did not entirely eliminate the possibility of the unborn child as motive, a theory which the sergeant found intriguing. He therefore spent several weeks in an attempt to trace the whereabouts and movements of Ursula Graf during the final eight months of her life.

The attempt was largely successful, but the result was a report of five words, 'Ursula Graf had no lover.'

'You go at things backwards,' complained the inspector. 'You should have started with Graf. He was having an affair. She found out and threatened to divorce him. That would have ruined him so he had her killed.'

The chastened sergeant went back to looking for lovers, this time for Manfred Graf, and, although he did not immediately find one, he did turn up some evidence of perfidy.

Graf, it seemed, was a passionate but little-talented golfer. He had rarely been home at weekends or holidays and Ursula's parents said that she had believed him to be playing in tournaments.

Graf really had played in some tournaments, but not nearly as often as he had been absent from home.

In fact, Graf's handicap was such that there was little possibility of his taking part in a serious tournament.

'The caddies say he couldn't hit a golf ball with a tennis racket,' said the sergeant, 'so he was, perhaps, engaged in other, less demanding sports as well.'

'Less demanding?' said the inspector, raising his eyebrows. 'Where and with whom?'

'I don't know that yet,' admitted the sergeant. 'He was very careful. Seems to have simply vanished.'

'Then he's probably still vanishing,' said the inspector. 'Put a tail on him and find out where he goes.'

Manfred Graf was still vanishing at weekends, and the

detectives assigned to follow him reported that he went to the airport in Frankfurt, but that he did not board any of the flights.

The sergeant was puzzled.

'He must be meeting the girl at the airport,' he said.

'To what purpose?' asked the inspector. 'So they can hold hands over a cup of tea in the airport cafeteria? You forget, Graf's rich. He either owns a plane himself or he charters one, and that means that his girl friend lives some considerable distance away.'

The sergeant went personally to Frankfurt, where he found that, although Manfred Graf did not own a plane himself, he had no need to charter one as there was a so-called executive air-taxi service available.

No more was required than a little discreet questioning of the air-taxi pilots, and the sergeant knew where Manfred Graf spent his weekends.

'Hanover,' he told the inspector. 'It must really be true love. It's not all that far. Just over five hundred miles, but the air taxis cost like fury.'

'Seen from the point of view of a sergeant of detectives,' said the inspector dryly. 'Or from an inspector's, for that matter. For a jeweller who's just inherited his wife's interest in the business, it may seem cheap. I presume that you'll have someone waiting for him in Hanover next weekend?'

'Me,' said the sergeant. 'I've always wanted to visit Hanover.'

Although the sergeant's expense account did not run to air-taxi service, he managed to get to Hanover ahead of Manfred Graf. He did not, however, return immediately as he had a good deal of work to do there first.

'A Miss Karin Best,' he reported upon his arrival back in Aschaffenburg. 'An affair between equals. She's a jeweller too and, if anything, richer than Graf. Hanover's a bigger city. Thirty years old and very good-looking, but she's not married and she's concealing the affair because she's engaged to somebody else.'

The inspector thought this over for a few minutes,

doodling idly with his pencil on the margin of the progress report form he had been reading.

'I think I see the picture now,' he said finally. 'Mr Graf and Miss Best are madly in love, but there was an obstacle to their happiness in the form of Mrs Graf. Miss Best is unwilling to break off with her present fiancé until Mr Graf is in a position to marry her, for fear of falling between two stools. Thirty is quite an age even for a handsome female jeweller. Mr Graf cannot, however, divorce Mrs Graf because it would ruin him and make him financially inferior to his beloved. He therefore decides, with or without the knowledge of Miss Best, to eliminate the obstacle and employs qualified professional help to carry out the sticky parts. The obstacle is eliminated. Miss Best can now terminate her engagement. She and Mr Graf are free to marry and live happily ever after.'

'And probably will, as far as I can see,' said the sergeant. 'The fact that Graf was having an affair with another jeweller doesn't prove that he murdered his wife, and I doubt very much that Miss Best knew anything about the murder beforehand or even now, but, if she did, she's not going to tell us.'

'We're going to have to take a chance,' decided the inspector. 'We're reasonably certain that Graf is responsible for the death of his wife and there's no real reason, apart from his statement, to believe that any other party was involved. You recall what the autopsy report said about the level of adrenaline in Mrs Graf's blood?'

The sergeant nodded.

'We thought it strange that she was not even excited over being held hostage,' he said.

'She was not excited because she was not being held hostage,' explained the inspector. 'She was simply sitting in her living room reading a magazine or watching the television when her husband picked up a chunk of firewood and smashed her brains out. She probably never knew what hit her.'

'And Graf staged the rest of the thing,' said the sergeant, nodding in agreement. 'He got the key from his parents' place, opened the safe, took out some things and hid them, drove to the rest area at Weiskirchen and locked himself in the boot. Probably knocked out the rear light before he even got into the boot, to be on the safe side.'

'Which means that it may still be possible to detect traces of blood on his clothing or in the car,' observed the inspector. 'Mrs Graf bled copiously, and Graf can't know how sophisticated the methods for detecting such traces have become.'

'So, the chance we take is to arrest him, charge him, bring his clothing and the car to the laboratory and hope we get something material,' said the sergeant. 'And, if we don't, we've blown it.'

'That's about it,' said the inspector.

Manfred Graf was taken into custody and furiously denied having murdered his wife. He demanded to see his solicitor and threatened to bring charges of false arrest and harassment against the police.

The inspector had arranged for the arrest to fall on a Friday evening and, as the courts were not open again until Monday, it was not possible for the solicitor to obtain a writ of habeas corpus immediately.

Manfred Graf, therefore, spent the weekend in the detention cells at police headquarters while the laboratory technicians worked frenziedly to find some tell-tale clue on his clothing or car.

They found three. Wool fibres on the chunk of wood which had been the murder weapon came from one of Graf's sweaters, and the housekeeper testified that it was she who had carried in the firewood and that the fireplace had not been in use yet that year. There was no reason for Graf to have handled it.

More important, a spot of blood the size of a coin was found on the inside of one of Graf's vests and, on the basis of the system by which the laundry was done, this would have been the vest he was wearing on the day after the murder. Having been laundered, the spot was invisible to the eye, but not to the instruments of the police laboratory.

Finally, several traces of blood were found in the boot of the car. They were of the same group as that of Ursula Graf, but, of course, also that of her husband. Graf had, however, been examined when he was brought to the station on the night of the murder and he had not been bleeding.

The experts' explanation of how the blood spot came to be on the inside of the vest was that Graf had presumably been splashed with his wife's blood and had washed and changed his clothing. The clothing he had been wearing had probably been burned, but, in washing himself, he had overlooked a spot of blood in his hair. When he pulled the vest on over his head, the blood was transferred to the inside of the vest.

Manfred Graf continued to protest his innocence and was still doing so when he was brought to trial in March 1988. As the evidence against him was slim and as his counsel fought a brilliant delaying and technical action on his behalf, the trial dragged on for over three months.

Graf never confessed to the crime, but he would not repeat in court his original statement to the police, and this was apparently seen as evidence that he feared contradicting himself.

Somewhat to the surprise of everyone, he was found guilty of manslaughter on 7 July 1988 and sentenced to fourteen years' imprisonment.

The inspector had been off by only one year.

There was no reason to believe that Karin Best had ever known anything of the murder of her lover's wife and she was not accused of anything.

2

SCOURGE OF HOTEL PORTERS

It was three-fifteen on the morning of 18 February 1983 and the lobby of the three-star Bristol Hotel facing the railway station in Lyon was empty except for two men.

One was a hotel guest who was waiting for his girl friend, a waitress in a night club, to get off work. The other was sixty-one-year-old Angelo Perret, night porter, watchman and receptionist.

The door to the lift slid open, a young man stepped out, made a circle of the lobby and re-entered the lift.

'The gentleman in 306,' observed Perret from his armchair opposite the guest.

The lift door opened again and the young man reappeared. He was carrying a small suitcase. Resting it on the desk, he opened it and took out a sawn-off shotgun, which he pointed at the startled men, and snapped out a string of orders in barely intelligible French.

A man with sharp reflexes, the hotel guest dived behind the nearest table, from which, peering over the top, he saw the gentleman in 306 lay down his gun, pull out a large dagger and rush upon Perret, whom he stabbed in the groin.

Perret groaned and staggered off in the direction of the door to the hotel linen room and the young man bent over his suitcase again.

The guest did not wait to see what he would take out now, but broke and ran for the stairs, climbing them three at a time, and locked himself in his room. Snatching up the telephone to call the police, he abruptly realized that he could not. To obtain an outside line, he had to be connected through the hotel switchboard, and Perret was not there to do it.

A quarter of an hour passed, during which the guest barricaded the door of his room with all the furniture he could move. Then the telephone rang.

It was his girl friend, who had finished with work and come to the hotel to meet him. There was no one in the lobby, she said.

The guest came down and, before even going to see what had happened to Perret, called the police. They found the night porter dead in the linen room. The knife had severed the femoral artery and he had bled to death.

The hotel guest was able to provide a reasonably detailed description of the murderer. He was, he said, young, under thirty, dark, rather frail-looking, and he had a thin black moustache. His black hair was combed down over his forehead in a fringe and he spoke French almost unintelligibly, with a Spanish accent.

According to the hotel register, room number 306 had been occupied by a Mr Fernando Dome, but, not surprisingly, both the name and the home address given turned out to be false.

At five-fifteen in the morning of the same day, two hours after the murder of Angelo Perret, twenty-three-year-old Alain Cardot, night porter at the Hôtel Ibis in Valence, sixty miles south of Lyon, was setting out the breakfast dishes for the guests in the company of a fifty-three-year-old waitress named Yvonne Fischer.

A young man with a black moustache suddenly appeared in the breakfast room and demanded a cup of coffee.

Before Miss Fischer had time to serve him, the man produced a sawn-off shotgun from inside his jacket, tied the hotel employees to chairs and gagged them with napkins.

His attempt to open the cash register failed because it was electronic and, not knowing how to operate it, he jammed the mechanism. Calm and in no wise discouraged, he untied Cardot from the chair and brought him, his hands still tied, to the cash register. Then he produced a thin, sharp awl, which he inserted in Cardot's chest, pressing it slowly and deliberately deeper in the direction of the heart until Cardot told him how to open it.

There was only three hundred francs – about thirty pounds – in the cash register, and this apparently irritated the robber for he struck Cardot and Miss Fischer several violent blows in the face with the stock of the sawn-off shotgun before departing.

His next appearance was on 23 February when he entered the underground car park of the Solhôtel in Cannes, a hundred and fifty miles southeast of Valence on the Côte d'Azur. Taking the lift to the roof, he jumped down on to a balcony and entered the room where Dutch tourists Jan and Katarina Smid were sleeping.

Jan attempted to resist, but gave up when he was stabbed painfully in the foot. The robber collected a small amount of jewellery, but only seven hundred francs (seventy pounds) which he found so unsatisfactory that he tore the couple's passports to shreds and trampled Mr Smid's glasses into the carpet. He then left through the door.

The following night, it was the Hôtel Palma in Cannes and the victim this time was a fifty-six-year-old receptionist named Robert Bergel, who annoyed the robber by refusing to open the safe.

The robber responded by tying him to a chair and stabbing him through the hand. He then began forcing the point of the knife into Bergel's thigh. Convinced that he could only yield or die, the receptionist hurriedly provided the combination of the safe, and the robber made off with five thousand francs (five hundred pounds).

Both cases were promptly reported to the Cannes police and, as the descriptions corresponded closely, a sketch was prepared by the police artist and distributed nationwide, together with details of the crimes.

Responses were promptly received from Lyon and Valence, and a special commission, headed by Chief Inspector Jules Grandin of the Cannes police department of criminal investigations, was formed.

It was immediately presented with a new case. On the morning of 1 March, the chambermaid coming to tidy room number seven of the Hôtel Brice in Nice, twenty miles further east along the Côte d'Azur, found the bathroom floor covered with blood.

The blood stemmed from fifty-seven-year-old Nicolas Defeo, a married father of two, who had been the night receptionist at the hotel.

The following investigation determined that the occupant of room number nine had been Mr Antonio Arrete, described as young, dark, frail and with a thin black moustache. He had spoken French 'like a Spanish cow'. He was, of course, no longer there.

'What we have here,' said Chief Inspector Grandin, 'is not a Spanish cow but a mad dog. He doesn't even bother to disguise his appearance and he's striking indiscriminately and at extremely short intervals. He's also moving around, so we are going to have to alert every police and gendarmerie unit in France to be on the lookout for him.'

A tall, flat-bellied man in his late fifties with penetrating pale-brown eyes and a grave, deliberate manner, Chief Inspector Grandin had brought the key members of his commission together for briefing and discussion.

'Is there any reason to believe that he'll confine his activities to the Côte d'Azur?' asked Inspector Paul Serreau, who had been appointed Grandin's second-in-command.

'None,' said the chief inspector. 'He started in Lyon, came south to Valence and continued to Cannes and Nice. It may be that he'll head back north now. He probably won't want to retrace his steps for fear that he'll run into someone who can identify him.'

'Are we going to run the sketch in the newspapers?' asked the fingerprint specialist.

'It could scare him out of the area,' said Inspector Serreau. 'Do we want that?'

'I think we'll have to chance it,' said Chief Inspector Grandin. 'He isn't concerned about showing his face, so he may be recognized when he checks into a hotel.'

By that same afternoon, police and gendarmerie units throughout France from Rennes in the northwest to Menton in the southeast went on alert. The Hotel Porter Killer had already killed twice. Unless he was taken quickly, he would kill again.

As the last two incidents had taken place on the Côte d'Azur, an effort was made to warn hotel personnel along the famous Mediterranean holiday coast individually, something which would have been impossible during the season when all the the many thousands of hotels were open. At the beginning of March, however, it was possible to cover most of the three-star hotels which the killer seemed to favour.

The precaution proved to be unnecessary. When the Hotel Porter Killer struck again, on 8 March, it was in the city of Grenoble, a hundred and fifty miles to the north.

The scene was the Savoie Hôtel and the victim was twenty-eight-year-old Brahim Mrabet, the Algerian night porter.

This time the killer was carrying a machine pistol rather than a sawn-off shotgun. He did not have to use it and, having bound Mr Mrabet hand and foot, he stuffed him into the telephone booth in the lobby and made off with two thousand francs (two hundred pounds) from the till.

The Grenoble police were in possession of the police sketch and the description of the killer's modus operandi, and he was tentatively identified by Mr Mrabet as the man sought by the Cannes commission. Who that man was, however, remained a mystery. Suddenly, he had appeared out of nowhere, robbing, wounding, murdering. He was almost certainly a foreigner, probably a Spaniard; but without fingerprints, the Spanish police could not identify him either, and no fingerprints that could be definitely ascribed to the killer had as yet been found.

Chief Inspector Grandin was informed of the latest crime in the series, and an investigations team was dispatched to Grenoble. They arrived at eight-thirty in the evening, and an hour later Mr René Foucher was shot through the leg in the basement garage of the block of flats where he lived.

Mr Foucher had heard suspicious sounds coming from the basement and thought that someone might be stealing his car.

He went to investigate and found himself confronted by a slender young man with a thin black moustache, who brusquely ordered him out of the basement in a mixture of French and Spanish.

Mr Foucher prudently withdrew, but then imprudently returned.

Whereupon the man shot him in the leg and left.

Foucher dragged himself to the lift and telephoned the police from his flat. The area around the building was sealed off, off-duty officers were called in and a house-to-house search was carried out. Details rushed to cover the railway station and the bus terminal, and fourteen persons were arrested and temporarily detained.

Several were found to be guilty of various offences, but they were all released when, on 9 March, the killer struck in Toulon, the French naval base twenty miles to the east of Marseille.

This time, the killer added rape and abduction to his crimes.

The time was seven o'clock in the evening and Marie-Christine Artus, a very attractive blonde shop assistant of eighteen, who was employed at a large department store, was returning home to her flat in a building located at 30 Boulevard de Strasbourg.

As she entered the lift, a young man with a thin black moustache got in with her. He was wearing jeans and a marine-blue sweat shirt.

No sooner had the lift door closed than he pulled out a gun, pointed it at her head and informed her in very broken French that she was taking him home with her.

Frightened nearly out of her wits, Marie-Christine had no choice but to obey, but, once inside the flat, she made a desperate attempt to frighten him off.

'My fiancé will be here any minute,' she said.

'Good,' said the man, smiling. 'We wait for him.'

Marie-Christine had not been lying and, a few monments later, her fiancé, Philippe Herr, did arrive, but immediately found himself looking down the barrel of the killer's gun.

'We're expected by friends,' he said in an ill-advised effort to scare the intruder. 'They'll be suspicious and call the police if we fail to turn up and we can't telephone them because our telephone hasn't been installed yet.'

'No problem,' said the killer calmly. 'I go to pay phone and say you have visit from friend. Cannot come. I take girl. You keep quiet or. . . .'

He placed the muzzle of the machine pistol under the terrified girl's ear.

Herr was left with no choice but to remain helplessly in the flat while the killer went off with Marie-Christine. What frightened him most of all was that he had been lying. He and Marie-Christine were not expected by friends and he had no idea what would happen when the man found that out.

The killer did not find it out because of Marie-Christine's presence of mind. Realizing that this was an opportunity to alert others to her predicament, she called not friends, but her parents, saying that she was detained and could not visit them that evening. As they had not been expecting her, she hoped they would grasp that something was wrong.

Indeed they did, but by the time they went to her flat, discovered the gibbering fiancé and called the police, it was already too late.

The killer did not bring Marie-Christine back to the flat, but searched her handbag and found the keys to her

Ford Escort. Forcing her to lead him to the car, he put her in the passenger seat and, taking the wheel, set off in the direction of Cavaillon, a town seventy miles to the north.

'Where are you taking me? Who are you?' sobbed the nearly hysterical girl.

'You'll see,' said the man. 'You can call me El Bandito.'

It was the first mention of a title that would soon become very well-known throughout France.

It meant nothing to Marie-Christine, who was convinced that the man was going to rape her, but she had made up her mind that, no matter what happened, she was going to survive.

Her sole hope for salvation, she decided, lay in not antagonizing the man and, as she had already noted that he seemed grateful for the opportunity to confide in someone, she strove to become the best of sympathetic listeners.

'I come from Uruguay,' said El Bandito, opening his shirt to the waist to reveal an enormous scar crossing his chest. 'I political dissident, freedom fighter. They catch me. Beat with barbed wire whip. I escape. Your friend lucky. He try anything, I cut off balls.'

'No one is going to try anything,' said Marie-Christine hurriedly.

Upon their arrival in Cavaillon, El Bandito took a double room at the Pergola Hôtel, where, after having remarked that he had not made love for a long time, he raped Marie-Christine several times – she lost count after the third.

The experience appeared to have a calming effect on him and he set off in good spirits early the following morning for Saint Raphael on the Côte d'Azur, ten miles west of Cannes, where he accepted Marie-Christine's suggestion that he go into the cathedral and pray.

His prayers completed, he drove to the railway station, released his prisoner, gave her two hundred francs (twenty pounds) to pay for her petrol, said, 'Please don't denounce me!' and disappeared.

The relieved but badly shaken Marie-Christine assured him that she would not and raced straight to the nearest café to telephone the police.

A very short time later, she found herself surrounded by most of the Saint Raphael police force. It had not occurred to her that her abductor was the notorious Hotel Porter Killer, but it had to the police.

Marie-Christine was able to add a number of new details concerning the killer's appearance – among them, the scars on his chest and another on his right thumb.

Despite the very prompt response of the Saint Raphael police, El Bandito escaped arrest. The railway station was a busy one and there were trains arriving and departing constantly. After an exhaustive canvass of railway personnel and such passengers as could be located without turning up a single witness, Chief Inspector Grandin began to suspect that driving to the railway station had been no more than a ruse. El Bandito had not taken a train. He had simply remained in Saint Raphael.

He did not remain there long for on 12 March he was in Marseille, where he tried to gain entrance to the flat of a pretty schoolteacher called Maryse Blanc, using the same system he had employed with Marie-Christine. Miss Blanc, however, quicker on her feet, managed to get inside and slam the door in his face. Attracted by her screams, two of her neighbours pursued El Bandito down the street, one of them firing blank cartridges after him.

The narrow escape failed to intimidate him for, that same afternoon, he attacked, handled in an intimate manner and robbed a Mrs Paule Lecornu in the basement garage of a block of flats only a short distance from the scene of the failed attempt on Maryse Blanc.

The author of both attacks was quickly identified as El Bandito and the Marseille police poured policemen into the streets until it looked as if half the population was in uniform, while the Cannes commission came racing down.

It was all in vain. As far as El Bandito was concerned, the police might as well have been ballet dancers. Making use of one of his favourite techniques of climbing over the roofs, he gained entry into a luxury block at 9 rue de la Visitation and by eight in the evening was holding captive Jean Coguillot, a retired army colonel, and his wife Yvette.

The Coguillots were slow to cooperate and El Bandito shot the colonel in the hip and his wife in the shoulder with a twenty-two calibre rifle fron which stock and barrel had been sawn off.

The Coguillots' daughter Thérèse, alarmed by the sound of the shots, came running downstairs and was forced to hand over two thousand francs (two hundred pounds) in cash, Mrs Coguillot's rings, some other jewellery and several watches.

El Bandito departed by the front entrance, and Thérèse called the ambulance and the police. They arrived within minutes, but he was already gone.

Chief Inspector Grandin was upset.

'This is incredible!' he muttered. 'The man robs, rapes, murders right under our noses. We have excellent descriptions of him. We know how he operates. We even have samples of his semen. And yet he goes about his business as if the police didn't exist.'

'And his French is so bad as to make him conspicuous the moment he opens his mouth,' added Inspector Serreau glumly. 'He must be insane to keep on like this.'

'Not in my opinion,' said Dr Yves Desmoines, the scrawny, slightly scruffy but highly-qualified medical expert assigned to the commission. 'If you discount all moral considerations, his actions are rational, purposeful and, you must admit, effective. It's the new, modern man, unhampered by any sense of social responsibility or feelings of pity for his victims. What he wants, he takes and, if anyone stands in his way, they're eliminated.'

24

'He's religious,' remarked the chief inspector. 'He accepted the girl's suggestion that he go and pray.'

'It would be easier if he wasn't a foreigner,' said the inspector. 'The man's surely got a criminal record wherever he comes from, but, without his name or his prints. . . .'

'Uruguay reported nothing on Fernando Dome or Antonio Arrete,' said the chief inspector, 'but they're obviously false names. We could try other Spanish-speaking countries, but I don't know what good it would do us to know his name anyway. He never uses it.'

Adding insult to injury, El Bandito followed his exploits in Marseille by returning to Cannes, the commission's headquarters, on the night of 17 March – his thirty-fifth birthday, although the police did not know this at the time. He clambered over the roof of a block of flats at 8 rue du Général Ferrie and entered the bedroom of Pierre and Paulette Cohen.

He was armed with a pistol and a dagger and he effortlessly obtained the elderly couple's total cooperation as their little granddaughter was sleeping in another room in the flat.

He was given three thousand francs (three hundred pounds) from the drawer of the night table, which did not, however, deter him from laying hands on Mrs Cohen's valuable collection of jewellery or pocketing another five thousand francs (five hundred pounds), two hundred thousand lire (one hundred pounds) and a cheque book from a wall safe which he forced Cohen to open.

Cohen signed a cheque for twenty thousand francs (two thousand pounds), then El Bandito announced that he would be staying the night as he wanted the Cohens to accompany him to the bank in the morning so that there would not be any problem about cashing it.

Business affairs thus successfully concluded, he became quite jovial and suggested that a little hospitality would not be amiss.

Still trembling secretly for their granddaughter, the

Cohens cooked and served him a light supper, following which he remarked that his hair had not been washed recently and as there was still a good part of the night to kill. . . .

Mrs Cohen obligingly gave him a shampoo, and on the following morning, she and her husband accompanied him to the bank, where he collected the twenty thousand francs. El Bandito brought them back to their flat, thanked them courteously for their hospitality, assured them that they were as good as dead if they breathed a word of his existence and disappeared.

The Cohens, who had been under some considerable stress, waited fifteen minutes and then reported the robbery to the police, who sealed off Cannes.

With no more results than in the previous cases. By noon of the same day, El Bandito was back in Saint Raphael in the rue Gounod, where he visited a jeweller's shop owned by Mr and Mrs Claude Veron-Roque and asked for an appraisal of Mrs Cohen's jewellery.

Mr Veron-Roque was not present and his wife suggested that El Bandito return later. She did not, of course, suspect that he was the famous El Bandito. Not many robbers sauntered into legitimate jeweller's shops for an appraisal of their booty.

While waiting for Mr Veron-Roque to turn up, El Bandito took room forty-one at the nearby Hôtel de Genève, owned by Mr Maurice Chenaud.

He had a rather good lunch at the hotel and struck up an acquaintance with a chambermaid. He took some photographs of her and, at his request, she took some of him. He then returned to the jeweller's shop.

Mr Veron-Roque was there and he assessed the value of two rings set with rubies at forty thousand francs (four thousand pounds). An emerald ring and two with diamonds were worth rather more.

'I sell them to friend in Marseille,' said El Bandito. 'Right now must catch train.'

The following morning, Mr Veron-Roque and Mr

Chenaud opened their newspapers almost simultaneously and, almost simultaneously, leaped from off their chairs.

Plastered across the front page of the *Saint Raphael Gazette*, as it was across the front page of every newspaper along the Côte d'Azur, was an easily recognizable police sketch of El Bandito.

While the chambermaid fell in a faint, both men rushed to telephone the police, and an enormous detachment immediately surrounded the hotel while a heavily armed squad of detectives stormed room forty-one.

El Bandito was not there, but he apparently planned to return for he had left his professional equipment, which included two twelve-gauge shotguns and a twenty-two calibre long-rifle carbine, all with sawn-off stocks and barrels, a dagger with brass knuckles on the hilt, various burglary tools, most of Mrs Cohen's jewellery and fifty thousand francs (five thousand pounds).

There was no indication of where he might have gone, but he had mentioned Marseille and a train to Mr Veron-Roque, and it was known that he often travelled by train.

The Saint Raphael railway station was staked out with dozens of plain-clothes officers, while another detachment remained at the hotel.

The Cannes commission had, in the meantime, been alerted and was rushing to Saint Raphael to take charge of the operation.

At a little before eight o'clock in the evening, a sharp-eyed plain-clothes inspector watching the passengers disembark from the train that had just arrived from Marseille saw a young man with a thin black moustache raise his arm to look at his watch and recognized the scar on the thumb described by Marie-Christine Artus.

Signalling to his men, he closed in and El Bandito suddenly found himself surrounded by detectives who seized his arms while the inspector held his service pistol within an inch of his nose.

'*Que pasa?*' cried El Bandito, limp with astonishment.

What was happening was a body search of the suspect. This produced a P38 pistol with a round in the chamber and, as the inspector opened the suspect's shirt, the terrible scar reported by Marie-Christine came to light.

Identification was positive. The career of El Bandito had come to an end.

Brought to police headquarters in Cannes, El Bandito proved cooperative and confessed to everything with which he was charged.

His name, he said, was Pedro Hechaugue, but he seldom used it for professional reasons. Although he had been born in Uruguay, he was a Spanish citizen and he was married to a Madame Maria Fernandez who lived in Madrid.

Not a word of this was true. El Bandito's real name was Fernando Alonso de Celada and he was born in Buenos Aires, Argentina.

Little was known of his parents, but his official record began at the age of thirteen when he was sent to jail for the first time. Since then, he had rarely been at liberty for more than a year.

On 13 February 1979, he contracted a marriage with a woman known simply as Azbiga, whose whereabouts were currently unknown.

He fled Argentina in 1980 – to escape his wife, he said – and went successively to Brazil, the Canary Islands and Spain, collecting prison sentences along the way, before arriving in France in January 1983.

Brought to trial on 2 November 1987, El Bandito offered an unusual defence for robbery, if not for rape. The victims, he said, had been consenting. Marie-Christine had practically forced him to have sex with her, and her charge of rape was merely to prevent her fiancé from finding out the truth. The Cohens had been so taken with him that they had cooked him a meal and Mrs Cohen had washed his hair. They had given him the money and jewels voluntarily.

What the bemused jurors would have made of this remains unknown for he was tried not for rape and robbery, but for the murders of Angelo Perret and

Nicolas Defeo, where his claims of consenting victims was less plausible.

Much of the trial was taken up with the testimony of a small crowd of psychologists, most of whom described Celada as sane, but the most dangerous criminal they had ever encountered.

The jurors thought so too and sentenced him to life imprisonment.

3

A FATAL ATTRACTION TO OLDER WOMEN

There were crowds in the via IV Novembre that Wednesday afternoon of 6 May 1987. Sicily, the big triangular island off the toe of the Italian boot, lies about as far south as any place in Europe. Spring comes early and, with it, the tourists.

What happened in the via IV Novembre at a little after three o'clock that afternoon was not a tourist attraction. It was a purely local matter concerning only the residents of Aci Castello, which, with a population of a little over fourteen thousand, is a large village or a small town, depending upon the viewpoint.

Apart from the castle which gives it its name, Aci Castello has little to offer other than the beaches of the Ionian Sea and proximity to Catania, a city of four hundred thousand, three miles to the south.

Catania is lively and dangerous, but Aci Castello is quiet and, normally, safe. Shoppers and strollers were therefore startled when a young man suddenly drew a pistol, fired four shots into the back of an older man standing beside a car, leaped into another car and drove rapidly away.

Everyone was, in fact, so startled that the police would later collect no less than nine contradictory descriptions of the assassin and seven of his car.

However, it was certain that he was a professional. The operation had been swift and efficient, and every shot would have been fatal by itself. The victim had hardly had time to realize what was happening before he was dead.

Such things are not good for the tourist business, upon which the Aci Castello economy is largely dependent, and the town's modest police department turned out en masse.

Rather pointlessly, it turned out. The victim was dead. The murderer had escaped. And the Aci Castello department of criminal investigations was neither equipped nor authorized to investigate murder cases.

The suburban homicide section of the Catania police was therefore notified, and arrived at four o'clock to find that the local police had erected a canvas screen around the corpse and collected the identity cards of forty-four potential witnesses.

As Inspector Giuseppe Lucca, a slender man with black hair, black eyes and black moustache, had been briefed on the circumstances over the telephone, he came with his full squad of medical officer, photographer, ballistics expert and half a dozen detectives for taking the witnesses' statements.

The scene having been photographed, Dr Damiano Milanese, a slender man with black hair, black eyes and black moustache, carried out a rather cursory examination of the corpse, while Detective Sergeant Luigi Bartolo, a slender man with black hair, black eyes and black moustache, searched the car for evidence of the dead man's identity.

The doctor's report was brief.

'Heavy calibre,' he said. 'Nine millimetre, I think. Expert marksman or improbably lucky. I can cover all four entry wounds with my hand. Dead less than an hour.'

The inspector had been expecting nothing more. He merely nodded and held out his hand to the sergeant, who was approaching with the papers he had found in the glove compartment of the car.

According to these, the victim's name was Concetto

Centurino. He was aged forty-five, unmarried and a professional lorry driver.

'Must have had other interests,' said the inspector. 'Who puts out a contract on a lorry driver?'

The question was not meant to be answered and the sergeant refrained from replying.

'I'll see what we're getting from the witnesses,' he said.

'Ran over somebody's dog with his lorry,' suggested the ballistics expert. 'No shell casings. Either it was a revolver or the witnesses picked them up for souvenirs.'

The suggestion was not entirely serious, but the inspector gave it some thought before discarding the idea. Sicilians are easily irritated. Killing somebody for running over a dog was not completely out of the question, but paying for it was. A man might murder somebody for such a trivial reason in anger, but paying out good money to a professional killer called for a stronger motive.

The chief of the Aci Castello police, who had been waiting discreetly in the background, came over and asked rather diffidently whether it would now be possible to remove the body. The via IV Novembre was in the middle of town, and the murder was making a bad impression on the visitors.

The inspector had no objections, and the corpse was whisked into the waiting ambulance and taken off to the police morgue in Catania.

The doctor had already gone and, after waiting only long enough to learn that the witnesses' statements were, as he had expected, confused and contradictory, the inspector returned to his office, leaving the operations at the scene in the hands of the sergeant.

The local police took away the canvas screen. A crew from the street-cleaning department washed away the blood stains. By four-forty-five, the strollers along the via IV Novembre had no reason to suspect that anyone had ever been murdered there.

At six-thirty, the sergeant returned to police head-quarters in Catania.

'A lead of sorts,' he reported. 'The man was a pimp.'

'I thought he was a lorry driver,' said the inspector.

'He was originally a lorry driver,' the sergeant explained. 'Apparently didn't bother to change his identification papers when he changed his profession.'

'Well, that at least explains the motive,' said the inspector.

'Not exactly,' the sergeant argued. 'If you're thinking that somebody was trying to take over his operation, it wasn't that. The man was only running one girl and he married her last week. She couldn't be taking in much, either. Big, blonde and reasonably good-looking, but she's thirty-eight years old and carrying about twenty pounds too much weight.'

'She must have put in a lot of overtime,' said the inspector. 'That car's a new Lancia Thema and he was wearing a suit I can't afford.'

'He's an unusual sort of pimp,' the sergeant told him. 'Hard-working. Supported himself driving the lorry. The girls only supplied the luxuries.'

'A hard-working pimp?' queried the inspector. 'Now, I've heard everything. I thought you said there was only one girl.'

'Only one at a time,' said the sergeant. 'He's had others before this one. The man was a real freak. Kept getting his whores pregnant so they couldn't work. He's got two grown-up daughters and a son of seventeen, all from whores and all illegitimate.'

The inspector leaned back in his chair and regarded his assistant pensively.

'You aren't making this up, are you, Luigi?' he asked. 'There are lots of people in the department who would like your soft, easy job.'

'I swear it, chief,' said the sergeant, who did not agree that his job was soft or easy, but did not want to lose it. 'I've got all the evidence on tape.'

The inspector sighed. He did not like outlandish,

incomprehensible cases, and this one was clearly as weird as any he had ever encountered.

'I'll listen to it later,' said the inspector. 'If you're sure that it wasn't the tarts, then he must have been mixed up in something else. Drugs maybe. Guns maybe. Holding out on the Honourable Society maybe. We might start with that.'

He did not say 'Mafia' but 'Honourable Society', a safer expression to use in Sicily. Both he and the sergeant were aware that, if the killer was a professional hit man, he could be operating only with the permission, or at least tolerance, of the local capo.

If that was the case and this turned out to be a Society affair, it was not likely that the murder would be solved.

The question could be answered easily enough. Catania was full of part-time police informers who were paid on a piecework basis and who were always short of money.

Not so short, however, that they were liable to forget their primary consideration of remaining alive. Accordingly, their information was not always completely accurate and a certain amount of interpretation and guesswork was required.

The sergeant was very good at this sort of thing and he was soon able to report that his original information was entirely correct. Centurino was a part-time pimp and a full-time lorry driver. He had not been mixed up in the drug or gun trade. He had stepped on no dangerous toes.

'In fact, he was very popular in Aci Castello,' said the sergeant. 'He wasn't hard on his girls. He was a handsome dog and they gave him the money voluntarily.'

Concetto Centurino had been a slender man with black hair, black eyes and black moustache.

'Maternal instinct,' said the inspector. 'All whores are like that. The better clothes and the more jewellery they can put on their pimps' back, the prouder they are of them. All right, so why was he killed if he was so popular?'

'Beats me,' said the sergeant. 'Not a clue. The informers say he didn't have an enemy in the world.'

'So he was murdered by his friends,' said the inspector. 'Well, it looks as if you're for it. Take about half a dozen of the people who aren't busy to Aci Castello and bring me back a run-down on Centurino and everybody who knew him well enough to call him by his first name. Keep an eye out for friends who own a nine-millimetre revolver.'

The four slugs which had killed Concetto Centurino had been recovered from his body by Dr Milanese during the course of the autopsy and sent to the ballistics department, which had identified them as nine-millimetre bullets fired from a gun that had never been in the hands of the police.

This had surprised no one. The ruthless efficiency of the murder, the accurate shooting and the cool-headed, swift getaway all pointed to a top professional. The gun would have been obtained new for the job and disposed of immediately afterwards.

The police did not regard the identity of the actual assassin as important. He had only been doing a job for which he was paid. What the inspector wanted to know was who had paid him.

The bullets had been the only result of the autopsy, but hardly anything else could have been expected. They had been fired into Centurino's back from a range of about twenty feet and had all passed through or near the heart.

For the next week and a half, the sergeant and his detail of investigators commuted back and forth between Catania and Aci Castello, and every evening the sergeant had something to add to the growing mass of information concerning the life of Concetto Centurino and the people around him.

They were mainly women and almost exclusively whores. None was outstandingly beautiful and none was very prosperous. They were local girls patrolling their beats on the streets of Aci Castello and hoping to run into a generous tourist. Their services were competent, if not inspired.

Not women to be careless with money; their own requirements were modest, which left enough over to keep Centurino in luxury cars and tailored suits.

'A very small-scale operation,' said the sergeant. 'If there is such a thing as a respectable, family-father pimp, Centurino was it. You want to know about his children?'

The inspector did. For all he knew, one of them might have put out a contract to murder him.

However, to begin with there was some question as to just how many children Centurino had.

A man who had, it seemed, developed an interest in the opposite sex at an early age, his oldest acknowledged child was Lucia, now aged twenty-eight.

The daughter of fifty-six-year-old Mathilde Sambataro, she went by her mother's name and was, like her, a professional prostitute. She not only knew that Centurino was her father, but was very proud of it.

Her sister, Anna Maria Sambataro, was two years older, but denied that Centurino was her father. So had he, but many others thought differently, although he would have been barely fifteen at the time of conception. Mathilde sometimes said that he was and sometimes that he was not. It was possible that she was not sure herself.

The mother of Centurino's seventeen-year-old son Franco was Grazia Contino, the woman whom he had married shortly before his death. Grazia, Centurino and Franco were all in agreement on the subject of his paternity and Franco had always gone by his father's name.

'Very complicated relationships and, as you can see, they go back for a number of years,' said the sergeant. 'Centurino has been switching back and forth between companions all his life. Everybody knew it. Nobody objected.'

'Not even the ladies?' said the inspector sceptically. 'If you ask me, that's the motive for the murder. Centurino switched once too often. Probably got mixed up with

36

some eighteen-year-old tart and his ex-girl friends took up a collection to hire a hit man.'

'There wasn't any eighteen-year-old tart,' said the sergeant. 'Half the population of Aci Castello would have been talking about it if there was. Anyway, Centurino doesn't seem to have liked them young. People were surprised that he married Contino. Everybody thought, if he married anybody, it would be Sambataro. They'd been going steady for years, so to speak.'

'Which Sambataro?' said the inspector. 'Mother or daughter?'

'Mother,' said the sergeant.

The inspector snorted.

'The man sounds crazy enough to have hired his own hit man. And that's all?'

'Except that he apparently knew there was a contract out on him,' said the sergeant. 'He's been living barricaded in his flat ever since he married Contino. Probably thought he was safe on a busy street in the middle of town.'

The investigation was stalled. Although the past histories of every person who had been on close terms with Concerto Centurino had been exhaustively investigated, no plausible motive had appeared.

The prostitutes with whom he had had sentimental and commercial relations at varying times might have resented his switching back and forth, but certainly not to the point where they would spend hard-earned money to have him murdered. Earning a living by any means in Sicily is not easy.

'Not even for hired killers,' said the sergeant, 'but one as good as this wouldn't come cheap. A hundred thousand lire (fifty pounds) minimum, but results guaranteed, of course.'

'Which is more than I'm getting from you,' grumbled the inspector. 'How is it that somebody can put out a contract on a man in a town of fourteen thousand and you can't find any trace of who it was?'

The sergeant shrugged.

'Low-grade labour,' he said. 'I'm not being paid any hundred thousand lire for this. Anyway, you're in charge of the case. You're supposed to tell me what to do.'

'Okay, okay,' said the inspector. 'I'll tell you what to do, but I have to think about it a little first.'

He would think about it a good deal more than a little, but the only conclusion he could reach was that the information on Centurino and his lady friends must be inaccurate and incomplete.

Although everything learned gave the impression of calm and reasonable behaviour on the part of all concerned, the inspector, a Sicilian himself, found such a lack of temperament jarringly abnormal. Two tough, lower-class prostitutes such as Mathilde Sambataro and Grazia Contino should have been clawing each other's eyes out rather than amicably sharing their pimp's favours.

Had Centurino maintained both of them simultaneously, there would have been nothing unusual in the arrangement. Many pimps had stables of two girls or more.

Concetto Centurino had, however, been the most improbable of pimps, a monogamous one. He had not added girls. He had simply exchanged them.

And many, many times. According to the sergeant, he had been switching girls for close to thirty years.

It could not always have been Sambataro and Contino. Thirty years earlier, Contino would have been eight years old, young to be working as a prostitute even in Sicily. Centurino himself would have been only fifteen. Obviously, there had been other women involved, probably many other women.

All things considered, there seemed to be little doubt that the person who had put out a contract on him was a woman, but why now? What had Centurino done to so enrage a woman that she had had him murdered.

As far as was known Centurino had done only one thing recently that differed from his usual pattern of behaviour. He had got married, and such a short time before the murder that it had not even been entered on his driving licence.

The motive then was the marriage. Centurino had been switching back and forth between a couple of ageing whores for years, and when he married one, the other, finally and irrevocably rejected, had had him murdered.

In that case, the murderess was Mathilde Sambataro, even if she had not pulled the trigger personally.

The inspector summoned the sergeant and told him so.

'Unfortunately, there's no evidence and I'm afraid there won't be,' he said, 'but it has to be her. Nobody else had a motive.'

'Do we drop it then?' the sergeant asked hopefully.

The inspector shifted uneasily in his chair.

'Maybe not quite so fast,' he said. 'Sambataro probably wouldn't have known a hit man of that calibre personally. She'd have to make a connection. You might be able to trace who she made the connection through.'

'I'm flattered by your confidence in me,' said the sergeant expressionlessly. 'Some people would think that was impossible.'

The inspector did not think that it was impossible to identify the contact between Mathilde Sambataro and the assassin, or even to identify the assassin himself, but he was aware that this would not solve the case. Knowing who he was was not enough. He had to be able to prove it, and with a dozen contradictory witnesses' descriptions and no material evidence, this seemed highly unlikely.

On the other hand, sending the case to the unsolved files without following up every possible lead looked bad in the record.

Although the inspector had suggested that he concentrate his investigations on Mathilde Sambataro, the sergeant had some ideas of his own, and he put a detail of his men to interrogating the neighbours in the block of flats where Centurino had lived. It occurred to him that, if the man had been barricading himself in, it was to keep someone out – and the other tenants might have seen this someone.

If any of them had, they were prudently disinclined to mention it to the police. None admitted to having seen any stranger in the building for years.

One did, however, mention something odd. Centurino, he said, had been receiving a great deal of mail prior to his death and, strangely, he had been refusing it.

The detective consequently went to the post office and questioned the postman who delivered to the building. He confirmed the tenant's statement. For a very long time before his death, Centurino had been receiving one or more letters a day which he had refused. They had therefore been returned to the sender – the same person in all cases. There had been no letters since Centurino's murder.

There was obviously some significance in this flood of refused mail, and the detective asked the postman if he could recall the name of the sender.

The postman could. Centurino lived on the fourth floor and he had been passably irritated by having to climb four flights of stairs only to have the letters refused.

The name, said the mail man, was Sambataro.

'Mathilde?' asked the sergeant.

'A. M.,' said the postman.

The puzzled detective went to report to the sergeant.

'I think it must mean something,' he said, 'but I can't imagine what.'

'Nor can I,' said the sergeant, 'but A. M. must be Anna Maria, Mathilde's daughter. If she was writing every day to Centurino, who some people think was her father, and he was refusing the letters, there's a reason for it.'

The inspector thought so too.

'Bring both the Sambataros in,' he ordered. 'I have the feeling we're about to get to the bottom of this.'

Mathilde and Anna Maria had been questioned previously and had said they knew nothing about the murder. They now repeated their statements.

The inspector did not believe them and, while they were being grilled mercilessly, a detail armed with a search warrant went through their flats.

Nothing was found in Mathilde's, but in Anna Maria's a dozen of the letters refused by Centurino were recovered.

Whatever others might believe, Anna Maria was clearly convinced that Centurino was not her father, for the letters contained some of the most erotic and seductive language that the inspector had ever seen.

Anna Maria had been hopelessly in love with her mother's pimp, lover and former fiancé, and she had been insanely jealous!

Shown the letters, Mathilde broke into tears and made a long and detailed statement in which she described the bizarre competition for the favours of Concetto Centurino which had pitted her, unwillingly, against her daughter.

'I would have let her have him!' she wailed. 'It didn't matter that much to me any more. God knows, I've had enough men to last me a lifetime. All I wanted was my peace.

'It was Concetto who wouldn't have it. He was very conventional and he was afraid that Anna Maria was his daughter. I don't know whether she is or not, but I swore that she wasn't so that he'd take her before something bad happened.

'She couldn't control herself. If she was alone with him for five minutes, she'd tear off her clothes and jump on him. I don't know how many times I came into the room and she was hanging around his neck stark naked. It was pitiful to see.'

'Pitiful is no word for it,' remarked the inspector. 'This Centurino was wasted in a place like Aci Castello. With that kind of sex appeal, he could have made it big in the movies.'

Anna Maria, said Mathilde, had made so much trouble

between her and Concetto that they had finally abandoned their plans to marry. She had simply worn them both out.

She had not known that Concetto was going to marry Grazia until she saw the announcement of the marriage in the newspaper.

The only sensation she had felt was relief, but Anna Maria had been hysterical with rage. Perhaps she had mentioned her problem to one of her more violent clients and he had decided to do her a favour.

This was a rather transparent attempt to save her daughter, but Anna Maria, her beloved Concetto lost forever, did not want to be saved and she not only confessed to hiring the killer, but provided the inspector with his name.

He was thirty-three-year-old Nunzio Ruscica, a professional hit man, well known to the police, but so competent at his trade that he had never been arrested or charged.

He was not charged this time either, for the only evidence against him was Anna Maria's unsupported word and, having made a statement in which he said he had never heard the names of Anna Maria Sambataro or Concetto Centurino and that he had never killed anybody, he was released.

Later invited to take part in a line-up, he cheerfully complied, but was not recognized by any of the witnesses to the murder; he was a man whom few would care to implicate.

Anna Maria Sambataro therefore faced the court alone when the case came to trial on 9 September 1988. Having not retracted her confession and having expressed great and unquestionably sincere contrition for her act, she was found guilty of inciting to homicide, granted substantial extenuating circumstances and sentenced to eight years' imprisonment.

4

INSTANT INHERITANCE

The young man who stumbled into the Lambrecht police station that cold Tuesday morning of 24 February 1987 was pale and shaking, obviously in the grip of some very strong emotion.

'Dead!' he croaked. 'My folks are all dead!'

The startled desk sergeant did not need to ask who his folks were. The Metzmanns were easily the most prominent residents in the little community of 4,290 persons, and nineteen-year-old Kai was their only son.

'Where did it happen?' he exclaimed, reaching for the microphone which was his link to the department's two patrol cars. He was assuming that the Metzmanns had been in a car crash.

'At home,' groaned the boy. 'Eighteen Freiherr-vom-Steinstrasse.'

The address was unnecessary. The sergeant knew very well the location of the Metzmanns' villa on the high slopes of the Forest of the Palatinate overlooking the green valley of the Speyer.

The accident, it seemed, was domestic and, as the first thing that occurred to the sergeant was fire he wasted no time with further questions, sent his patrol cars racing to the scene and called out the fire department and emergency ambulance in Neustadt-an-der-Weinstrasse, three miles away.

He had just taken Metzmann into the back room, given him a stiff shot of brandy and made him lie down when one of the patrol-car officers came on the radio-telephone, half out of his wits with excitement.

43

'They're all dead!' he yelled into the instrument. 'The whole blasted family's been murdered!'

Scarcely able to believe his ears, the sergeant turned out the chief of the Lambrecht police and called the Neustadt department of criminal investigations.

Neustadt-an-der-Weinstrasse – a name meaning the New Town on the Wine Street and used in its entirety only when necessary to distinguish it from the many other Neustadts not on the Weinstrasse, a road running along the eastern slopes of the Palatinate Mountains, where some of West Germany's finest white wines are produced – has a population of fifty thousand and takes care of such emergency services as Lambrecht, a largely residential community, lacks.

Neither the fire department nor the ambulance arrived in Lambrecht, because their missions were aborted by Police Chief Walter Reinert immediately following his arrival at the villa. There was no fire and the Metzmanns were in no need of an ambulance.

A detachment from the Neustadt department of criminal investigations did arrive, but found the case so serious that it was decided to call in the Ludwigshafen police.

Ludwigshafen, a city of over two hundred thousand at the junction of the Rhine and Neckar rivers twenty miles to the northeast, has one of the best equipped and staffed departments of criminal investigations in central West Germany.

It was, however, nearly noon before Ludwigshafen homicide commission of some forty officers, detectives, specialists and technicians arrived in Lambrecht. The central European winter was at its worst. The roads were covered with ice, and driving was rendered the more difficult by a persistent freezing fog which reduced vision to near zero.

In charge of this detachment was Inspector of Detectives Werner Kreissauer, a grey-haired veteran of twenty years' criminal investigation work. A straight-backed man with the ruddy complexion of someone who spent a good deal of time outdoors, it was he and medical expert Dr Leopold Graf who first entered the house.

The inspector's second-in-command, Sergeant of Detectives Peter Falken, a lean, hawk-faced man with dark, very deep-set eyes, had remained at the Lambrecht police station to tape-record the statement by Kai Metzmann, sole survivor of the massacre, concerning his discovery of the bodies. Kai was no longer excited and, indeed, little short of comatose as the duty sergeant had been pouring brandy down him with a liberal hand.

The corpses of the rest of the family were in the big, luxurious house in Feiherr-vom-Steinstrasse. Forty-seven-year-old Renate Metzmann lay on the double bed in the master bedroom, her forty-nine-year-old husband Willi lay on the floor, ten feet away, and their twenty-five-year-old daughter Silke lay sprawled in the study. All three were wearing nightclothes.

The doctor, a substantially overweight man with a close-shaven head and nickel-rimmed glasses, began with the body of Metzmann.

He was, however, unable to determine the immediate cause of death.

'Shot several times in the chest and upper abdomen with what looks like a fairly heavy-calibre gun,' he said. 'Probably would have been ultimately fatal, but his skull is also fractured and there are multiple stab wounds. I'll have to perform the autopsy before I can tell what it was that killed him.'

'Not immediately important to the investigation,' the inspector told him. 'What about the woman?'

'Single bullet in the centre of the forehead,' said the doctor. 'Same apparent calibre and she's been stabbed several times. Bayonet or a very large knife.'

'Was she raped?' asked the inspector.

'No sign of it,' said the doctor. 'Where's the third body?'

'The chief said the study,' remembered the inspector. 'It's a big house. We'll have to look for it.'

The study was at the other end of the house, but easily located for the door had been smashed in.

Silke Metzmann lay on the floor near a desk, her limbs sprawled wide. Her short, transparent nightgown was bunched up under her armpits and her naked body was covered with blood and stab wounds.

'Also shot,' said the doctor. 'There's no point in my continuing here. We're going to have to get them back to the morgue. There are a great number of wounds on all these bodies and it's going to take time to arrive at any conclusions.'

'Can you give me an approximate time?' asked the inspector. 'I suppose it's the same for all three?'

'Close, at least,' the doctor agreed. 'Call it between midnight and two in the morning. I can't be any more exact until I've done the autopsy.'

'It'll have to do then,' said the inspector. 'I'll send them over as soon as I can. I'd like the report on the girl first, if possible. I have a hunch she may be the motive for all this.'

The doctor grunted in agreement and left the house. He was rather out-of-sorts as he was driven back to Ludwigshafen. He did not like driving and he did not even like riding in a car in such weather.

The photographer was already at work in the bedroom, making the official pictorial record of the crimes and, as he passed on to the study, the detection specialists moved in, searching for clues and dusting for fingerprints. They worked silently and efficiently, trained and experienced in their profession.

The direction which the investigation would take depended largely upon their findings, and the inspector left them to it and went to join the sergeant at the police station.

The sergeant had by now assembled a good deal of information concerning the victims from the local police, who were in something of a state of shock. In so far as anyone could remember, this was the first homicide ever to have taken place in Lambrecht.

'The most prominent family in the area,' the sergeant told the inspector. 'Metzmann was a self-made man who started off as a simple mechanic and became a millionaire. He was the owner of a flourishing firm dealing in welding equipment, and a village councillor. Owned a weekend house in the forest, a stable of riding horses and a string of expensive cars.'

'Family problems?' the inspector wondered. 'Mistresses? Lovers?'

'Not that the police here know about,' said the sergeant. 'They'd been married for twenty-six years and 24 February would have been the wife's forty-eighth birthday. She had worked with her husband in the family firm and apparently contributed a good deal to his success. There's never been any gossip.'

Silke and Kai had also worked in their father's company, Kai as an apprentice welder and Silke in the bookkeeping department. Neither was married and both were still living at home.

'Conspicuously wealthy family and somebody decided to rob them,' said the inspector. 'Does the chief know whether they kept large sums of cash in the house?'

The chief did not; but the question was of no consequence, for the technicians reported that nothing appeared to have been stolen.

'There are forty-odd thousand marks (fourteen thousand pounds) in a safe in the office and various smaller sums elsewhere in the house,' they reported. 'The safe wasn't even locked properly and both the mother and the daughter had valuable jewellery lying out exposed, but, as far as we've been able to determine, nothing's been stolen.'

The motive for the murders had apparently not been robbery after all, and the other conclusions of the technicians were equally unexpected.

The murder weapons appeared to have come from the Metzmann household itself. Two hunting rifles were believed to be missing from the rack in the hall, for there was twenty-seven and thirty-calibre ammunition and accessories, but no guns. A large kitchen knife was missing from a set in the kitchen and, of two crossed cavalry swords hung on the wall of the living room as a decoration, only one remained.

According to the deductions of the specialists in their reconstruction of the crimes, two people had entered the Metzmanns' house sometime during the night of 23–24 February. They had either had a key or picked the lock – or one of the doors or windows had not been locked.

Willi, Renate and Silke had all been in bed asleep, the parents in the master bedroom and the daughter in her room down the hall.

The intruders had entered the master bedroom and shot Renate in the forehead, killing her instantly. Willi, aroused by the sound of the shot, had leaped out of bed and charged the killers, but had been shot down in turn.

The killers had then fallen upon the victims, stabbing them with the sword and the kitchen knife and smashing their skulls in with the gunstocks.

In the meantime, Silke, alarmed by the sound of the gunshots, had fled to the study and locked herself in. She had presumably tried to telephone the police because the instrument was out of the cradle, but the killers had broken down the door and shot her before she could dial the number.

The three murders accomplished, they had immediately left, taking nothing with them but the murder weapons.

'And where was the son while this was going on?' said the inspector.

The question was directed to the Lambrecht chief of police, who said he did not know. Kai was by now nearly unconscious from the effects of shock and brandy, and he had been taken to his own home as the police chief did not know what else to do with him. Kai could not return to the villa while the investigation was in progress.

Questioned later that day by the sergeant, Kai said he had been at an all-night party in Neustadt and volunteered the names and addresses of some of the other guests.

The sergeant, who was not a man to accept unsupported statements, contacted them, and several recalled seeing Kai and his best friend, eighteen-year-old Juergen Lischer, leave the party at around eight-thirty in the morning. As Kai had appeared at the station in Lambrecht shortly before nine, his statement was largely confirmed.

'Interesting party,' the sergeant reported back to the inspector. 'A whole bunch of kids from wealthy families riding the punk trend. Crazy haircuts, nutty clothes, safety-pins in the ears, anything to shock their elders. There must have been fifty of them.'

'Any of them seem homicidal?' asked the inspector. 'Like, say, with an expensive drug habit?'

'Homosexual, yes,' said the sergeant. 'Homicidal, no. They're probably all on something, but they can afford it, or at least their parents can.'

'I'm almost ready to accept a band of multisexual punks as suspects,' said the inspector. 'The autopsy report hasn't helped matters at all.'

The autopsy report made for bloody reading, but failed to throw any light on the motive for the murders or the identity of the murderers.

Renate Metzmann had been killed by a single thirty-calibre rifle bullet fired into her forehead at close range. Her corpse had been subsequently stabbed a total of eleven times, three times with the sword and eight times with the kitchen knife, and her skull had been fractured in four places by violent blows with what was assumed to be the rifle butt. She had not been sexually molested and she had probably been asleep at the time as the adrenaline level in her bloodstream was below normal.

The adrenaline level in her husband's bloodstream had been extremely high, an indication that he had been angry or frightened at the time of his death. Metzmann's right eye had been shot out and there were six other thirty and twenty-seven-calibre bullet wounds in his chest and stomach. He had been run completely through with the sword and his skull had been smashed with repeated blows of something smooth and heavy.

Silke had also been shot twice in the chest, and her body displayed a total of forty-four stab and slash wounds, many made by the sabre. Damage to the genital area was so extensive that the doctor was unable to say whether there had been sexual activity or not. However, no traces of semen on or in the body were recovered.

The time of death of all three victims was fixed at between twelve-thirty and twelve-forty-five in the morning of 24 February 1987.

'I think our problem here is the motive,' said the inspector. 'It wasn't robbery and I doubt that it was sex. That leaves only emotional grounds: hatred, envy, revenge. The Metzmanns started out poor and, in clawing their way to the top, they may have made enemies.'

'If so, we should be able to identify them,' said the sergeant, 'but wouldn't that mean that they came to the house with the express intention of murdering the Mertzmanns?'

'Obviously,' said the inspector.

'Then why did they come unarmed?' the sergeant wondered. 'Why only the weapons they found in the villa?'

'A very good point,' said the inspector thoughtfully. 'Ballistics says that all the bullets recovered from the bodies match the type of twenty-seven and thirty calibre ammunition found in the gun cabinet. Of course, as they don't have slugs known to have been fired from Metzmann's missing rifles, they can't say with certainty that they were from them, but it seems more than probable.'

'The whole affair strikes me as so irrational that I wonder if it wasn't a couple of kids high on some kind of a weird drug,' said the sergeant. 'They gained entry to the villa by some means or other and were snooping around, not even intending to steal anything and . . .'

'. . . and they were surprised by the Metzmanns and

went into a killing frenzy,' finished the inspector. 'Only they weren't surprised by the Metzmanns. Mrs Metzmann was definitely the first to be killed and she was asleep in bed.'

'I'm out of theories,' said the sergeant. 'I don't think we'll ever solve the case.'

'Possibly not,' agreed the inspector. 'The motive is certainly obscure. However, if we could determine that, I think the identity of the murders would become immediately apparent, so that is what we are going to work on.'

The sergeant shrugged.

'A business competitor then?' he suggested.

'It's hard for me to believe that competition in the welding-equipment business is that savage,' said the inspector, 'but I suppose you might as well begin there. God knows, I can't think of anything better.'

Neither could the sergeant and, although he was not much impressed with his own suggestion, he applied himself to the business affairs of the Metzmann welding-equipment company. He soon learned that the Metzmanns had indeed had a very bitter enemy, who was no longer a competitor as he had been forced into bankruptcy several years earlier.

His name was Boris Andower and he had been in the welding-equipment business long before the Metzmanns. Now sixty-two years of age and in very reduced circumstances, he blamed his misfortunes on what he termed the unfair competition of Willi Metzmann.

'In fact, it doesn't appear to have been unfair,' said the sergeant. 'Metzmann was simply a better businessman and he kept up with new developments in the field. Andower couldn't adapt and he went under, more due to mismanagement than anthing else.'

"But he had a grudge against the Metzmanns?' queried the inspector.

'To put it mildly,' said the sergeant. 'He's been threatening to get even with them for years.'

'There were two killers in the Metzmann murders,' said the inspector.

'Andower has an old foreman named Karl Bursch, who lost his job when Andower's firm went bankrupt,' said the sergeant. 'He's made threats against the Metzmanns too.'

'But the women?' the inspector objected. 'They wouldn't have had anything against the women.'

'The whole family worked for the firm,' said the sergeant. 'There was an incident last June. Somebody shot at Metzmann while he was in his car. The bullet lodged in the upholstery and the Lambrecht chief of police says it was twenty-two calibre, long rifle. The bullet's gone. Metzmann took it and he refused to prefer charges. The chief thinks he knew who it was.'

'Two old men who believed that they had been ruined by the Metzmanns,' mused the inspector. 'Well, I suppose it's possible. Dammed unlikely suspects though.'

'They're what we have,' said the sergeant. 'I've got Max, Albert, Joachim and Ulrich over in Neustadt trying to determine where Andower and Bursch were on the night of the twenty-third.'

Max, Albert, Joachim and Ulrich were among the department's top investigators, but they were not able to determine anything definite regarding the whereabouts of the suspects on the night of the murders.

'Andower is a widower and Bursch has never been married,' said the sergeant. 'They both live alone and they're not interesting enough for the neighbours to pay any attention to their comings and goings.'

'So they could have done it, but there's no evidence that they did,' said the inspector. 'I still don't think much of them as suspects, but it is possible, I suppose. A couple of bitter old men nursing a grudge, they could have lost touch with reality. There have been other cases like that.'

'It still doesn't answer the question of why they came to the villa unarmed,' the sergeant pointed out.

'Maybe they were armed, but, when they got into the

house, they found the guns and the sabre and knife and decided to use them because they couldn't be traced back to them.'

'In that case, taking the murder weapons with them was pure madness,' said the sergeant. 'They'd be the sole evidence of their connection with the murders and, if they were found on them . . .'

'If they were crazy enough to take them, maybe they were crazy enough to keep them,' said the inspector. 'Apply for a warrant and we'll search their homes.'

Boris Andower and Karl Bursch were arrested and brought to police headquarters in Ludwigshafen, where they denied vehemently any connection with the deaths of the Metzmann family, although both admitted having made threats against them.

However, the search of their homes turned up a thirty-calibre hunting rifle in Andower's garage and there were traces of what appeared to be blood on the stock.

The gun was taken to the police laboratory, and subsequently to the ballistics department for test firing and comparison with the bullets recovered from the bodies of the victims.

Asked about the gun, Andower said it was his, but that he had not fired it for years. The blood, he thought, might have come from a chicken he had killed in the garage the preceding Sunday.

The inspector was inclined to believe him, and a few hours later, when the results of the laboratory and ballistics tests were handed in, Andower's statement was confirmed. The blood on the rifle stock was chicken blood; the gun had not been fired for a long time and the marks made by the rifling on the test bullets did not match those on the ones taken from the bodies of the victims.

Nothing else suspicious was found in either man's home and they were released for lack of evidence.

The inspector began casting about for other potential suspects.

'We still don't have the right motive,' he told the sergeant, 'but I'm convinced that there was one. The people weren't insane. The murders were a deliberate attempt to wipe out the entire Metzmann family, and the only reason the boy wasn't killed too was that he wasn't there.'

There was a short, thoughtful silence.

'Wasn't he?' said the sergeant.

The inspector gave him a startled look.

'You checked his whereabouts at the time of the murders,' he reminded him.

'Maybe I wasn't thorough enough,' said the sergeant. 'It seems to me that Kai is a mighty lucky boy. He misses out on the massacre and now he's sole heir to the family millions. Doesn't even have to split with his sister.'

'A theory like that could destroy my last illusions about German youth,' commented the inspector, 'but I'm very much afraid you may be right. We've been looking for a motive. The boy had one.'

'He had a key to the house,' said the sergeant. 'He knew where the guns and other weapons were kept. He didn't steal anything because it was all his own property.'

'How good is his alibi?' said the inspector.

'I don't know,' admitted the sergeant. 'Half a dozen of the kids said he and Lischer left the party at around eight-thirty that morning.'

'But not if it was the only time they left the party,' said the inspector. 'It wouldn't take long to drive to Lambrecht and back. A big party like that, they wouldn't even have been missed.'

'If they weren't, we haven't a case,' observed the sergeant. 'We're not going to get a confession out of a punk cold-blooded enough to wipe out his entire family for the inheritance.'

'You overestimate modern youth, Peter,' said the inspector dryly. 'Don't forget, they were stupid enough to take the murder weapons with them, and I would be willing to bet they still have them. Before we proceed to arrests, however, I want you to run down every person who was at that party and get exhaustive statements from

54

them – what time the party started, times they saw Metzmann and Lischer, how drunk or drugged they were, and so on. I don't want to bring charges and then be presented with an alibi we can't break.'

The sergeant found this a difficult assignment. He already knew something of the atmosphere which had reigned at the party. It had begun at around eight o'clock in the evening and, by ten o'clock, most of the revellers had been high on marihuana, hashish, alcohol or some combination of all three. Worse yet, it was the carnival season and several other parties had been going on at the same time. There had been a certain amount of switching back and forth.

'You know how it goes,' he said. 'People come in, get a drink, smoke a joint, lay somebody maybe and move on. Later they may come back or they may not. Considering the state they were in, I don't think their testimony would hold up in court.'

'But then, neither would any statements in support of Metzmann's and Lischer's alibis,' said the inspector. 'See what you can get and we'll bring them in for questioning.'

All that the sergeant could get was negative evidence. No one could be found who would swear to having seen Kai Metzmann or Juergen Lischer at the party between the hours of eleven-thirty and one-thirty in the morning.

'Fine,' said the inspector. 'Now, bring them in and we'll talk to them.'

He did not say 'question' because he did not intend to question the young men. Instead, he explained to them precisely why he suspected them of having murdered Kai's family.

'Yours was the only motive,' he said. 'You benefited by the murders and no one else did.

'You could enter the house because you lived there and you had a key.

'You knew where the guns and other murder weapons were kept so you brought no weapons with you.

'You stole nothing because, with all other members of your family dead, it was your property anyway.

'All of these things point to a member of the family, and you are the only surviving member.'

'That's no proof,' said Kai sullenly.

'The proof will be the murder weapons,' the inspector told him. 'We know that you have them and we will find them.'

'I don't have any murder weapons,' said Kai, but he looked uneasy.

The inspector sighed.

'We have enough evidence right now to keep you under interrogation for months,' he said. 'It's very tedious for us and for you. Sergeant, would you read Mr Metzmann and Mr Lischer the German Juvenile Criminal Code?'

'All of it?' asked the sergeant in a startled voice.

'Only the sections on sentencing and possibilities of early release,' said the inspector.

'I know them,' said Kai hurriedly. 'Ten years max and out in under five if you stay clean.'

'I thought you might,' murmured the inspector. 'Are you prepared to make a statement now?'

Kai Metzmann was. In a brisk, businesslike manner, he dictated a confession to the murders of his mother, father and sister. Juergen Lischer, his best friend, had been invited to take part in return for a slice of the inheritance. They had simply left the party, carried out the murders and returned to the celebrations.

'I was sick of welding,' he said. 'What's the good of being rich if you have to work all the time? I had to take Silke too, because otherwise I'd have had to split the estate with her.'

His confession having been confirmed by Juergen Lischer, the young killers led the police to the point on the Speyer river, a comparatively modest stream, where they had thrown the murder weapons into the water. Both rifles, the kitchen knife and the sabre were recovered.

On 22 January 1988, Kai Metzmann and Juergen Lischer appeared before the juvenile criminal court in Ludwigshafen, pleaded guilty to wilful premeditated homicide and were sentenced to ten years' juvenile detention each. Under normal circumstances, neither will remain in prison for more than five years, so Kai will be free and rich at the age of twenty-four.

'Not a bad deal by present-day standards,' remarked the inspector, leaving the court with the sergeant. 'Now, if your parents were rich and you were under twenty-one. . . .'

But, of course, they were not and he was not.

5

AFFLUENT LIFE STYLE

Afterwards, no one was quite sure of the exact time, but it was shortly before midnight of Wednesday 12 May 1982 when the residents of the little Swiss village of Seelisberg were torn from their television sets or their beds by a series of agonized screams.

Dashing out of their houses, they found that the screams, which were continuing and growing even louder, were coming from somewhere along the road to the east of town.

The entire ambulant population of Seelisberg began to run down the road in the direction of the sounds, some dressed but in slippers and others in their nightclothes.

It was a clear night. The full moon was still high in the sky, but the road at the entrance to the village was bordered on either side by steep rock walls, so it was only as they rounded the curve a hundred yards from the first houses that they were confronted with the most ghastly sight any of them would ever see.

Stumbling along the road towards them, turning and twisting in a gruesome dance of death, was a human figure wrapped in flames!

The villagers came to an as abrupt halt as if they had run into the rock of the mountain, but their hesitation lasted only a few instants. Tearing the clothing from their own bodies, they rushed forward to fling it over the burning human in an effort to smother the flames.

The effort was successful and the villagers hastened to pick away – in some cases, with singed fingers – the pile of clothing from what was eventually revealed as the body of a woman.

She did not look much like one as the fire had burned away her hair, eyebrows and eyelashes. Not a thread of her clothing remained, and the skin of her entire body was black or, horribly, blood-red where the raw flesh lay exposed.

Incredibly, she had not lost consciousness and she continued to writhe and scream feebly, mouthing out several times what sounded like the name 'René'.

Most of the appalled villagers, afraid to move her, afraid even to touch that pitifully roasted flesh, could do nothing but weep and wring their hands, but one or two cooler heads ran back to the village to telephone for the ambulance, while some others went further down the road to where something was throwing huge orange flames into the night sky.

The object turned out to be a little Austin Mini, its nose crumpled against a signpost and burning like a torch. It was not possible to approach closely enough to see whether there was anyone in it, but if there was, they were beyond saving.

The car was standing on a steep rock slope leading from the road to the Vierwaldstaetter See and, had it not been for the post, would obviously have continued on down, to plunge into the mountain lake's deep, dark waters.

The villagers backed away, apprehensive of the explosive petrol tank, and, indeed, a few moments later it did explode, flinging sparks and burning debris high in the air to arc hissing into the lake below.

The woman had still not lost consciousness but her screams had been replaced by a whimpering, whining sound, even more heart-rending. Some of the women clapped their hands over their ears and others broke and ran for their houses, traumatized as much by their inability to help as by the terrible suffering of the victim.

Professional help was, however, already on the way, and the siren of the emergency ambulance, responding to the frantic telephone calls, could be heard in the distance. Switzerland is a rich country and the public services around Lucerne, the big city on the western end of the Vierwaldstaetter See, are among the best in the world.

The ambulance came, not from Lucerne, but from Altdorf, a smaller but much closer community, and with it came a car from the highway patrol. The villagers who had called the ambulance had described the situation as a traffic accident.

Although no member of the ambulance crew believed that the woman would survive the trip to the hospital, the first consideration was to relieve her suffering and the paramedic immediately injected her with a quick-acting anaesthetic.

The woman lost consciousness instantly and the crew eased her on to a plastic sheet, lifted the sheet on to a stretcher, slid the stretcher into the ambulance and set off at top speed for Lucerne, which had better hospital facilities than Altdorf. If the woman was to die, it would not be because of negligence on their part.

Even before the wail of the siren had faded away, the highway-patrol officers had begun taking statements from the villagers, but stopped once they learned that there had been no actual witnesses to the accident. The car and woman were already burning before anyone arrived.

Although the car was no longer burning as fiercely as before, it was still too hot to approach, but the explosion had blown off the doors and it was clear that there was no one else in it.

The highway-patrol officers sent the villagers back to their homes and began going over the scene of the accident, taking measurements and examining the pavement for tyre marks.

It immediately became apparent that the cause of the accident was obscure. There were no indications that a second vehicle had been involved or that the Austin had skidded or braked. It had simply gone off the paved, well-maintained road in a straight line rather than follow-ing the curve.

It could not, however, have been travelling very fast or the impact would have snapped off the signpost.

The most probable explanation was, therefore, a mechanical or driver failure. The woman had had an attack of some kind, or she had been drunk or she had been driving for a long time and had simply dozed off. Such accidents were not uncommon, particularly at that time of night, but the most difficult question to answer was how the car had come to catch fire through simply running into a post at low speed.

The highway patrolmen made mention of this in their report and suggested that the possibility of suicide could not be ruled out.

Suicide or attempted suicide is a criminal offence and, as a result, the report was routed to the desk of Inspector Anton Bieler of the Altdorf department of criminal inves-tigations, who read through it and found the circum-stances as puzzling as had the highway patrolmen.

Obviously, the person who could most easily solve the mystery was the driver herself, and he sent his assistant, Detective Sergeant Bernard Deichmann, to the hospital in Lucerne to see if she was still alive.

Contrary to all expectations, she was, but in a coma from which the doctors doubted she would emerge. Everything possible had been done, but the woman had suffered second and third-degree burns over sixty per cent of her body.

'They say that seventy per cent is almost invariably fatal,' reported the sergeant, a stoic, blond man with a snub nose and a short haircut. 'Her underwear and part of the safety belt were literally burned into her flesh. They think there's little chance that she'll ever regain consciousness and even less chance of her being able to make a statement if she does.'

'Has she been identified?' asked the inspector.

He was a trim, clean-cut, rather handsome man with

a black close-clipped moustache and streaks of grey at the temples.

'The car is registered in the name of Erika Ackermann,' said the sergeant, 'but that may not be the woman in the hospital.'

'Get the missing-persons reports checked,' said the inspector. 'Do you think she could be identified by sight?'

'Not by her own mother,' said the sergeant. 'Fingerprints, maybe. I didn't think to ask if she has any left. The doctors say she may have been drenched with petrol.'

The inspector looked up sharply, but said nothing for a few moments.

'Possible homicide then,' he observed finally.

'Or suicide,' said the sergeant. 'Unusual modus though.'

The inspector did not think it had been suicide. There were people who doused themselves with petrol and burned to death in imitation of world-weary orientals, but, if that had been the case, why go all the way to Seelisberg to do it?

'And why drive the car off the road?' he said. 'Even if she was planning to run the car into the lake and drown, there was no reason for her to burn herself up. She could have simply run down the slope and jumped in. No, it was either an accident or murder.'

'Attempted murder,' corrected the sergeant. 'She's not dead yet.'

'We'll start the investigation immediately anyway,' said the inspector. 'See what you can do about identification, and put some people to investigating her private circumstances, assuming that the identification is positive.'

The identification was positive. Not many of forty-two-year-old Erika Ackermann's fingertips were capable of yielding fingerprints, but enough remained to determine with certainty who she was.

The prints for comparison came from her toilet articles, provided by her husband, forty-seven-year-old René Ackermann to whom she had been married only since 21 February of that same year.

The couple lived in the town of Kriens, a mile to the south of Lucerne, and Ackermann had reported her missing on the morning of the thirteenth.

In his report to the missing persons department in Kriens, he said that he had picked Erika up at shortly after six o'clock at the Lucerne department store where she worked and that they had had dinner together at a restaurant.

Following dinner, she had set off for Kriens in her second-hand Austin Mini, which he had bought her only the week before, and he had gone to visit a friend.

He had returned home at four-thirty in the morning to find no sign of Erika or her car. After waiting until eight-thirty on Thursday morning on the off-chance that she might be spending the night with a girl friend, he had reported her missing to the police.

Brought to Altdorf for questioning, he repeated this statement and provided a summary of his wife's background, in so far as he knew it. He had not, it seemed, known her very well as they had met only the preceding year, in the department store where she worked.

Ackermann, who described himself as an independent builder, said that Erika was originally German, born in Biberach, a village thirty miles to the north of the Swiss border. For reasons which he did not know, she had to flee Germany during the war and spent part of her childhood in Switzerland.

Following the end of the war, she returned to Germany where she married and subsequently divorced, before returning to Switzerland and finding work in the department store in Lucerne. He did not know her ex-husband's name or address.

Ackermann had also been married, but divorced four year earlier. His ex-wife retained custody of their two daughters.

There was nothing in this rather prosaic account to

explain why anyone might have wanted to murder Erika Ackermann, but it was obvious that there was much in her past history that Ackermann had not told the police and, perhaps, did not know himself.

'It's hardly probable that they would have managed to get on such bad terms within three months of marriage that he would try to murder her,' said the inspector, 'so, unless there's money involved, I think we can exclude Ackermann as a suspect. Check with that friend he's supposed to have visited anyway, just to be on the safe side.'

Ackermann had not mentioned his friend's name and, when the sergeant went to ask him, he returned with the rather intriguing news that the friend was female.

'Cornelia Riffel,' reported the sergeant. 'Thirty-four years old. Divorced. Lives in Stans. Very attractive. Swears Ackermann was with her from eleven-thirty to four in the morning.'

Stans was another small community on the lake to the south of Lucerne.

'Oh-oh!' said the inspector. 'This is beginning to look bad! How does Ackermann explain this fortunate visit just at the time his wife was being burned to a crisp?'

'He says Miss Riffel is his mistress,' said the sergeant.

The inspector's initial reaction was to have Ackermann arrested and charge him with suspicion of attempted homicide.

On second thoughts, however, it occurred to him that the man had a sustainable alibi and that there was nothing to support the charge. If Cornelia Riffel stuck to her story, it would not be possible to obtain an indictment.

'The whole thing's becoming weird,' he said. 'Take as many men as you need and get me a detailed run-down on all these people. Ackermann must be a freak of some kind. Married less than three months and already a mistress? There has to be money in this somewhere.'

Astonishingly, it turned out that René Ackermann had had his mistress longer than his wife. He and Cornelia had been living together since 1976, years before he even met Erika.

In fact, their affair had been the grounds for both his and Cornelia's divorces.

'Which explains why he's so open about it,' said the sergeant. 'It's all here in the divorce-court records.'

According to these, Cornelia Riffel was no less eccentric in her marital arrangements than her lover. Born in the town of Romanshorn on Lake Constance, she married a widower of fifty-four at the age of twenty-one, and not even for money as the widower had none.

The marriage was, apparently, happy, and the couple lived a quiet, almost secluded life up until the death of Cornelia's father, when she came into a substantial inheritance.

She used some of the money to build the two-family house in Stans, where she still lived, and she acquired a horse and a boat.

As she knew nothing about boats, she took sailing lessons from René Ackermann, who had previously bought a boat with money inherited from his father.

The lessons were extended to include matters having little to do with boats, and the lovers rented a secret love-nest in Kriens.

Unfortunately, it was not secret enough, and the affair came to the attention of their respective spouses, who promptly filed for divorce. René's children remained with their mother and Cornelia was awarded custody of her six-year-old son.

After a short stint as a nanny for a doctor in Lucerne, Cornelia took a job at an aircraft factory in Stans, where she remained for several years. At the moment, she and René were managing a restaurant at the sports field of the football club in Buochs, another town on the lake, where Ackermann was born.

Ackermann, very much of a good-time Charlie, was popular in Buochs. A man who never missed an opportunity to celebrate anything and everything, he was famous for standing drinks all round, regardless of how many were present. Although only modestly talented musically, he played the cornet in the Buochs marching society and band and the trumpet in the Buochs nine-man dance orchestra, and he was a much appreciated goalkeeper for the Buochs Seniors Soccer Club.

Ackermann's father had been the owner of a small building firm, and René started out in the construction business, but quickly switched to insurance salesman, to sales representative for a scaffolding company, to fore-man in a flooring factory and finally to manager of the restaurant at the Buochs sport centre.

René and Cornelia, although not married, were prominent socially and thought to be wealthy as they owned jointly two motor boats, five luxury cars and property in Lucerne, Stans, Buochs and Kriens.

'That must have been some inheritance,' remarked the sergeant. 'They have a life style like a Greek shipowner.'

'And similar domestic arrangements,' said the inspector. 'The man's actions don't make sense. He's been living with Miss Riffel openly for years. They're associated in a dozen projects. And they've been going around socially as a couple even after his marriage. So why did he want to marry somebody else?'

'It wasn't for money,' said the sergeant. 'I've looked into Mrs Ackermann's background. She didn't have any. Her job at the department store in Lucerne was her sole source of income.'

'Then it was insurance,' decided the inspector. 'There has to be an angle of some kind.'

It was, it seemed, insurance. Erika Ackermann, who had already had a life-insurance policy for the equivalent of thirty thousand pounds in Germany at the time of her marriage, had taken out a policy for another sixty thousand immediately after the wedding. Both listed René Ackermann as sole beneficiary.

Ackermann, however, remained out of reach of the police. Cornelia had sworn in her statement that he had been with her in the flat in Stans at midnight on 12 May, which would have made it physically impossible for him to have been outside Seelisberg at the time of the accident.

'Which means one of two things,' said the inspector. 'Either there was an accomplice or Miss Riffel is perjuring herself.'

The possibility that it really had been an accident had never been seriously entertained. The hospital had confirmed that Erika Ackermann had been liberally doused with petrol, and no petrol container had been found in the remains of the burned-out car, which had been brought to the police garage in Lucerne for examination by police experts.

Their conclusions were that not only Mrs Ackermann but the entire interior of the car had been drenched in petrol, and that the car had been pushed rather than driven off the road as the ignition key had been turned off.

For the inspector, the case was completely clear. René Ackermann or an accomplice had poured petrol over his wife and the interior of her car, set fire to it and pushed it off the road with her at the wheel. The motive was the insurance.

'Undoubtedly married her for that specific reason,' he said. 'You say he's in a bad financial situation?'

'Catastrophic,' said the police accountant who had been delving into the finances of René Ackermann and Cornelia Riffel. 'Bankruptcy within weeks. They've both been spending money like politicians.'

There was a chance that René and Cornelia might yet escape bankruptcy, for the police had still not been able to assemble enough evidence to bring a charge when, on 19 May, Erika died and the insurance policies came due. She had never fully recovered consciousness and the only word she had ever uttered was her husband's name.

'She was probably trying to say he did it,' said the inspector glumly, 'but defence counsel would say that she was just calling for her beloved husband.'

The inspector had reason to be glum. Although he was morally certain that René Ackermann had murdered his wife in the most cruel manner imaginable, he was beginning to despair that he would ever be able to prove it.

The three main obstacles which he had not been able to surmount were Cornelia's sworn statement placing René elsewhere at the time of the murder, the failure of the police to identify an accomplice and the lack of any explanation of why Erika had remained sitting docilely in the car while her husband poured petrol over her, set her on fire and pushed the car off the road.

'She definitely went down the slope in the car,' said the specialist from the police laboratory who had been in charge of the investigations at the scene. 'She was burning so fiercely that she left a trail of charred clothing and skin from the car up to the road.'

'Couldn't the car have been set on fire after it went down the slope?' asked the inspector. 'Ackermann had a fresh burn on the back of his right hand which he claimed he got putting a dish in the oven.'

'It was set on fire up on the road,' said the specialist. 'The way it was tipped on the slope, there would have been more damage to the rear of the car than to the front, and that wasn't the case. It went down burning.'

'And you have no suggestion as to why she remained in the car and let herself be set on fire?'

'Nothing other than a half-empty bottle of sleeping pills in the glove compartment, which was in the original report,' replied the specialist, 'but I understand the medical opinion was that they weren't strong enough for a half-bottle to put her under.'

'Not prescription,' said the inspector, 'and, anyway, why would she have taken sleeping pills before driving?'

The specialist shrugged.

'Maybe the restaurant is only a short distance from their home,' he suggested. 'Where was this restaurant anyway?'

The inspector was embarrassed. He did not, in fact, know where the Ackermanns had dined that evening. It was one of the minor oversights that could crop up in the course of any investigation. No one had thought to check.

A review of Ackermann's statements showed that he had not mentioned the name of the restaurant, but also that he had not been asked.

He was asked now, and named an expensive restaurant in Lucerne. Although it was feared that, considering the length of time, no one would remember who had dined there on that evening, the sergeant hurried to the restaurant. There he found a waiter who remembered Erika and René Ackermann's dinner on the evening of 12 May very well. Ackermann was a regular at the restaurant and he was a heavy tipper.

Mrs Ackermann, said the waiter, had drunk rather too much and complained of a headache. Her husband ordered a glass of water and gave her some pills from a bottle. The waiter thought it a very large dose.

They left the restaurant shortly after eleven and drove off in an Austin Mini with René at the wheel. Mrs Ackermann appeared to be decidedly groggy.

'The time fits,' said the sergeant. 'If they went directly from the restaurant to the scene of the accident, they would have arrived at a little before midnight.'

'Something else doesn't fit,' said the inspector. 'Ackermann said his wife went off to Kriens and he went to his mistress in Stans, but Kriens is on the way to Stans, so he would have had to be in his own car and, anyway, Seelisberg is beyond both places. I think there's enough evidence of falsehood in his statement now for us to bring formal charges.'

It was still not going to be easy.

Brought to police headquarters in Altdorf and charged with the murder of his wife, Ackermann had a ready explanation for the discrepancies in his statement.

'I was driving the BMW,' he said, 'but I couldn't find a parking space in front of the restaurant so I parked in the car park down the street and we took Erika's car from there. When we left, I drove her back to the car park and got my own car.'

It was, like all his statements, a perfectly plausible explanation, but René Ackermann had just made his first serious mistake.

For the inspector believed him. He believed that Ackermann or someone had been driving the BMW that evening. There would have been too great a possibility of the police determining that the car had not been in the car park for him to lie about it.

And, if he had been driving the car on the night of the murder, perhaps there was still something in it to connect him to the crime.

The BMW was consequently brought to the police garage and two extremely important clues were found in it.

One was an empty five-gallon reserve cannister for petrol.

The other was a pair of men's gloves. The right-hand one was badly burned on the back.

Although Ackermann denied that the gloves were his, they fitted him perfectly and, when the right glove was placed on his hand, the hole burned in the back matched precisely the scar of the burn that he claimed to have received putting a dish in the oven.

Even then, Ackermann did not give up. He now admitted that the gloves were his, but said he had been wearing them to put the dish in the oven.

The glove was so badly burned, however, that he would have had to hold his hand under the grill for some time, and he was indicted on a charge of wilful homicide.

Cornelia Riffel, who continued to swear to Ackermann's alibi, was indicted on a charge of acting as an accomplice to homicide.

At the trial in the spring of 1985, the prosecution charged that, having drugged his wife with a combination of wine and sleeping pills, Ackermann had strapped her into the driver's seat of her car, drenched her with petrol and pushed the burning vehicle off the road. He had then been picked up by Cornelia Riffel in his BMW.

Both defendants pleaded not guilty and René Ackermann never did confess to anything.

Cornelia eventually broke down and admitted to having picked René up on the road outside Seelisburg, but denied all knowledge of the murder.

The jury believed neither her nor him and, on 10 May 1985, sentenced René to life imprisonment and Cornelia to seventeen years.

6

EXTENDED FAMILY

This is the true story of the very short life and very hard times of a little boy who died an appalling death over twenty years ago.

His name was Andreas Neumann and he was not born in some backward, third-world country, but in one of the most highly civilized and socially conscious countries in Europe, West Germany.

There are, of course, backward areas even in West Germany. The isolated little villages buried deep in the Black Forest. The lonely farms lost in the great moors of the Lueneburger Heide. The empty coastal plains of Ostfriesland. In such places strange things sometimes happen. Murders for which no man knows the motive. Women stoned and burned as witches. Human sacrifices . . .

Andreas, however, lived out his short life in a rich and densely populated area of West Germany, the fertile plains east of the Upper Rhine.

To the north, the east and the south lie the teeming cities of the Ruhr, the mightiest concentration of industry in Europe. To the west is ultra-modern Duesseldorf, a consumer's paradise of three-quarters of a million inhabitants, high among the wealthiest communities in the country.

So Andreas starved to death, not quickly, but slowly, and with the tantalizing aroma of warm food in his nostrils and the sight of a full plate inches from his eyes.

Andreas could not, however, eat the food, although no one restrained him from it.

What restrained him was his own body. Andreas was born handicapped. How severely handicapped is no longer possible to determine, but, according to some medical opinion, probably not so severely handicapped that therapy and training could not have enabled him to live a near normal life.

It is certain that he knew what the food was and wanted it, for, until he had lost so much of his body fluid that there was no saliva left in his mouth, he drooled and made whimpering, pleading noises.

Andreas never learned to speak properly and he could not, at the age of three, walk, but these things were not fatal. That he was incapable of grasping a spoon or fork was.

Andreas had two brothers and two sisters, Karl-Detlef, who was seven, Dagmar, who was six, Olaf, who was four, and Michaela, who was two. They were not too handicapped to feed themselves.

At each mealtime, Andreas's mother, Hermine, set out five plates for the children and one for herself. Husband Carl-Heinz, a long-distance lorry driver, was rarely at home.

Each child was given his or her portion of food, and this included Andreas, but, whereas the other children could and did feed themselves, Andreas could not.

When the meal was ended, Hermine took away the plates, all empty except Andreas's, which she emptied into the rubbish pail.

Slow starvation is a cruel enough death for a child, but starvation with a full plate of food and in the presence of five others eating to their heart's content is a torment which the world's many professional torturers would find hard to match. The smell of the warm food, the sounds and sight of the brothers and sisters eating, must have resulted in some of the most hideous suffering ever inflicted on a child.

Why did Andreas's mother do this and why did the father permit it?

Hermine would later say that it was because her husband did not give her enough money to feed the family.

But she admitted that she had emptied Andreas's full plate into the rubbish pail after every meal.

Hermine said that her husband drank and beat her.

But he actually drank rather less than many of the men in his social class and, according to her children, he beat he scarcely at all.

Hermine complained that Andreas had stunk abominably.

But if he stank, it was because his mother did not wash him.

Carl-Heins made fewer excuses. It had taken all his time to support such a large family, he said. Caring for the children had been Hermine's responsibility.

It was a responsibility which she apparently enjoyed, for she continued to have children. Christian, Astrid, Reinhild, Randolf . . . In the end, there were eight. Although she had borne nine, one was missing. Andreas.

Andreas Neumann was born on 23 May 1962 and he died on 22 February 1965. The date was easy to remember. It was his father's thirty-second birthday. There was a cake.

Andreas did not quite make it to his third birthday, but there would have been no birthday cake even if he had. There had been none for his first and second birthdays, but that hardly mattered as he would not have been able to eat it anyway.

His parents did not bother to put him into a box or even wrap him in a blanket, but simply carried him out into the garden, dug a hole less than a yard deep and, having dropped him into it, filled up the hole with earth and trampled it down firmly.

Andreas had taken quite a long time in dying and his body was as dried out and brittle as a stick. Most of his ribs and some of his other bones were broken in the process. Carl-Heinz and Hermine were heavy people and there is little strength in the bones of a child who has died of malnutrition.

From her kitchen window, Hermine could gaze upon her son's grave while she was preparing dinner. Presumably, it was not a very attractive sight. In February, the depth of winter, the trees and bushes were bare. An icy wind whined through them, and the low-hanging, leaden clouds racing inland from Holland gave promise of snow.

It was warm in the house though, and fortunately the ground had not been frozen too hard for digging. Indeed, the exercise had stimulated the appetite.

Physically, Andreas was gone, but administratively he lived on. On the first of every month, Hermine collected a hundred Deutschmarks for his support from the social welfare service.

West Germany is a country with a negative birth rate. It has been estimated that, with no increase in the number of births, by the year 2500 or so, there will not be enough Germans left to field a hockey team.

There is disagreement over the reasons for this. Usually, the materialistic society is blamed. A man alone can no longer support a family. Married women are forced to work to maintain the approved level of family affluence. Children cost money, and many couples find a second car or a swimming pool a better investment.

Unfortunately, this applies mainly to the wealthier and better-educated sectors of the population. Among those who have little hope of acquiring a second car or a swimming pool, producing children is simply an easy way of making a living.

For them, children are profitable because the West German government, faced with a future without taxpayers, does everything in its power to encourage reproduction. The parents of each child receive an allowance for as long as the child is a minor, and the more children, the higher the allowances. Hermine Neumann, with nine children on the books, scarcely needed her husband's salary.

Of course, the Kindergeld (child money) is not pure profit. The children have to be fed and clothed.

If they are alive. Andreas was not, and what he

brought in was net. Over the years, his parents would collect 17,780 Deutschmarks or slightly more than four thousand pounds, taking the average exchange rate.

Obviously, the Neumanns were on to a very good thing and, had they been motivated solely by profit, they could have done away with the rest of their children and prospered greatly.

In fact, money appears to have played only a secondary role. Andreas was allowed to starve simply because it was too much trouble to take care of him, and they could not stop drawing his allowance from the social welfare because they would have had to report his death.

West Germany is, however, a country in which everything is precisely and minutely reported and recorded. If Andreas was dead, there had to be a death certificate, a registration of burial, confirmation that he had been removed from the rolls of the local community administration, and many other formalities. As it was impossible to obtain any of these necessary papers, Andreas lived on.

Having reached the age of six, his parents were legally required to enrol him in school, and this could have presented a problem, had he not, fortunately, been certified mentally and physically handicapped at an early age by an official from the Health Department.

Hermine was therefore able to present the certificate showing that Andreas was in no condition to attend school, as, indeed, he was not, although not for the reasons stated.

For the next twelve years, Andreas continued his career of disembodied welfare recipient until, having reached the hypothetical age of eighteen, it was time for him to report for his military service.

When he failed to do so, a civil servant from the Department of Defence came round to find out why.

Hermine was embarrassed. She did not dare produce Andreas's certificate of mental and physical disability as the civil servant might ask to see him.

She therefore branded him an ungrateful son and a runaway.

'We were never able to keep track of him,' she said sadly. 'He was always running away. Somebody said he was in the DDR.'

So the official wrote, 'Fled to East Zone' on the draft notice, and Andreas was now not only handicapped physically and mentally, but out of the country as well.

However, having reached the age of eighteen, according to his birth certificate, the Kindergelt from the government automatically ceased.

The Neumanns were in the clear. Their phantom little boy was duly registered with all of the various departments of the government necessary, and no one would come looking for him.

It was a perfect murder, which is not such an uncommon occurrence as might be thought. There is reason to believe that a great many murders are never recognized as such by anyone.

Except, of course, the murderer or murderess.

Andreas's brothers and sisters did not know that he had been murdered. Four of them were born after his death. The other four had been young at the time. The two oldest knew that he was dead, but they thought he had died of natural causes because he did not eat. They did not know where he was buried.

The neighbours, of which there were not a few in this heavily populated area, had noticed nothing. In a family the size of the Neumann's, it was hardly possible for the parents to keep track of the children, let alone outsiders.

Time passed. The house which the Neumann's had rented, an old, half-timbered and picturesque but rotting ruin, was torn down and the garden became part of a cow pasture. The family moved on to different, but only marginally better, housing.

By the beginning of 1985, Dagmar, the second oldest of the children, had reached the age of thirty-one and was, regrettably, still single, although there had been one or two near misses.

Suitable males in their late thirties and early forties being rare, she had been on the verge of despair when, rather miraculously, Arthur Schmiedt appeared on the scene.

Arthur was a trifle young. He was only thirty, but he was serious, a moderate drinker and even quite handsome, with a fine drooping blond moustache. A crane operator, he was in a position to support a wife, and he liked Dagmar.

He was, consequently, warmly welcomed into the Neumann household, where he was soon going in and out as if he had lived there all his life. He came to know well Dagmar's mother, her brothers and sisters, her father, although he was seldom home, and the family dog.

After dinner, he was often regaled with pictures from the family album, some of which were rather daring shots of Dagmar at a tender age, and, by a stroke of bad luck, someone took it into their head to show him the Neumann family book.

Like all German families, the Neumann's had a family book in which were registered all important events in the family such as births, deaths, marriages and outstanding achievements by its members.

'Curious,' said Arthur to Dagmar. 'There are nine children entered in your family book, but I have met only eight. One appears to be missing.'

'Oh, that was Andreas,' said Dagmar carelessly. 'He died and I guess Pa and Ma buried him.'

'Pa and Ma?' said Arthur.

Private interments are verboten in West Germany.

'It was a long time ago,' said Dagmar. 'I don't know the circumstances. Nobody ever talked about it.'

Obviously, she did not consider the demise and unorthodox burial of her little brother a matter of importance.

Astonishingly, Arthur Schmiedt did.

If there is one universal rule of conduct in modern civilized societies, it is: Don't get involved.

It was none of Arthur Schmiedt's business what had

happened to the Neumann's fifth child or how he had been buried. He did not know that the child had starved to death. He did not even know when he had died, only that, according to Dagmar, it was a long time ago.

None the less, in a sort of throwback to the moral values of a less enlightened age, or, perhaps, merely because of a Germanic distaste for deviations from regulations, Arthur felt himself impelled to do something.

He mulled the matter over for several days and then went to the Duesseldorf police.

'I wish to report a missing child,' he said.

'When did the child disappear?' inquired the sergeant on duty in the department of missing persons, reaching for the appropriate form.

'I don't know,' said Arthur. 'A long time ago.'

The sergeant put down his pencil and gazed at him in thoughtful silence. In a city the size of Duesseldorf, there were many people whose contact with reality was none too secure. Arthur did not, however, look as if there was anything very seriously wrong with him.

After a short pause, there followed a rather guarded conversation, during the course of which the sergeant gradually came to the conclusion that Schmiedt was neither mentally disturbed nor under the influence of narcotics, but was actually reporting what he believed to be an illegal burial which had taken place many years earlier.

Although the sergeant had fielded some very far-out reports in his time, this one was outside his experience and, coming to the conclusion that it was also outside his competence, he sent Schmiedt to the department of criminal investigations.

For the duty officer there, the situation was clear. There had been an unreported death and an unauthorized burial of a human being. It was a case for the homicide squad.

As a result, on 5 January 1985, Inspector of Detectives Johann Brecht found himself assigned to the investigation of a case possibly as much as twenty years old.

The inspector was not pleased. An officer-in-charge of Homicide East-Two, he had quite enough current cases to investigate without going back to a period before he had even joined the department of criminal investigations.

He had, however, no choice in the matter so, summoning his assistant, Sergeant of Detectives Peter Baden, he handed him the first information report from the missing persons section and told him to check it out.

The sergeant, an otherwise reasonably handsome young man who had had the ill-advised idea of growing a fringe of beard running from ear to ear but without moustache, did as he was told and presently reported that, according to the records, Andreas Neumann was still alive.

There was, however, an inconsistency in the records. According to the departments of Health and Education, he was too handicapped to attend school. According to the Department of Defence, he had been able-bodied enough to flee to East Germany.

'No,' said the inspector. 'If he was handicapped, the East Germans wouldn't take him. They sell us their handicapped persons, but they don't take any of ours.'

West Germany, for political reasons, at that time paid East Germany large sums for the release of East Germans into the West. This permitted the East Germans to rid themselves of many of their criminals, lunatics and generally undesirables.

'We continue then?' said the sergeant.

'We have to,' said the inspector. 'I can't close the report like this. See what else you can turn up without contacting the family.'

A methodical man with a long, mournful face and a badly receding hairline, he kept, like all successful civil servants, as closely as possible to the regulations.

'We may be wasting our time,' said the sergeant.

'How so?' asked the inspector.

'Statute of limitations,' said the sergeant. 'If the boy's

been dead over twenty years, there'll be nothing we can do about it.'

'Schmiedt doesn't know when he died,' said the inspector. 'You might begin by trying to determine that.'

This was rather a tall order. Over the years, many of the Neumanns' former neighbours had moved or died, and those who had not could recall little about the family other than that they had had a great many children.

With former schoolmates of the Neumann children, the sergeant had more luck. Many of them remembered the family as for many years there had been at least one Neumann in almost every class.

Some even remembered that there had been another Neumann who had been excused from school by reason of mental deficiency.

'According to the birth register, the boy was born on 23 May 1962,' said the sergeant, 'and I've found people who recall seeing him as late as the beginning of 1965. My guess is that he died in January or February of that year.'

'Then it's very close to the statute of limitations,' said the inspector. 'The girl told Schmiedt that the boy was buried somewhere. If we could do it without the Neumann's knowledge, I'd like to dig up their garden.'

'No problem,' said the sergeant. 'They've moved since then and even the house has been demolished.'

'Good,' said the inspector. 'Tell the men to go down about four feet. It won't be much deeper than that.'

It was not that deep. The Neumann's old garden, fortunately, was not large and, after only a modest amount of digging, the investigators brought to light the skeleton of a small child.

For the first time, there was concrete evidence of a crime, although not necessarily of homicide, and the inspector moved quickly to intensify the investigation. There was still no certainty that Andreas had died of anything other than natural causes, but the illegal burial and the evidence that his mother had lied to the school and draft authorities made the matter highly suspect.

The most vital question was, of course, the time of death. It was now 10 January and, if the boy had died before that date in 1965, the statute of limitations had expired. Even if the Neumanns confessed to having drawn and quartered their little boy, there was nothing that could be done about it now.

The skeleton was turned over to Dr Friedrich Krause, a forensic bone specialist, for urgent determination of the date and, if possible, cause of death.

The doctor spent twelve hours in the examination of the skeleton and reported that the exact cause of death could not be established, but that there were indications of extreme malnutrition. Many of the bones were broken, but he thought this to have taken place after death and to be the result of the rough burial.

'The time of death,' stated the doctor, 'was between 15 January and 20 February of 1965 with a potential error of twenty percent.'

'We'll ignore the potential error and try for 15 January,' said the inspector. 'Arrest the whole family and begin interrogation.'

The entire Neumann family was taken into custody, but Christian, Astrid, Reinhild and Randolf were immediately released. Christian had been a baby at the time of Andreas's disappearance and the others had not even been born.

The older children were also eventually released. Karl-Detlef and Dagmar remembered Andreas, but they did not know what had happened to him. He had simply disappeared one day, but, by a stroke of luck, they both recalled that it had been their father's birthday.

'Which makes it 22 February,' said the sergeant to the inspector, 'so we have over a month yet before the statute of limitations expires.'

'That may not be enough,' said the inspector. 'We've no evidence that the child was murdered and he was officially certified handicapped. The death could have been due to natural causes.'

'And we've no way of proving that it wasn't,' said the sergeant. 'Is there anything we can do?'

'Not unless they confess,' said the inspector. 'We'll charge them now with illegal burial, obtaining child allowance money under false pretences and making false statements to the school and draft authorities. That may shake an admission out of one of them.'

Indeed, it did. First Carl-Heinz and then Hermine broke under interrogation. They became more and more confused and contradictory in their statements and ended by confessing to the murder of their son.

'It wasn't my fault,' said Carl-Heinz. 'Hermine was supposed to feed the kids. I wasn't even there most of the time.'

'It wasn't my fault,' said Hermine. 'I gave him food, just like the others.'

'But you knew he wasn't able to feed himself,' the inspector pointed out. 'Who fed him up until that time? He didn't just suddenly lose the ability to feed himself.'

'I did,' said Hermine, 'but he was nearly three years old. It was time he learned to feed himself.'

'How long was it from the time you stopped feeding him until he died?' asked the inspector, who needed to establish intent or lack of it.

'Two weeks . . . three weeks,' said Hermine vaguely. 'I don't remember.'

'Then you must have been giving him water,' insisted the inspector. 'The child could not have lived more than a few days without water.'

'Oh, I did,' said Hermine. 'He could drink out of a bowl.'

'On the table?' asked the inspector.

'On the floor,' said Hermine.

'But you knew that he would die if you didn't feed him,' said the inspector. 'You deliberately deprived your child of food until he died.'

'I didn't deprive him,' Hermine argued. 'I gave him food. If he didn't eat it, it wasn't my fault.'

Although neither Hermine nor Carl-Heinz appeared

to regret their act or even to be aware that what they had done was wrong, the psychologists who kept them under observation while in detention reported that they were competent to stand trial. They were not insane. They had merely had many children and they regarded one more or one less as a matter of little importance.

Neither was, however, sufficiently shrewd to maintain that Andreas had died of natural causes, a claim which would have been impossible to disprove.

They did deny any physical mistreatment, and the charges on which they were eventually tried were gross negligence resulting in the death of a dependent minor.

The court, apparently unmoved by the vision of a little boy slowly starving to death with a full plate of food in front of him while the others ate, were more compassionate with the Neumanns than the Neumanns had been with their son and, on 11 September 1987, sentenced them to three and a half years' imprisonment each. The length of time they can expect actually to serve will be shorter than Andreas's entire life.

On the subject of the child allowance money which the Neumann's had illegally received, the court was stern. They were sentenced to repay every pfennig of it with interest.

7

FAMILY VISIT

At one o'clock in the afternoon of 9 September 1982, Roger Duc telephoned the gendarmerie post at La-Côte-Saint-André.

'I'm concerned about my parents,' he said. 'I've been trying to reach them since yesterday and they're not answering the telephone.'

The officer manning the switchboard asked for details and was told that Eugène and Thérèse Duc lived on a farm at Millières, a hamlet near La-Côte-Saint-André. Eugène was seventy-four, his wife ten years younger. Both were in good health, as far as Roger knew. He himself lived in Grenoble, the winter sports centre in the French Alps, thirty miles to the southeast.

The switchboard officer took Duc's telephone number and said that someone would be sent to his parents' farm to check up on them. It was a routine job. The little farming villages of France are filled with old people whose children have grown up and gone to the cities. If the children are unable to contact their parents, they call on the gendarmerie for help.

Although routine, the matter was taken seriously. Old people could be ill or suffer accidents.

Or they could be dead. Fifteen minutes after the gendarmes arrived in Millières they reported over the radio-telephone that they were at the scene of a double homicide. They had found Eugène and Thérèse Duc lying bound, gagged and dead in their own cellar.

Tragically, this too was almost routine. France is also full of mostly very young people who have expensive addictions to finance or who wish to live on a grand scale with the money of others. Old people, living isolated and alone, are one of the easiest sources to get it.

This often leads to situations of the purest horror. Some old people refuse stubbornly to reveal where their savings are hidden, with the result that they are tortured barbarously.

In other and worse cases, they have no savings or, exceptional for France, they have placed them in a bank. They are then tortured to death in the belief that they are merely more stubborn than most.

Strangely, the Ducs had not been tortured. Both had suffered severe head injuries and both had been so savagely gagged that the corners of their mouths were split, but there were no signs of burns, cuts or even beating on the bodies.

'The cause of death seems to have been asphyxiation in both cases,' said Dr Yves Dunoyer, the dark, slender, rather boyish-looking gendarmerie medical officer. 'The gags were forced into their mouths so violently that they choked on them. Both, however, suffered multiple skull fractures which would ultimately have proved fatal as well.'

'Can you give me an estimate of the time of death?' said Lieutenant Gérard Pauly, chief of the La-Côte-Saint-André gendarmerie homicide section.

He was a comparatively young man, short but muscular, and broad in the shoulder. His black hair was cut close and he carried himself very straight in a military manner.

'Saturday evening,' said the doctor. 'I'll be able to determine the time more exactly when I've finished with the autopsies.'

It was now past noon on Monday, which meant that the Ducs had been dead for close to forty-eight hours.

'No point in beginning an immediate search then,' remarked the inspector. 'They've had plenty of time to clear out of the area.'

'They?' said Sergeant Claude Brousseaux, the lieutenant's second-in-command. 'You think it was more than one?'

The slim, blond, tousle-headed sergeant, who was making a valiant effort to grow his first moustache, had graduated from the gendarmerie criminal investigations training centre only three months earlier and this was his first homicide case.

'Probably,' said the lieutenant. 'These old farmers are tough, the women as much as the men, and I doubt that a single person could have overpowered them. See if the technical people are finding anything.'

The specialists, who had been going over the house and, indeed, nearly the entire farm, had found something of significance to the investigation in the laundry room.

It was a section of tree branch ninety inches long and as thick as a man's forearm. The club was liberally stained with black dried blood in which a number of white hairs were sticking.

'Picked up in the woods on their way here,' said the lieutenant. 'Evidence of premeditation. Will you be able to lift any prints off it?'

The specialist shrugged.

'We'll try when we get it back to the lab,' he said. 'The bark is pretty soft and rotten.'

'And otherwise?' asked the lieutenant.

'Blood stains and hair on the tiles at the foot of the stairs,' said the technician. 'The head of one, maybe both, of the victims had been pounded on the floor. The scarves with which they were gagged appear to have been theirs. No indications that the murderers brought anything with them other than the tree branch.'

'And what did they take?' asked the sergeant.

'Whatever money they found,' said the specialist. 'There's none here now. No way of estimating how much.'

'They had to hunt for it?' said the lieutenant shrewdly.

'No,' replied the specialist. 'They knew where it was.'

'But that would mean . . . !' exclaimed the sergeant.

'Right,' said the lieutenant. 'It was probably some-body who knew them well, possibly family.'

'Good God!' muttered the sergeant.

He knew from his training that much violent crime took place between people known to each other or even related, but he was still shocked. Such things happened in big cities like Paris or Marseille or even Lyon, but not in the peaceful country around Grenoble.

The lieutenant knew better. He had handled more than one such case in his district. Old people were one of the highest-risk groups in France, preceded only by prostitutes and cab drivers.

That the Ducs had been murdered by members of their own family would, however, only become probable if it turned out that they were more wealthy than they seemed. Murders of old people by relatives are nearly always in connection with an inheritance, and they are comparatively easy to solve as the motive led to the murderer.

Murders involving people well known to each other but not related are more difficult. Motives in such cases are often obscure and may go back to some real or imagined injury which took place years earlier.

'We'll divide the investigation, Claude,' said the lieutenant. 'You work up a list of relatives and I'll see what local gossip there is about feuds in the village involving the Ducs. You'd probably better begin by getting the accountant to run a check on their finances. If they didn't have anything, the relatives are poor suspects. I'd appreciate the laboratory and autopsy reports as soon as convenient.'

The last remark was directed at the doctor and the specialist, both of whom nodded in understanding. The lieutenant was a thorough, methodical investigator. The actual investigation would not begin until he had had an opportunity to study all the available data.

The laboratory report was handed in first, as it did not contain much information. It had been possible to determine that the Ducs had had dinner guests for their last meal as there were unwashed dishes for four in the kitchen sink.

Whether these dinner guests were the murderers was doubtful, for a threatening letter had been found between the pages of Thérèse's Bible. It was neither signed nor dated and read, 'You, the fat sow. You'd better send us a cheque. If you don't, you're going to catch it. A farm burns good. Your animals will make a nice barbecue.'

Someone had clearly been trying to extort money from the Ducs and it seemed unlikely that it had been a relative or even a close acquaintance, for either would have known that the couple's sole income was an old-age pension amounting to less than a hundred and fifty pounds a month.

However, the demand for a cheque did show that the extortionist knew the Ducs had a current account with a Grenoble bank, although the balance was trifling.

The chequebook was one of the things that had been stolen and the bank reported that, although no cheques had been paid out prior to the Duc's murders, no less than a dozen had been issued immediately afterwards. The signatures had been carefully forged and the total amount was in excess of two thousand pounds.

All the cheques had been cashed in hotels and restaurants in and around Grenoble, and the sergeant, who had now completed his list of friends and relatives, went off to collect descriptions.

In the meantime, the autopsy report had been handed in. The difference in the times of death was too small to determine who had died first. Both had been strangled by the gags forced nearly a foot into their throats. Both had suffered multiple skull fractures. Both had died within half an hour of eating dinner. The time had been approximately nine-thirty in the evening of Saturday.

'There are a number of mysteries here,' said the lieutenant. 'If the two people who dined with the Ducs on Saturday evening were not the murderers, why don't they come forward? We've canvassed the whole village and no one admits to having even seen the Ducs on that day. Secondly, if the murderers knew the Ducs so well that they knew where they kept their chequebook and savings, how is it that they didn't know there was no money in the account?'

'They didn't care,' suggested the sergeant. 'As long as they got the money, it didn't matter if the cheques weren't covered.'

'That must have been it,' said the lieutenant. 'None of the relatives are plausible suspects. The older ones didn't stand to inherit even what little there was, and the sons were better off financially than their parents.'

The Ducs had three sons, Roger, forty-eight, Marius, forty, and Lucien, twenty-nine. All were married, Lucien only since June of that year. He and his bride, twenty-two-year-old Christine Jacquin, lived in Saint Marcellin, twenty miles south of Grenoble. The two older brothers lived in Grenoble.

'Isn't it possible that the murderers didn't know the Ducs at all and simply tortured the location of the chequebook and what cash they had out of them?' suggested the sergeant.

'Then who wrote the letter and who had dinner with them?' said the lieutenant. 'We end up with more coincidences than we can accept in a criminal investigation.'

The captain in charge of the La-Côte-Saint-André gendarmerie post, who had summoned the lieutenant to his office to explain why there had not been more progress in the case, agreed.

'The evidence is contradictory,' he said. 'If the people didn't know the Ducs, why did they pick on them to send extortion letters? There are dozens of poor farmers living around Millières who would do as well. And the people who came to dinner must be mixed up in this. Farmers like the Ducs don't invite just anybody to dinner. They were either relatives or such close friends that they were practically members of the family.'

'There's reason to believe they intended to stay the

night,' murmured the lieutenant unhappily. 'The bed was made up and turned down in the spare bedroom.'

The captain was not finished.

'Somebody was sending the Ducs threatening letters,' he said, 'trying to extort money that they didn't have out of them. Why didn't they report it to the police? Or, if they didn't want to do that, why didn't they tell their sons?'

The lieutenant was unable to answer any of these questions and, having spent a very uncomfortable half-hour, returned to his office, where the sergeant greeted him with the information that he had developed a new theory of the case.

'The murderers were insane,' he said. 'They were dangerous psychopaths and the Ducs knew it. They'd been threatening them so they invited them to dinner in the hope that they could convince them how poor they were, but the psychopaths ate the dinner and murdered them anyway.'

The lieutenant gazed at him silently for several minutes and then got up and went home without a word. He was afraid that, if he said anything now, he would later regret it.

The following morning, the sergeant made no further mention of his new theory of the crime and contented himself with a report on his investigation of the hotels and restaurants where the cheques had been cashed.

They had been big places doing a lot of business and the descriptions were sketchy. A young couple. The girl was pretty.

'Anyone like that among the relatives?' asked the lieutenant. 'There are no couples that you'd call young in the village.'

'The youngest son and his wife,' said the sergeant. 'All the others are older.'

'Is the wife pretty?' said the lieutenant. 'People tend to remember pretty women.'

'Not bad,' admitted the sergeant. 'Sort of frail. It's

hard to imagine her beating her in-laws over the head with a club.'

'Lucien pretty hefty?' persisted the lieutenant.

'A wreck,' said the sergeant. 'He looks as if it took all his strength to lift a glass.'

'Which is pretty often, I take it,' surmised the lieutenant. 'Run me up a background on him and his wife. Finances. How he makes his living. Why they're living in Saint Marcellin. Whether they're on drugs. Have you checked for police records?'

'Not yet,' said the sergeant.

'Do it,' ordered the lieutenant, 'and see what you can do about establishing the whereabouts of all three sons on the night of the seventh.'

'You consider them suspects?' said the sergeant in surprise. 'They knew the parents didn't have any money.'

'They're all we have,' said the lieutenant, 'but make certain they don't realize they're being investigated. We don't want their lawyers on our backs.'

The sergeant began by requesting assistance from the Grenoble police in tracing the whereabouts and activities of Roger and Marius, while he went to Saint Marcellin to see what he could learn about Lucien.

The result was the removal of Roger and Marius from the list of even possible suspects. Both were respectable, hard-working fathers of families. Roger was a skilled construction worker. Marius drove a lorry. Neither had any serious financial problems and both had occasionally helped out their parents.

On the evening of 7 September, Roger and his wife had entertained friends at their home. It would have been physically impossible for him to murder his parents.

Marius was not quite as clear. He had been making a late run with his lorry on that Saturday and it would have been just possible for him to race in his car to Millières, murder his parents and race back in time to return his lorry. This was, however, so improbable that he too was removed from the list of possible suspects.

There remained Lucien, but, although Saint Marcellin was so small that it had neither a policeman nor a gendarmerie post, the sergeant found that no one there knew anything about him. He had only moved into the somewhat dilapidated cottage at 1 rue Jean-Baillet at the beginning of June and had had almost no contact with the other members of the community, most of whom were older people.

On the subject of Christine Jacquin, there was, however, a wealth of information, much of it in the records of the social welfare department.

Born on 3 May 1963, she had never known the identity of her father and, according to her own statements, neither had her mother.

As her mother had neither the means nor the inclination to care for her daughter, Christine was placed with foster parents, Robert and Agnes Rodet, at the age of eight days.

On 28 June 1965, her mother married René Jacquin, who, although he could not have been Christine's father, acknowledged her as his own.

She lived with the Jacquins until the age of seven, when she was returned to her foster parents at her own request. Jacquin had taken to beating her mother so violently that she was afraid to live in the house.

At the age of sixteen, she was taken away from the Rodets and placed in an institution for orphans and unwanted children. Robert Rodet, she charged, had been molesting her sexually over a period of more than two years.

Whether the sexual contacts had resulted in actual intercourse was not clear and, although Rodet was initially charged with statutory rape of a dependent minor, the charges were subsequently dropped and the case never came to trial.

This unfortunate childhood had had such a disastrous effect on Christine that, by the age of eighteen, it was necessary to transfer her to the psychiatric clinic at Saint Eygreve.

There, she had made substantial progress up until 15 April 1982, when she ran away with Lucien Duc.

As she was now legally an adult and as she had not been committed under court order but at her own request, no effort was made to bring her back.

She and Lucien moved to Saint Marcellin immediately following their marriage on 2 June 1982, in order to eat free at her mother's home, it was said.

The couple had to eat free somewhere, for Lucien was unemployed and Christine had never held a job of any kind.

Lucien had. The youngest of the three brothers, his upbringing was the complete opposite of Christine's. He was the pampered baby of the family, and his parents gave him everything they could afford and more.

Although an indifferent student, he managed to pass his entrance examination for the lycée, the grammar school, but dropped out after two years.

He then found a job as a cutter with a textile firm, where he worked for two years.

Although he was highly regarded by his supervisors, he left and took a job with another textile firm called Gillibert.

He remained only a short time with Gillibert and quit to become an agricultural labourer, but, after a year of this, went back to Gillibert where he subsequently had to leave to avoid being fired for absenteeism.

Lucien also had a police record. On the night of 16 November 1977, he set fire to the farm buildings of one of his former employers and nearly burned the house over their heads. It was only the furious barking of an alert farm dog which brought the family out in time to save themselves and their animals.

Lucien was not suspected as it was over a year since he had worked at the farm and his relations with his employer had been good. Although he had remained there only a little over two months, the farmer had given him an excellent reference.

'Ah-ha!' said the lieutenant when the sergeant reached this point in his report. 'The extortion letter to the Ducs threatened to burn down their farm. Did he also try to extort money out of the farmer?'

'No,' said the sergeant. 'The farmer wouldn't even believe he'd done it until his shoes matched prints in the mud at the farm and he confessed.'

'An act without a motive,' said the lieutenant. 'Is he legally sane?'

The sergeant had already asked the question of Dr Michel Guillomin, the director of the psychiatric clinic at Saint Eygreve. Lucien had been sent there because he could not explain why he had burned down his former employer's farm.

'The psychiatrist says he's sane when he's sober,' said the sergeant. 'He's one of those people who can't tolerate alcohol. Normally, he's just lazy and not much interested in anything, but when he's drunk, he's capable of anything.'

'Including murdering his parents,' said the lieutenant grimly. 'Should make a great defence. He was drunk so he wasn't responsible for his acts.'

'Can we prove it?' asked the sergeant.

'Not without a confession,' said the lieutenant. 'Even if we can show he was in the house, there's no reason for him not to be. He was family.'

'His wife wasn't,' the sergeant pointed out, 'but according to Guillomin, she's a stronger personality than he is and she's probably dominant in the marriage.'

'Let's hope she's not too strong a personality,' said the lieutenant, 'because if we can't get a confession out of him, we'll have to get it out of her. Bring them both in.'

Lucien and Christine Duc were arrested and brought to gendarmerie headquarters in La-Côte-Saint-André, where they denied all knowledge of the murders.

However, although Christine stuck to her story, saying

that her mother would confirm that they had been in Saint Marcellin on Saturday night, Lucien very quickly broke down and confessed to the murders.

'We needed money,' he said, 'and Christine said that was the place to get it. They'd given us five thousand francs [five hundred pounds] for the wedding, but we'd already spent that in restaurants. When I asked them for more, they said they had hardly enough to eat and they couldn't give me any.'

'Christine thought if we wrote them the letter, it would scare them, but Mum just wrote back that if I didn't stop trying to get money out of them, she'd show my letter to Roger and Marius.

'Christine said that if they were going to be unreasonable, we'd have to take it.'

'And you found nothing wrong with that?' said the lieutenant.

'Well, we needed the money and they wouldn't give it to us,' Lucien explained. 'What else could we do?'

'Some would have considered working,' said the lieutenant. 'Continue.'

'I rang Mum up and said we'd like to come for dinner on Saturday,' said Lucien. 'We'd been eating at Christine's mother's all the time, but she isn't much of a cook and she was beginning to complain a lot.

'Mum said it would be all right and, if we wanted, we could stay the night.

'On the way, we picked up a good, strong club in the woods and left it outside the house so they wouldn't see it.

'After dinner, Mum and Dad went up to get the room ready for us and we got the club and waited at the foot of the stairs. We didn't know which one would come down first, but it was Mum.

'I hit her over the head with the club and she fell on the floor, but she wasn't dead and she was groaning so I hit her some more, but she still didn't die.

'Christine brought me the scarf from the hall rack and said to stuff it in her mouth so she'd be quiet.

'We tied her wrists then and dragged her into the laundry room.

'A few minutes later, Dad came down and I hit him with the club. He fell on the floor and I started pounding his head on the tiles.

'I was kneeling on him and he said, "I'm not old yet. I want to live. Don't kill me."

'Christine brought me another scarf and I stuffed it in his mouth. Afterwards, we dragged both of them down to the cellar. They were still moving and trying to say something.

'We only found three hundred francs [thirty pounds] in the house, but we got the chequebook, so that was all right. We never had any trouble cashing the cheques.'

Having listened to a tape recording of her husband's confession, Christine Duc added her own, which was identical in every respect except that she said the murders had been Lucien's idea and she had only gone along because she was afraid of him. She was, she said, four months pregnant, so she would have to be released.

In this she was mistaken. Both she and Lucien remained in detention for over a year, and it was in the police clinic that her baby was born.

Although she had almost certainly been the instigator of the murders, Lucien gallantly swore that she had taken no physical part in them, with the result that she was found guilty only of aiding and abetting homicide. On 16 June 1985 she was sentenced to ten years' imprisonment.

Lucien did not get off too badly either and was sentenced to a mere eighteen years for the brutal murders of his mother and father. The court found his claim to have drunk most of a bottle of brandy that evening an extenuating circumstance.

8

THE CASE OF THE CODED KNOCK

On the evening of 15 October, 1982, fifty-three-year-old Adolf Wachter arrived home at the attic flat that he shared with his mother and, as usual, found the door locked.

As he did not have a key to the flat, he applied his knuckles to the door in a precise series of sharp knocks and pauses.

To his consternation, there was no response from within the flat and, having repeated the series twice, he went downstairs to his car and drove back to the farm where he was employed.

'I'm afraid that Mother may have had a heart attack,' he told farmer Georg Heilmann. 'She isn't answering the door.'

Heilmann immediately followed him in his own car back to the building at 14 Schwarzenbergstrasse in Bamberg, a town of some eighty thousand inhabitants in the southeast corner of West Germany, and together they climbed the stairs to the third floor.

Heilmann began to ring the bell and pound on the door, but Wachter stopped him.

'Mother's afraid of letting strangers in, so we have a special code for knocking,' he said. 'Let me try again. Maybe I got it wrong the first time.'

The coded knocks produced no more response than before.

'We'll have to break it down,' Heilmann decided. 'She may have had an accident.'

'Let me,' said Wachter.

He was a big, enormously powerful man who earned his living sometimes as a furniture mover, sometimes as a lorry driver and sometimes as a farm labourer. Under the impact of his thick-muscled shoulder, the tongue of the lock tore through the wood of the door jamb and the door slammed back against the wall.

Eighty-eight-year-old Maria Wachter lay on the floor of the little entrance hall and it was immediately obvious that there had been neither accident nor heart attack, for the floor was covered with an enormous pool of the blood which was still pouring from gaping wounds in her head and her neck.

The horrified Heilmann stumbled backwards and ran yelling down the stairs in search of help, but it was past eight o'clock of a Friday evening and the street was deserted. It was only when he reached a tavern a street away that he was able to telephone for the ambulance and the police.

Returning to the building, he was amazed to see a police car already standing at the kerb. Wachter, with greater presence of mind, had telephoned from the flat itself and had gone to wait at the front door for the emergency services to arrive.

Although the police officers did not doubt that the woman was dead, regulations required them to search for signs of life and, having found none, they took Heilmann and Wachter into custody and informed the station that they were at the scene of a homicide.

The emergency ambulance had arrived in the meantime, but remained only long enough for the crew to determine that Maria Wachter was beyond help and had, in all probability, been murdered.

There followed a wait of over three-quarters of an hour before the arrival of the homicide squad, some of whose members had not been in the station.

An examination of the corpse was carried out by Dr David Diederich, a pale, aesthetic-looking man with an aquiline nose and fluffy red-gold sideburns down nearly to the corners of his mouth.

'She was killed within the past two hours,' he said. 'Multiple fractures of the skull and the carotid has been severed. You'll have to wait for the autopsy for anything more.'

'Who reported it?' mumbled Inspector Peter Altbauer around the short black cigar lodged permanently in the corner of his mouth. A small but thick-bodied man in his middle fifties, he needed to shave twice a day, but generally did so only once.

'Her son and his employer,' said Detective Sergeant Joachim Hart. 'They're downstairs in the patrol car.'

His appearance contrasted sharply with that of his chief as he was young, rosy-cheeked and looked too healthy to be anything other than utterly depraved. He was, however, as wholesome as he looked.

'I'll see what they have to say,' said the inspector, heading down the stairs on short, surprisingly nimble legs. 'You stay here and see to it that the technical people don't miss anything.'

The sergeant assumed a responsible look and went into the living room, where the police photographer was setting up his camera to take a shot of the hall with the corpse lying in it. Three laboratory technicians in white smocks were going through the drawers of the sideboard and dusting appropriate surfaces for latent fingerprints.

In the patrol car downstairs, the inspector looked briefly at the identity cards which Heilmann and Wachter, like most Germans, carried. He informed them that their statements were being taped and began asking questions.

'How is it you don't have a key to your own flat Mr Wachter?' he asked when the man had concluded his account of the discovery of the murder.

'Mother is . . . Mother was always at home,' said Wachter. 'Didn't need it.'

'You say you had a secret code of knocks,' continued the inspector. 'How many people knew it beside you and your mother?'

'Nobody,' said Wachter.

'Did anyone other than your mother have a key to the flat?' said the inspector.

'Nobody,' repeated Wachter. 'There was only one key.'

'You are under arrest on suspicion of homicide,' said the inspector formally. 'I call upon you to accompany me to police headquarters. You are warned that anything you say will be taken down in writing or recorded on tape and may be used against you. Do you wish to make a statement?'

'Yes,' said Wachter. 'You're crazy. Why would I murder my own mother?'

'I don't know,' said the inspector, 'but, on the basis of your own statements, no one else could have got into the flat.'

The stunned and disbelieving Georg Heilmann was sent home and the inspector took Wachter to police headquarters, where he booked him on suspicion of homicide and turned him over to a team of detectives for interrogation.

He then returned to the flat in Schwarzenbergstrasse, where the technicians had by now largely completed their work and were bringing the body down the stairs in a metal coffin. A police car with the corpse-transporter, a low, closed trailer used mainly for transporting the bodies of victims of car accidents, was waiting at the kerb.

Sergeant Hart was supervising the operations or getting in the way, depending upon the point of view, but the doctor had already left.

'There are signs that the flat was searched,' reported the sergeant. 'No estimate of what was taken. The victim had the key in her hand and they think she'd just opened the door when she was murdered.'

'False clues, probably,' said the inspector. 'According to the son, she'd open the door only to a coded knock and nobody but them knew the code.'

'You mean he confessed?' asked the sergeant. 'Did he say what the motive was?'

'Denies it,' said the inspector, 'but he admits that no one else could have got into the flat. The lab people find any signs of a struggle?'

The sergeant shook his head.

'As far as they can tell, she was knocked down the minute she opened the door,' he said. 'Unless the son is completely insane, I don't see why he'd do that.'

'Nor I,' agreed the inspector, transferring the cigar to the opposite corner of his mouth. 'Nor can I understand why he'd search his own flat unless the whole thing is an elaborate scheme to throw off suspicion. Did they find anything that looks like a murder weapon?'

'Nothing,' said the sergeant. 'He must have disposed of it when he went to get Heilmann.'

'If Diederich can give us some idea of what to look for, we'll search the ditches along the route between the farm and the flat tomorrow,' said the inspector, 'assuming that Wachter doesn't make his confession tonight.'

Wachter did not confess to anything, but, at eleven o'clock the following morning, Dr Diederich included a partial description of the weapons in the preliminary autopsy report.

The victim's skull was fractured in nine places by sixteen extremely violent blows with a hard, smooth, slightly tapering object approximately two inches in diameter. Several small beech splinters were embedded in the scalp, indicating that the object was made of wood.

The victim was stabbed three times in the throat. One of these stab wounds severed the carotid artery, resulting in death within a matter of forty or fifty seconds due to the cessation of the blood supply to the brain. She was, presumably, unconscious from the blows to the head at this time. A curious feature of the wounds in the throat is that they are straight stabs made as in butchering a pig and not the usual transverse slashes.

The victim was frightened and aware of the danger, for the

level of adrenaline in the bloodstream was abnormally high. Otherwise, the body functions were normal, with the exception of some indications of arteriosclerosis. The underwear was not displaced and there are no indications of a sexual motive.

Time of death was between seven and seven-fifteen in the evening of 15 October 1982.

The report from the laboratory was much shorter. There was no evidence of forceful entry other than the door which Wachter had broken down in Heilmann's presence. There was no trace of the murder weapons and no fingerprints other than those of the victim and her son.

'I imagine that wraps it up,' said the inspector. 'Only Wachter could have got into the flat and the times fit.'

Adolf Wachter had said and Georg Heilmann had confirmed that he left the farm at a few minutes before seven and returned at approximately twenty-five to eight. Driven at high speed, the trip took around fifteen minutes, meaning that he would have had no more than ten minutes to commit the murder, but this was a time which the laboratory considered to be ample for the purpose.

However, the times also corresponded to Wachter's version of the events, which was that he had driven home rather slowly and had spent some time trying to get his mother to open the door.

'Why didn't you call the fire department?' asked the inspector. 'The fire department has specialists for opening doors. Didn't you know that?'

'I knew it,' said Wachter. 'I just didn't think of it.'

The inspector left him with the interrogation team and returned to his office.

'Wachter is a moron. Wachter is a criminal genius,' he said to the sergeant. 'Which do you prefer?'

'Neither,' replied the sergeant. 'What are you getting at?'

'Because he'd have to be a moron or incredibly devious to commit a murder like this,' said the inspector. 'He still insists that his mother wouldn't let anybody in who didn't know the code and that he was the only one who knew it. He might as well accuse himself of the murder.'

'I see,' said the sergeant slowly, 'and, if he's devious, he thinks this display of candour will convince the court of his sincerity. He could pull it off. We still don't have a clue as to the motive.'

'Worse, it's hard to see what the motive could be,' the inspector elaborated. 'The old lady didn't have much and she was eighty-eight years old. If he wanted her dead, all he'd have to do was wait a couple of years and she'd have died of natural causes. The only thing that occurs to me is a quarrel. He hit her harder than he meant to and, when he saw what he'd done, he panicked and finished her off.'

'It would have been a pretty brief quarrel,' said the sergeant. 'She never even got out of the entrance hall.'

'Too brief,' agreed the inspector, sounding annoyed. There were too many mysteries to the case for his liking. 'But, if it was someone else, he'd have had to leave the apartment only minutes before Wachter arrived, according to the time of death fixed by the autopsy.'

'Maybe he was in the flat when Wachter arrived the first time,' said the sergeant, 'and he left while Wachter was going for Heilmann.'

'Damnation!' said the inspector, sounding more annoyed than ever. 'It's quite possible. And the search parties never found either weapon . . .'

It was decidedly a case which left a great many questions unanswered.

Time would not answer them either. Adolf Wachter never confessed to the murder, but, on the strength of his own insistence that no one else could have got into the flat, he was indicted for unspecified homicide and, on 12 July 1983, brought to trial.

The prosecution was unable to suggest a motive for the crime. The murder weapons had not been found. The clothing Wachter was wearing on that day had been examined thread by thread in the police laboratory and no traces of blood had been found, although experts testified that it would have been impossible for anyone to commit the murder without getting blood on himself. Eight witnesses stated that Wachter and his mother had been on good terms.

The response of the prosecution was to call to the witness stand Wachter's ex-wife, who stated that Wachter had once hit her over the head with the leg of a chair in 1963 and that she therefore thought him capable of violence. They had not, however, divorced until 24 April 1967, and she admitted that she had returned to live with him from 1970 to 1973. The Wachters' three sons, aged twenty-four, twenty-three and fourteen, were not called upon to testify.

Maria Wachter's family doctor stated that he had, on three occasions, treated her for bruises resulting from what she described as falls. He had also treated her for a black eye which she claimed to have received from the cork of a wine bottle opened under pressure.

Asked by the prosecution whether such injuries could have been the result of beatings, the doctor said that they could.

Asked by the defence if they could be the result of what Mrs Wachter had said they were, the doctor said that they could.

A neighbour in the same house, sixty-year-old Helga Auernheimer, stated that she had heard Maria cry out 'Ouch!' on several occasions, but she admitted that some of the times, at least, had been when Adolf was at work.

The newsboy who had delivered the newspaper to the Wachters' flat, told the court that Mrs Wachter had sometimes complained that she was not happy and that her son was not good to her.

The evidence against Adolf Wachter was, therefore, something short of overwhelming, and he would presumably have been acquitted had it not been for his own insistence that no one else could have got into the flat.

This was tantamount to an admission that no one else could have committed the murder and, after nine days of confusing statements, the charge was reduced to manslaughter, Wachter was sentenced to eleven years and six months' imprisonment and his lorry driver's licence was revoked.

His only comment was to repeat that he was innocent and that he thought the revocation of his licence unreasonably harsh. He had, he pointed out, not been convicted of any violation of traffic regulations.

The verdict was promptly appealed to the German High Court, which found a great many errors in the conduct of the trial and ordered a new hearing to take place on 8 February 1985.

The result of the second trial was an acquittal which left the prosecutor on the verge of tears. Standing in the middle of the courtroom, he pointed an accusing finger at the cringing defendant and cried in a voice trembling with rage, 'Very well, Mr Wachter. You have managed to get away with it, but I know and you know that you are the murderer of your own mother!'

The spectators thought so too and there were cries of 'Shame!' and 'Hang the bastard!'

The cries did not cease after the trial either. Bamberg, a picturesque town located at the junction of the Rhine-Main-Danube canal and the Regnitz river, is not large enough for a man accused of murdering his mother to remain anonymous.

His situation was not helped by the fact that, although he had spent nearly two years in prison, he was denied compensation on the grounds that he had made conflicting statements to the police.

Adolf Wachter was free; but not very comfortable, as everyone he encountered thought he had murdered his mother. So too did the farmers for whom he worked, but they were only interested in his muscles and cared little who he murdered in his spare time.

Inspector Altbauer cared, but by now he was much inclined to think that Adolf Wachter had not murdered his mother, and he often pondered the question of who had. Although Wachter had been acquitted, meaning that someone else was the murderer, the case was dormant for lack of further avenues to explore.

The inspector's interest was immediately aroused when, less than a year later, a report arrived on his desk in which other potential suspects in the Wachter murder were named.

Neither of the suspects had been mentioned at Wachter's trials, and the offence which had led to this report had nothing to do with a murder.

It had been a sordid but not terribly unusual affair. Two apprentice butchers, twenty-three-year-old Thomas Schaubert and twenty-one-year-old Herbert Friedemann, had taken an eighteen-year-old girl to Schaubert's flat and spent most of a night alternately raping her.

The girl had gone straight to the police upon her release, and Schaubert and Friedemann were arrested. Evidence of the night's activities was found in the flat and, following their confessions, they were convicted of rape with violence and sentenced to four years' imprisonment on 30 April 1986.

As German penal authorities tend to be more sympathetic to people in their twenties than to common labourers in their fifties, they could, under normal circumstances, expect to serve less than half of this.

Unfortunately, Friedemann suffered from a very immature appearance and had not yet succeeded in growing a beard. He was fearful that his fellow prisoners would not regard him as a fully accredited criminal, so he began to boast of a murder that he and his friend Thomas had committed.

This, in itself, was unexceptional. Young prisoners often like to regale their fellow inmates with colourful accounts of their imaginary crimes, but Friedemann went further. He named names, dates and details, all of which corresponded to the officially unsolved murder of Maria Wachter.

And, by mischance, there was, among his listeners, an opportunist who had read of the case, was intrigued by Herbert's detailed knowledge of it and suspected that this might be a means of gaining a reduction of his own sentence.

He was quite right and, on 17 July 1986, he was brought to Inspector Altbauer's office, where he repeated the statements made by Herbert Friedemann in the prison.

The inspector was impressed. The statements contained details known only to the police and the murderer.

He was, however, a man with a suspicious nature, and the first thing he did was determine where the informer had been at the time of the murder. The statement was unsupported and it was possible that he knew the details because he had committed the murder himself.

Fortunately for him, he had been in detention on another charge at the time, showing that, in this case at least, crime did pay. His sentence was reduced and his identity was never revealed.

For the first time, the inspector had two plausible suspects, but he still had no explanation of how they had gained entry to the flat. There was no reason to believe that Maria Wachter had known them, and two young, husky strangers would have been the last people in the world for whom she would have opened the door.

There was, the inspector thought, one person who might be able to solve the mystery. He drove out to the farm where Adolf Wachter was cutting hay and asked if he knew a Thomas Schaubert or a Herbert Friedemann.

Wachter said that he knew both. They were apprentice butchers and, when they had any money, which was not often, they drank in the same tavern as he did.

This was enough of a connection for the inspector, and he had the two men brought to headquarters, where they were interrogated separately.

Schaubert said he had never heard the name of Maria Wachter nor that of Adolf Wachter either. There were many men who drank at his favourite tavern and he did not know all of them.

Friedemann, who was as immature as he looked, was more easily intimidated and, having listened to a tape recording of the statement made by his fellow prisoner, panicked and confessed to the murder, saying, however, that the idea had been Schaubert's.

They had, he said, been short of money. A butcher's apprentice was not paid very much and they both had fines because of convictions for cruelty to animals.

They had therefore decided to rob Maria Wachter, not because they knew her or had any reason to believe that she had money, but because they had accidentally learned the code of knocks for getting into the flat.

Wachter had once performed some work for Schaubert's parents and had mentioned the knock code. Schaubert, who was eighteen at the time, had followed Wachter home and listened to the knocks from the stairwell.

On the evening of the murder, they rode to the flats on their bicycles, Schauberg carrying a plastic bag with one of the knives used for sticking pigs, and Friedemann a sports bag containing two pairs of plastic gloves, a length of cord and a heavy chair leg.

As they did not intend to kill their victim, Schaubert tied a handkerchief over his nose and mouth and pulled his cap down over his eyes, while Friedemann covered his face with the hood of his parka.

Having put on the plastic gloves, they rapped out the code on the door and, when Mrs Wachter, who was expecting her son at that hour, opened it, they rushed in.

Mrs Wachter screamed and tried to flee, but Schaubert struck her violently over the head with the chair leg and she fell to the floor.

Friedemann then took over and continued to beat the now unconscious woman's skull.

They had previously agreed that, whatever one did, the other would do likewise so that the guilt would be equally shared and neither could betray the other.

Their search of the flat having turned up neither money nor anything they thought they could sell, they were on the point of leaving when they noticed that

Mrs Wachter was still breathing and beginning to make moaning noises.

Schaubert consequently took the long, narrow, razor-sharp slaughterer's knife out of the bag and thrust it into Mrs Wachter's throat in the same manner in which he would have butchered a pig.

Friedemann repeated the gesture and the murderers left the flat, pulling the door shut behind them. They had barely cleared the building when they saw Adolf Wachter drive up in his car.

Even though the murder of Maria Wachter had brought in not a penny, the newly ordained killers felt that the event called for a celebration. Having managed to steal a little money from Friedemann's parents, they repaired to the tavern, where they spent the evening in gales of laughter at the thought of Wachter's consternation when he discovered his mother's corpse.

It had not occurred to them that he might be suspected of the murder and they were delighted and more amused than ever when he was.

Confronted with his associate's detailed confession, Thomas Schaubert added his own.

The confessions were identical and the fact that they were astonished the police.

As a rule, when two people confess to involvement in a murder, their confessions tend to exonerate themselves and lay the entire blame on the other.

Neither Schaubert nor Friedemann ever made such an attempt, but accepted the responsibility equally.

Of course, neither had much cause to worry. They were eighteen and sixteen at the time of the murder; under the German Juvenile Criminal Code, the maximum sentence possible was ten years, and they could expect to serve no more than half.

Their immunity from any serious punishment made for an interesting trial, as the young men described frankly and with apparent relish how the blood had spurted from Maria Wachter's head and throat to drench their hands and clothing.

They had washed the clothing, burned the chair leg and returned the knife to its function of sticking pigs, the technique of which was discussed at some length by Schaubert, holding his finger to his own neck in illustration.

'It's the same for pigs or people,' he said. 'If you put the point of the knife in here, you can feel when it cuts through the artery and then you have to look out because the blood is going to squirt. Pigs squeal if they haven't been stunned.'

'Did Mrs Wachter squeal?' asked the prosecutor who had branded Adolf Wachter a parricide.

Schaubert shook his head.

'She'd been stunned,' he said.

On 18 June 1987, Thomas Schaubert and Herbert Friedemann were found guilty of murder, but were granted extenuating circumstances, although it was never specified what these were, and were sentenced to eight and a half years' juvenile detention each.

9

DOMESTIC COMPLICATIONS

Angélique Rousselle was twelve years old when her mother committed suicide. She had gone off to school that morning as usual and, when she returned home at three in the afternoon, there was Georgette in the bathtub, the water a horrid deep red with the blood from her cut wrists.

Angélique called the emergency ambulance and it came quickly, but there was nothing to be done. Georgette Rousselle's life had ended at the age of thirty-one.

Angélique went to live with her father and his mistress, Danielle Demeirleir, who was, perhaps, the cause of her mother's death. Marcel Rousselle had abandoned his family to live with the twenty-three-year-old Danielle four years earlier. He was thirty-seven at the time and his wife had said that he was trying to recapture his youth.

Considering what his youth had been, that seemed an unlikely ambition. Born the son of a miner, he had gone into the mines himself before he was sixteen and had worked underground for close to twenty years, but, although a big, burly man, he had a weak heart, and, after two serious heart attacks, he was pensioned off in 1983, the year after he left Georgette.

His marriage to her had been his second and, had she not killed herself, would have ended with his second divorce. At the age of twenty, he had married a girl of seventeen named Colette and they had had a son, Jacques, who was now a full-grown man and had gone off somewhere, possibly to France.

Many young men in Namur did. Wallonie, the eastern, French-speaking half of Belgium, was economically depressed.

Following the divorce, Colette had remarried and produced three more children. Although she was the mother of Angélique's half-brother, Angélique had never met her or the children. Namur is a city of over a hundred thousand and people do not run into each other the way they would have in a village.

Marcel, Danielle and Angélique lived in Danielle's house at 213 rue Salzinnes-les-Moulin, which was on the Sambre river not far from its junction with the larger Meuse. Where the two rivers join, the land runs away in a sharp, high, rocky point crowned by the great walls of the Citidel, an impressive fortress which has long guarded this strategic site, but which has now been converted into a hotel and tourist attraction.

Although the hotel was reputed to have a fine restaurant, it was expensive and Angélique had never dined there, but she could see part of the curtain wall of the Citidel from her bedroom window and she sometimes went for walks in the park surrounding it.

Angélique was not happy in her new home. She missed her mother and she found the domestic arrangements confusing. Danielle had married Antoine Harcourt when she was only fifteen, had borne him a daughter named Solange who was now eleven, but had then run away with Jean-Pierre Roubaix. She had since become the mother of a son named Jonathan, now aged three, whose father was believed to be Marcel.

Marcel had met Danielle through Antoine, who had enlisted his help in trying to get his wife back from Jean-Pierre. Marcel had succeeded in the task, but, rather than returning her to her husband, he had moved in with her himself.

Antoine, however, had not given up and came round rather often, particularly when Marcel was not at home. There was also Alain Bara, a man with a beard, who came round when neither Marcel nor Antoine was there. Danielle, it seemed, liked company.

But not Angélique's. On 9 July 1987, she turned up on the doorstep of forty-two-year-old Odette Rousselle, Marcel's sister. She was carrying a small suitcase which contained all of her worldly possessions. Danielle, she said, had put her out of the house.

'And your father let her?' demanded Odette indignantly.

'He isn't there,' said Angélique. 'Mr Bora moved in yesterday evening. I haven't seen Daddy for two days.'

Odette took Angélique in. The child had nowhere else to go and she was, after all, her niece. She then set about trying to contact Marcel, but she was unsuccessful.

Danielle, when questioned, appeared to be little concerned over his whereabouts. Marcel was, by now, forty-four years old and in poor health, so that some of the magic had gone out of their relationship. She thought he had gone away somewhere, possibly France.

On 1 October 1987, having failed to find any trace of her brother, Odette went to the police and reported him missing. She had contacted the social security office where he drew his pension and he had not drawn it since 1 July. As it was his only source of income, he would have starved to death by now, she said.

A sergeant of detectives from the missing persons office was assigned to the case and went to the rue Salzinnes-les-Moulins, where he took statements from Danielle, Alain Bara, a thirty-three-year-old construction worker when he was working, which was not often, and thirty-seven-year-old Maurice Ballotin, who was also living in the house, which was becoming rather crowded.

Maurice had four children aged five, nine, eleven and fourteen, but no wife, as she had deserted her family two years earlier.

The statements were similar. Marcel had gone off somewhere around the first week in July, no one knew where. The general impression was that no one cared. Danielle was expecting again and Bara apparently thought himself the father, for he volunteered the information with obvious pride.

The sergeant subsequently spoke to the civil servants at the social security office and the doctor who had certified Marcel for his disability pension. The doctor was categoric: Marcel was incapable of holding a job involving physical effort and he lacked the education to hold any other kind.

'Rouselle has not drawn his pension for three months,' wrote the sergeant in his report. 'As he has no other known means of support, the possibility of foul play cannot be excluded. Further investigation by the department of criminal investigations is recommended.'

The following morning, this report turned up in the in-basket of Inspector Yves Martin, a small, busy man with a short, not very stylish haircut and a mouth which turned up naturally at the corners so that he appeared perhaps more cheerful than he was.

The inspector looked at it and passed it on without comment to his assistant, Detective Sergeant Paul Soubry, who was tall, thin, bald on top, had a long, sorrowful sort of nose and did not look cheerful at all.

The sergeant assigned two of his detectives to look into the matter. They went over much the same ground as the sergeant from the missing persons office, and collected a photograph of Marcel from his sister and arranged for an appeal for information in the local newspapers.

This resulted in three reports from the public, all of which turned out to be cases of mistaken identity.

'We have exhausted all possibilities,' said the sergeant, reporting back to the inspector on the case. 'Accident victims, amnesia patients, prison and psychiatric institution inmates. All blank. Rousselle, in so far as we have been able to determine, suddenly disappeared on the night of 7 July and we have found no one who admits seeing him since. The conclusion is that he has either left Belgium or is dead.'

'He couldn't leave Belgium without money,' said the

inspector, 'and if he's dead, there are several possibilities: natural causes, freak accident, suicide or homicide. All, however, in some place where the body has not yet been found. What do you think?'

'Suicide or murder,' said the sergeant. 'The man was living with a woman who changes her partners more often than her underwear. He'd deserted his family for her, and his wife later committed suicide, probably because of it. The woman is now living with another man and expecting his child, and according to Rousselle's daughter, he moved in the day following Rousselle's disappearance. I find the circumstances sinister.'

'So do I,' said the inspector, 'but we'll start with suicide. Have the area searched for Rousselle's body. Did he have transport?'

'No,' said the sergeant. 'Walking distance from the rue Salzinnes-les-Moulins should be enough. It's not likely that he'd take a bus to go and commit suicide. And then?'

'And then, if you don't find it, see what you can find out about Alain Bara,' said the inspector. 'If he replaced Rousselle in the affections of the lady, he may have arranged for the vacancy.'

An intensive search covering a circle with a radius of a mile and centred on the house at 213 rue Salzinnes-les-Moulins resulted in the discovery of some scraps of men's clothing in a thicket at a place known as Grand Leez. The clothing had been burned, but Angélique tentatively identified it as having formed a part of her father's trousers and shirt.

The centre of the search was shifted to Grand Leez, and a red anorak was found which Angélique said had been worn by her father the last time she had seen him. The police laboratory reported that the anorak bore extensive traces of human blood. The group was the same as that of Marcel Rousselle.

The anorak had been hidden under a pile of brush, but there was no indication who had put it there.

In the meantime, a detachment of detectives had been

looking into the background of Alain Bara, which turned out to be unexceptional by the standards of the time and place.

The son of a male nurse attached to the psychiatric clinic in Daverdisse, a few miles to the east of Namur, and a French woman, Bara had two brothers and a sister. The family was respectable and he had completed his secondary schooling at Saint-Servais on the outskirts Namur.

In 1965, when Bara was ten years old, his father moved the family to Marseille. The boy had apparently not liked Marseille for, in 1971, he ran away and made his way back to Namur, where he was living in the streets until rescued by a parish priest who turned him over to a Madame Berthe Mathot.

Alain found not only shelter with Madame Mathot, but also love in the form of Madame Mathot's daughter Armande, who was one year younger than himself. His sentiments being reciprocated, they began sharing bed and board, although without going to the expense of marriage, in 1975.

Armande produced three children and Alain worked in a rather desultory fashion as a window-cleaner, a factory production-line worker and, finally, construction labourer. Although the family was not rich, they were apparently happy, and there was even some talk of legitimizing the children.

Alain's working days and happy family life ended simultaneously when he was introduced to Danielle Demeirleir by Marcel Rousselle towards the end of 1986. Three months later, Armande moved out, taking the children with her.

'Miss Demeirleir apparently falls in love easily,' said the sergeant, 'and she seems to have a devastating effect on the men she meets. As a result, situations arise in which there is an element of conflict.'

'To say the least,' said the inspector dryly. 'However, if Rousselle was murdered, I should think it would have been Bara or Ballotin. Miss Demeirleir doesn't strike me as a woman capable of concentrating on one man long enough to murder him.'

The Marcel Rousselle case had been officially classed suspected homicide following the discovery of the blood-stained anorak and burnt garments.

'Bara is the most likely suspect,' said the sergeant. 'He's the only one with a plausible motive. Ballotin only moved in after Rousselle disappeared. No question of robbery. Rousselle didn't have anything. Jealousy is out. His wife was probably jealous, but she committed suicide before he disappeared.'

'Even Bara didn't have much of a motive,' said the inspector. 'We know that Miss Demeirleir is more inclined to increase the number of her companions than to replace them, and Bara had been coming around for some time.'

'So had Harcourt, who's still legally her husband,' said the sergeant, 'and God knows how many others. The woman is very active.'

'We'll have to check on Harcourt too,' said the inspector, frowning. 'Maybe the best way to start is to try to determine just how many close friends Miss Demeirleir has. There could be some unstable people among them.'

'I should be surprised if there was anything else,' said the sergeant glumly. 'Actually, Rousselle had more reason to murder the others than they him.'

'True,' said the inspector, 'but, if anybody was murdered, it was Rousselle.'

So far, it could only be assumed that Marcel Rousselle had been murdered. Although the burnt and blood-stained clothing indicated violence, there was no evidence of how he had died nor even any concrete proof of his death.

It was therefore of vital importance that the body be found and, on the supposition that the clothing would have been left not far from the corpse, the searches were concentrated in the area around Grand Leez.

Hundreds of off-duty police and firemen and a smaller number of volunteers combed the patches of brush and forest for a distance of several miles from the point where the anorak had been found, but without success. No corpse was found, or anything else that might have a connection with Rousselle's disappearance.

All the residents near the rue Salzinnes-les-Moulins were questioned about someone transporting a large parcel through the streets on the nights of 6 or 7 July. No one reported having seen anything.

'Bara has a car,' said the sergeant. 'He could have taken the body away late at night, but, with so many people living in the house, somebody would surely have noticed something.'

'No doubt,' said the inspector, 'but they're not going to tell us. I think we're going to have to do more than simply question them.'

'You can't search the house without a warrant,' said the sergeant, 'and you can't get a warrant without charging one of the occupants.'

'We'll charge Bara with suspicion,' said the inspector. 'It won't hurt to put a little pressure on him.'

The charge and his arrest made no very profound impression on Alain Bara, who not only denied any connection to Rousselle's disappearance, but expressed doubts that he was dead.

'He was pretty old and he had a dud ticker,' he said. 'Danielle's not the girl for an old man. He'd been talking about going to France for quite a while. I think he just went.'

'Stopping first to burn his clothes in the woods and hide his bloody anorak,' said the inspector.

'Probably cut himself accidently,' said Bara, 'and threw the stuff away. He was careless with things.'

'Such as drawing his pension,' said the inspector.

Bara shrugged.

'Maybe he had an accident in France,' he said, 'and they don't know who he is.'

The inspector was slightly startled. What Bara said was improbable but possible. Rousselle could have gone to any of the countries of the Common Market with nothing more than his identity card and, if he had not had it on him when he was killed, his body could have remained unidentified.

In the end, the inspector had no alternative but to release his suspect. There was insufficient evidence to warrant holding him, and the search of the house had produced nothing more than a few drops of blood on the living-room carpet. They were too small and too old to determine the blood group, and Danielle said they came from her finger, which she had cut while peeling an apple.

The explanation was a mistake, for the laboratory said that the blood was months old and Danielle claimed to have cut her finger only the week before. As there was no sign of a cut on any of her fingers, she was taken to police headquarters and questioned rather intensively, but proved to be remarkably vague and evasive.

The incident with the cut finger had, perhaps, taken place much earlier, she said. Time passed quickly when one was busy and she had taken no special notice of the date she cut her finger. Anyway, maybe she hadn't cut her finger after all. It might have been one of the children. They were always cutting themselves.

The inspector was unable to get anything definite out of her, but he did succeed in boring her and, apparently not realizing that he was on the point of releasing her, she offered him a suspect or two.

'Antoine never forgave Marcel for moving in with me,' she said, 'and neither did Jeane-Pierre. I don't believe anything's happened to him, but if it has, they're the two you want to investigate. They've both been in jail.'

The inspector was already aware of this and he did not like it. He still regarded Bara as the most probable suspect because he had been living in the house, but either Harcourt or Roublaix had had a better motive for murdering Rousselle. Both had been rejected because of him and Bara had not been rejected at all.

Indeed, looking at the records, it was hard to see why

neither one had not murdered, or at least tried to murder, Rousselle before.

Harcourt had been convicted of assault with a deadly weapon and grevious bodily harm in 1979, when he had nearly beaten a man's brains out with a hammer, and Jean-Pierre Roublaix had been charged with attempted murder in 1982.

Danielle Demeirleir had been the motive in both cases.

Harcourt's record showed only the one offence, which involved a carpenter's helper who apparently believed that his help was required in a field other than carpentry.

Harcourt surprised him and Danielle in what the court described as a compromising situation, and took the hammer to him.

The young man, who had a solid skull, escaped with concussion and filed criminal charges against Harcourt, who, at his trial, told the court that he would repeat the treatment on him or anyone else he found playing around with his wife. He was sentenced to eighteen months' imprisonment, but the sentence was suspended because of his previous clean record and the fact that there had been, in the opinion of the court, considerable provocation.

It was while Antoine was in pre-trial detention that Danielle ran away with Jean-Pierre Roublaix, an unemployed pastry cook with a much more extensive criminal record.

Roublaix was repeatedly involved in barroom brawls and was twice charged with robbery, in addition to the attempted murder charge.

He was acquitted on one robbery charge and convicted on the other, for which he was sentenced to four years in prison. He served nineteen months and was then released on parole in June 1978.

He had no further contacts with the law up until May 1982, when he tried to stab a man with a butcher's knife.

The man was Marcel Rousselle.

Despite his past record, Roublaix was acquitted. He had not actually stabbed Rousselle and he claimed that the much bigger and stronger miner had threatened him when he refused to leave the house at 213 rue Salzinnes-les-Moulins.

Curiously, although she was then living with Rousselle, Danielle had supported Jean-Pierre's statement. Rousselle, she said, had threatened to kill him.

'None the less, I think Harcourt is the better suspect,' said the inspector. 'He was married to the woman – still is, for that matter – and he must have regarded Rousselle's actions in taking her over himself as the worst kind of betrayal. After all, he'd asked Rousselle to help in getting her back.'

'We haven't a scrap of evidence against him,' said the sergeant.

'Nor are we likely to get any at this late date,' said the inspector, 'but bring him in. He sounds like an honest man, so maybe he'll confess.'

Antoine Harcourt did not confess, but, in the rather carefree manner of Belgian newspapers, the press branded him the murderer in headlines an inch high. The case had already received attention out of proportion to the supposed victim's social importance because Danielle's romantic adventures made interesting reading.

They were apparently followed even by people who knew about them already, for the next morning, Maurice Ballotin came to police headquarters and asked to see the inspector.

'You've got the wrong man,' he said earnestly. 'I saw Alain Bara carry the body out of the house that night and I saw him come back an hour later and take away Rousselle's red anorak. There was blood on it.'

'Well, why the devil didn't you say something before?' demanded the inspector angrily. 'I ought to charge you with acting as an accessory after the fact. This investigation has tied up half the department for close to a year.'

'Bara said he would rape my kids if I said anything,' said Ballotin. 'I was afraid.'

'Two of your children are boys,' said the sergeant.

'He said he wouldn't make any exceptions,' said Ballotin. 'I can't let an innocent man go to jail, though. . . .'

Alain Bara was rearrested, formally charged with
homicide and confronted with Ballotin's statement. He
denied the accusation, claimed that it was Ballotin who
had murdered Rousselle, and said Ballotin was trying to
get him sent to jail so that he could have Danielle to
himself.

The inspector was not convinced by his story and the
interrogation continued for a week, by which time Bara
had become so entangled in contradictions and conflicting statements that he had no choice but to confess.

Rousselle, he said, had attacked him and he had killed
him accidentally in self-defence. He had wrapped the
body in an old blanket and left it in the municipal dump
at Bonneville.

As there was no evidence to the contrary, his claim of
self-defence would have to be accepted by the court, and
sixty police officers spent the next five days turning over
the hundreds of tons of rubbish that had been deposited
in the dump since the beginning of July.

No body was found, either because Bara was lying
about what he had done with it or because there was too
much rubbish.

The inspector was not ready to give up, however.
Danielle Demeirleir was arrested and charged with
acting as an accessory to homicide after the fact and
concealing information in connection with the investigation of a felony. Convinced of the seriousness of her
situation, she abruptly became less vague and admitted
that she and Bara had planned the murder together in
advance.

'Marcel kept hanging around and whining,' she said.
'He wouldn't go away and he stood in the way of our
love, so we had to get rid of him.

'On the evening of 7 July, I put a dozen ground-up
sleeping tablets in his coffee and he fell asleep in front
of the television.

'Alain was supposed to take him somewhere else and

kill him, but, when he started to move him, the sleeping pills weren't strong enough and he began to wake up.

'Alain went down to the basement and got a maul we used for splitting wood and smashed his head with it.

'We took his clothes off so he couldn't be identified and Alain took them and the body away in an old blanket. He told me that Ballontin had seen him, but that there wouldn't be any trouble. He would take care of him.'

Alain Bara eventually admitted that Danielle's account of the murder was correct and, on 24 February 1989, he was sentenced to life imprisonment. Danielle, because she had not taken part in the actual killing and because of her cooperation with the police, was sentenced to twenty years.

The body of Marcel Rousselle was never found.

10

CARD SHARK

As he did every working day of the week, forty-six-year-old Robert Farouelle left his house at a little before seven-thirty in the morning of Thursday 2 October 1986 in the company of his dog Lucky, an animal of good character but dubious ancestry.

Farouelle was on his way to work, but Lucky would be spending the day with Farouelle's mother-in-law, seventy-nine-year-old Lucienne Grandjean. Micheline, Farouelle's wife, also had a job. Paul, their twenty-two-year-old son, was studying near Paris and Thierry, a year younger, was out seeking work. There was therefore no one at home to look after Lucky.

The Farouelle home at 9 Cours Albert Premier was only two streets away from 9 rue Giorne-Viard, where Mrs Grandjean lived, and Farouelle arrived at almost precisely seven-thirty.

Had he not been on his way to work, he would have willingly taken longer. It was an exceptionally fine autumn day in Nancy, a city of a hundred thousand in the northeast of France, and far better suited to walking than working.

Lucky, however, was in a hurry. He was very attached to Lucienne, who since becoming a widow in 1953, had lavished her affection on dogs, stray cats, the children in the kindergarden where she still worked as a cleaning woman and her grandsons, Paul and Thierry.

Farouelle was consequently astounded when Lucky came to a halt before Mrs Grandjean's front door, put back his head, howled mournfully and braced his feet against the pull of the leash.

Normally, Farouelle was considerate of Lucky's whims, but he had to get to work. Picking the dog up bodily, he started up the two steps leading to the front door of the two-storey building.

The action produced such frantic struggles that Lucky got away altogether, slipped his collar and disappeared off down the street in the direction of home, whining and whimpering as if his heart was broken.

Farouelle stared after him in amazement and, now alarmed in spite of himself, tried the door.

It was locked.

'Lucienne?' he shouted, hammering on the door panels with his fist. 'Are you all right?'

The old woman had always enjoyed excellent health, but she was, after all, nearly eighty. She could have had a heart attack.

There was no response to his call and Farouelle ran off in the direction of home himself. He had a duplicate set of keys to the house there, so that he could get in and find out what was wrong.

Lucky was at home, hiding under the front steps, his habitual refuge when disaster struck.

Farouelle had no time to deal with his problems, but dashed back to the rue Giorne-Viard and let himself into the house.

There was a short hall with stairs at the end leading up to the first floor and a door on the right opening into his mother-in-law's flat. It was not locked and he entered, calling out her name.

An instant later, his voice died in his throat and he stood paralysed with shock and horror, staring at a scene which his mind was momentarily unable to comprehend.

There were three bodies lying on the living-room floor, unquestionably female, for their skirts were bunched up around their waists and the underwear torn or cut away. Blood-stained objects projected stiffly from between sprawled thighs. Streaks and splotches of black dried blood formed hideous patterns on the livid flesh, and from gaping cuts beneath the chins, blood had gushed and squirted over clothing, carpets, walls and furniture.

He could recognize none of the three, for the faces were black, blue, yellow, green and swollen out of all human resemblance, but he realized that one of them must be his mother-in-law. Who the others were, he had no idea.

The unexpected shock was so violent that for a few moments Farouelle lost touch with reality. Unable to believe the evidence of his own senses, he thought that he was dreaming or hallucinating.

It was the sudden remembrance of Lucky's strange behaviour which brought him back to the real world. Incredibly, the dog had known! Through the solid walls of the house, through two closed doors, he had sensed death and had been terrified.

Robert Farouelle realized in that moment that he too was terrified. It was not the fear of being murdered. His mind was clear now and he knew that it would have taken hours for the blood to dry so black and hard. The murderer was no longer in the house. What terrified Farouelle was the unpredictability of life itself, the brutal awareness that anything could happen at any time and that it could be horrible beyond belief.

Walking unsteadily back to his house, Robert Farouelle felt a strong urge to join Lucky under the front steps, but he was a man and not a dog so he called the police instead.

The police were nearly as shocked as Farouelle. As French towns go, Nancy is not particularly given to violence, and the bestial rape and murder of three elderly women was unprecedented in the annals of the department of criminal investigations.

Dr Marcel Loup, the young and bearded specialist in forensic medicine, had only read of such cases in the text books.

'The most savage type of sex psychopath,' he said. 'Sadism, perverted sex, fetishism – it's all here. I can't believe that such a person would be at liberty unless he's just escaped from some institution.'

'You'll check on that possibility, François?' called Inspector Charles Lebeau to his assistant, Sergeant of Detectives François Mocky, an olive-skinned man with a sleek muscular body and a sharp pointed face, who was on his knees peering under the furniture for a possible murder weapon.

'For the east or for all of France?' asked the sergeant, getting up and going into the bedroom. 'Looks as if he got her savings. There's an empty tin box lying on the floor here.'

'All France,' said the inspector grimly. 'This is an all-round man: murder, robbery, rape. It couldn't be his first offence.'

The autopsy would, however, show that both he and the doctor had been led astray by appearances.

'None of them was raped in the conventional sense,' said the doctor, dropping into the chair in front of the inspector's desk and accepting a cigarette and a mug of coffee from the sergeant.

It was eight o'clock on Friday morning and he had been up most of the night working on the three autopsies.

The specialists had not completed their work at the scene or released the bodies until three in the afternoon and there had been a great deal of medical investigation involved.

'What do you mean by "not in a conventional sense"?' queried the inspector. 'The murderer didn't achieve orgasm?'

He was a big man, with the brown hair and brown eyes common to the north of France and a heavy brown moustache whose points drooped below his jaw line so that he looked a little like a pirate.

'Not only was there no orgasm,' said the doctor, 'I doubt that there was penetration with anything other than the various objects forced into the victims' sex organs – a brush handle, a wooden spoon and the pendulum of a cuckoo clock, among other things. There are no traces of semen on or in any of the bodies. Either he's incapable of orgasm or this had nothing to do with sex.'

The inspector looked gravely thoughtful.

'I see,' he said slowly. 'A simulated sex crime to throw off the investigation. That will make things more difficult. Anything else?'

'Times of death were too close together to establish an order,' reported the doctor, 'but approximately nine in the evening of Wednesday, plus or minus half an hour for all three.

'All of them were struck violently and probably rendered unconscious with repeated blows to the face delivered by a bare fist. It's almost certain that he cut his knuckles, although I was unable to find any traces of blood of a group different to that of the victims.

'The stabbing and sexual mutilation took place while they were unconscious, and none of them regained consciousness thereafter.

'There is reason to believe that Mrs Grandjean was the first victim, for the level of adrenaline in her bloodstream was normal, meaning that she did not realize she was in danger. The level in the bloodstreams of the other two was abnormally high, which could mean that they were witnesses to her murder.

'The throats of all three victims were cut nearly to the backbone and all suffered multiple stab and slash wounds, seventeen in the case of Mrs Grandjean and eleven and fourteen respectively in the cases of Odette and Michele Gatinot.

'The weapon in all cases was the butcher's knife found sticking in Odette Gatinot's body.'

Sixty-one-year-old Odette Gatinot, the owner of a small grocer's shop in the nearby rue de la Colline, and her sister, Michèle, who was fifty-seven and a high-school teacher of history and geography at the Lycée Chopin, had been identified as the other victims. They had occupied the first-floor flat above Lucienne Grandjean.

'The butcher's knife has been identified as Mrs Grandjean's by her son-in-law,' said the inspector. 'A weapon of convenience, showing that he did not come to the house armed or intending to kill.'

'No, he was in a frenzy of some kind,' said the doctor. 'Maybe psychotic. Maybe drugs. Maybe simply drunk. The knife was bent so badly that I had to saw through her ribs to get it out.'

'A cool head for somebody in a frenzy,' remarked the sergeant. 'He cleaned everything out of the flat that was worth anything.'

'Sounds to me like a kid on drugs,' said the inspector. 'We've been averaging a killing a week of old people here in the northeast and it's almost always teenagers after money for drugs. The only difference with this case is the number of victims and the degree of violence.'

'Could have been a matter of necessity,' suggested the sergeant. 'He came to rob Mrs Grandjean, but the Gatinot sisters heard something and came down to investigate. He may have thought three witnesses were too many and that they'd be able to identify him, so he killed them.'

'That sounds reasonable,' said the inspector. 'No escaped lunatics, you say?'

'Not within the past six months,' replied the sergeant. 'Records are pulling the files on addicts with a history of acts of violence now.'

There were a dismaying number of these. Unemployment is high in France and so is drug abuse by the young unemployed – a dangerous combination as drugs cost money and the unemployed have little.

Most of the young addicts, however, engaged in rolling drunks or mugging women and elderly people rather than burglary and homicide.

'He probably didn't intend it,' said the inspector. 'It was just a situation that got out of hand. The strange part is that she let him in at nine o'clock at night.'

'Well, apparently not,' the sergeant told him. 'We've been talking to the neighbours and they say she'd let anybody in. She'd lived there almost her entire life and she felt she was safe.. She was particularly trusting with young people.'

'A dangerous attitude in this day and age,' commented the inspector. 'Any suspects that you particularly fancy?'

'There aren't any real suspects at all yet,' said the sergeant. 'We've got about five who are possibilities and we're trying to find witnesses who saw any of them in the area that night. The fingerprint section hasn't come up with anything useful so far.'

The investigation was proceeding in a routine manner. The presumed motive of robbery being the only factor known, the sergant's detectives were trying to identify everyone who might have wanted money desperately enough to be willing to murder three old ladies for it. Practically speaking, this meant heavy drug addicts.

Although the list of potential suspects was not yet complete, other detectives were already attempting to trace the whereabouts of those without alibis for the time of the murders. Normally, most would be eliminated, leaving only a manageable number to be investigated more intensively.

Eleven complete or partial fingerprints had been found at the scene, but none corresponded to those of the potential suspects, nor were any of them on record with the police.

The fingerprints were not regarded as being of great importance in any case. None had been recovered from the tin box in which Mrs Grandjean had kept her savings or from any other place that could tie them directly to the murders.

The inspector was not, therefore, disappointed when the fingerprint section reported that all the prints recovered were from members of the family.

'Her son-in-law, her daughters and her grandsons,' said the sergeant. 'The rest are children's prints. I suspect that the murderer didn't leave any. If he was smart enough to fake a sex crime, he was smart enough to be careful about prints.'

Mrs Grandjean had had two daughters, but Jeanine, although married, had no children. Neither, for that matter, had the Farouelles. Thierry and Paul were both adopted.

Fingerprints were not, however, the only clues recovered at the scene, and the technicians reported that the murderer had spent a considerable length of time in the flat following the murders.

Towels in the bathroom were stained with blood and, when the technicians disassembled the drains, they found such quantities of blood and other matter as to indicate that the murderer had taken a bath before leaving the house. He had carried out his search for money and valuables first, for there were traces of blood on the tin box believed to have contained Mrs Grandjean's savings, estimated at several thousand francs, and her two-thousand-franc (two-hundred-pound) old-age pension, which she had collected on the day she was murdered.

'He got himself clean,' said the inspector, 'but what about his clothes? With such butchery, they must have been drenched with blood. He couldn't have gone out like that. The first person he encountered would have noticed it.'

'Maybe he took her grandson's clothes,' suggested the sergeant. 'Farouelle says that she did Thierry's laundry, and there was male clothing in one of the cupboards.'

'Ask the boy if there's anything missing,' said the inspector. 'If there is, we have a rough indication of his size.'

Thierry Farouelle confirmed that the clothing in his grandmother's house was his, but said that nothing was missing.

By this time, all the potential suspects had been investigated and, although several had no alibi, none had injured knuckles nor was there any evidence against them.

The investigation was at a standstill and the inspector called a conference of the officers working on the case.

'This is what has been deduced so far,' he said. 'Sometime during the evening of 1 October, Mrs Grandjean let a man into her flat.

'Either she knew him or he had a plausible reason to come in. There was no forced entry.

'The man struck Mrs Grandjean a number of extremely violent blows to the face with his bare fist and she lost consciousness quickly, for the autopsy found no defence bruises on the hands or arms.

'Whether the Gatinot sisters were present at this time, or came down later because they had heard a noise, is an open question. In any case, they too were knocked unconscious.

'The man then got the butcher's knife from the kitchen, stabbed and slashed the unconscious woman, cut their throats, exposed the lower part of their bodies and inserted various objects from the flat in their sex organs with the intention of simulating a sex crime.

'Following the murders, he searched the flat for money and valuables, finding several thousand francs in the tin box in which Mrs Grandjean kept her savings and collecting a number of small objects of value, mainly jewellery.

'Before leaving, he took a bath and, apparently, changed clothes.'

'That doesn't make sense,' said the head of the police laboratory. 'The murder weapon was one of convenience. He didn't come equipped to kill, so why would he bring a change of clothes?'

'Precisely,' said the inspector, 'and there are other inconsistencies. Cutting the throats of three old women and mutilating them sexually are abnormal acts. Yet the search of the flat was systematic and he took rational, effective steps to conceal his identity and the true motive for the crimes.'

'There was a similar case in Strasbourg last year,' volunteered one of the senior detectives. 'Kid on some combination of drugs that produced sudden violent personality changes. One minute, he was completely rational and the next a raving maniac.

'He broke into an old woman's house wanting to rob her, but he flipped and nearly murdered her. Then he reverted to normal and did such a good job of covering up that they wouldn't have got him at all if he hadn't gone to pieces under interrogation.'

'Did the victim survive?' asked the sergeant.

'Yes,' said the detective, 'but she couldn't identify him.'

'It wouldn't be the same one here,' objected the inspector. 'That one must be still in jail.'

'I wouldn't count on it,' said Dr Loup.

'Check on it, François,' ordered the inspector. 'What was the fellow's name?'

'Beni El Daba,' said the detective. 'North African. Algerian, I think.'

'The desk had a telephone call the day after the murder from somebody who said his grandmother had been murdered,' added another of the detectives. 'They couldn't trace it, but the dispatcher said it sounded like a foreigner.'

'Check on that too, François,' said the inspector. 'Anything else?'

There were a few other suggestions, some of which the inspector ordered to be followed up, and the conference ended.

'Nothing very useful,' he grumbled. 'An anonymous telephone call and a North African in jail in Strasbourg.'

The North African was not, however, in jail, as a telephone call to the Strasbourg police quickly determined.

The doctor had been right. Beni El Daba was young, poor, non-European and a drug addict. A compassionate judge had found the combination so irresistible that he had released him without bail.

He had not been seen since.

The sergeant requested a copy of his record, which

arrived the following day, Strasbourg being only ninety-odd miles west of Nancy.

'We may have something here,' he said cautiously, laying the file on the inspector's desk. 'El Daba seems to be pretty mixed up. He didn't even know the old woman he savaged, but he told the police it was his grandmother.'

'Let's listen to the tape of the anonymous call,' said the inspector.

The call was short. 'My grandma's been killed,' it went. 'I guess . . . somebody's killed grandma. . . . It wasn't me. . . . In the rue Gio . . . the rue Général de Gaulle. . . .'

'There's no rue Général de Gaulle in Nancy,' said the inspector. 'There's a Place Général de Gaulle.'

'It was investigated,' reported the sergeant. 'They didn't find anything.'

'Because it was rue Giorne-Viard,' said the inspector. 'You can hear how he started to say Giorne and changed it to Général.'

The anonymous telephone call, the fact that El Daba's behaviour was known to be violent and unpredictable, and the confirmation that he had not been in custody at the time of the murders, placed him high on the list of potential suspects; but questions remained.

Although the officer taking the anonymous call had said that the man sounded like a foreigner, neither the inspector nor the sergeant could detect any trace of accent.

The Strasbourg police reported, however, that El Daba spoke relatively fluent French when he was calm, but had a strong Algerian accent when he was excited.

'The man who made the call sounded excited, but he didn't have any accent,' said the sergeant.

'Well, if it was El Daba, he's an addict and he had money, so Narcotics should be able to trace where he spent it,' said the inspector. 'That's one area where we don't lack informers.'

The response was negative. The narcotics section had

very good sources of information on who was buying what on the drug market, and there had been no major purchases by anyone resembling Beni El Daba.

'In fact, they say they don't believe he's in Nancy,' said the sergeant. 'The drug scene isn't so big here that a stranger with money doesn't stand out.'

'Or even a local man with five or six thousand francs [five or six hundred pounds],' agreed the inspector. 'He must have got at least that much. Still nothing on the jewellery?'

'Hasn't turned up at any of the usual outlets for stolen goods,' said the sergeant. 'Maybe it was a mental case who thinks all old women are his grandmother?'

'Strikes me as an unusual delusion,' remarked the inspector, 'and, if that was so, why stop at three? There hasn't been a murder of an older woman since.'

'Meaning that Mrs Grandjean was a specific victim?' said the sergeant. 'What about the Gatinot sisters?'

'Killed to avoid exposure,' asserted the inspector. 'I think she knew him and I think they knew him.'

'That doesn't leave many possibilities,' said the sergeant thoughtfully. 'Besides her family, she knew mostly young children.'

'Then inside it,' said the inspector. 'How thoroughly were the male members investigated?'

'Not very thoroughly,' admitted the sergeant. 'No apparent motive.'

'Money is a motive for everybody,' said the inspector. 'Find out whatever you can about all of them, women included.'

'Women?' queried the sergeant.

'There were no traces of semen at the scene,' said the inspector.

Lucienne Grandjean's female relatives were quickly eliminated as possible suspects. Their whereabouts at the time of the murders could be ascertained.

'I didn't think it could be a woman,' said the sergeant. 'Not with all that punching in the face with the bare fist.'

'There are things that leave marks like a bare fist and aren't,' said the inspector cryptically. 'Loup isn't infallible. What about the men?'

'It was neither of her sons-in-law,' reported the sergeant, 'nor the nephew nor any of the four cousins.'

'That leaves the grandsons,' said the inspector. 'Well?'

'Mrs Grandjean didn't have any by blood,' the sergeant reminded him. 'Both the boys are adopted. Paul is out of the question. He was at the university two hundred miles from here.'

'You're saying that Thierry is the murderer,' said the inspector.

The sergeant looked uncomfortable.

'I'm saying that if anybody in the family did it, he's the only one who could have,' he admitted. 'We've eliminated the others.'

'And?' said the inspector, beginning to sound a little impatient.

'I can't see him as a suspect in this kind of a murder,' argued the sergeant. 'He's got no police record. He's not on drugs and he's no drinker. Didn't do as well at school as his brother, but he was promoted to corporal while doing his military service. After he got out, he had a job as a watchman, but was fired for possession of an unauthorized pistol. Theoretically he's been looking for work ever since, but in fact he spends most of his time playing cards in a café called Chez Jean.'

'For money?' said the inspector.

'For money,' confirmed the sergeant, 'and he's a rotten player. He couldn't win playing against the Coco Girls.'

The Coco Girls were a popular quartet of young and sexy maidens who appeared in French television. They were not noted for card-playing.

'Nobody could,' said the inspector, 'but I'm afraid you may have found the motive.'

'I'm afraid of it too,' the sergeant agreed, 'but I don't see how we could prove it.'

'Skinned knuckles and jewellery,' said the inspector. 'The knuckles will be healed by now, but there'll be people who remember seeing them; and we know he hasn't sold his grandmother's jewellery yet, so he must still have it. Put some people to checking on his financial situation before and after the murder.'

'I already have,' the sergeant told him. 'He was broke before and he paid off his gambling debts the day after.'

'Good,' said the inspector. 'Get somebody to sit in on his card games and report when he's lost his money. He'll try to sell the jewellery then and we'll take him.'

'Supposing he wins?' asked the sergeant.

'He won't,' said the inspector. 'The boy's a born loser.'

Five days later, the detective assigned to play cards with Thierry Farouelle reported that he had begun gambling on credit.

Other detectives took him under surveillance and he was arrested the following evening while trying to sell his grandmother's engagement ring to a bartender.

Thierry Farouelle denied the murder and said that his grandmother had made him a present of the ring. However, the laboratory was able to find traces of human blood on it, and the scars on his knuckles were even now not completely healed.

In the end, he confessed. He had run out of credit with the other card-players and asked his grandmother for a thousand francs (a hundred pounds) to get back in the game.

She had never refused him before, but he had never told her the truth about why he wanted the money before.

Lucienne had indignantly refused to finance his gambling and he had knocked her unconscious with his fists.

In ransacking the flat for money, he had made so much noise that the Gatinot sisters came down to investigate. As they knew him, he had to murder them to avoid exposure.

Although Thierry Faraoulle appeared to have few regrets for the murders, he obviously did bitterly regret being caught, and his trial was characterized by arrogant abuse of the judge and attempts at physical attacks on court officials, journalists and witnesses.

This did not make a favourable impression on the jury and, on 24 July 1987, they sentenced him to life imprisonment.

11

DOWN THE DRAIN

Whether Katharina Kornagel died on Nikolaus Day or earlier could never be determined precisely. Certainly no one ever saw her after 6 December 1987 and, as she was a gregarious person with many friends and neighbours, it was probably not later.

If she had to die, Katharina might have found Nikolaus Day a good day to do it. Nikolaus Day is when German children receive their Christmas presents, Christmas itself being more of a religious holiday, and she was very fond of children, although she had none of her own.

At the time, Katharina was seventy-four years old and enjoying life as she was in good health and financially very comfortably off.

Ethnic Germans, she and her mother had emigrated to West Germany from Russia in 1978 and had received a substantial cash settlement from the government in compensation for losses suffered during the Second World War. Five years later, her mother had died at the respectable age of eighty-seven, leaving everything to Katharina.

Since then, she had lived quietly and happily in the two-room ground-floor flat at Auwiesen Way 3 in the pleasant little town of Wangen im Allgaeu, fifteen miles north of Lake Constance, the body of water separating West Germany from Switzerland.

Katharina's absence was soon noticed, particularly by Maria and Georg Weh, who lived two floors higher in the same nine-family building. They belonged to her age group; Maria was sixty-seven, and Georg seventy-four and had been a prisoner of war in Russia, which gave them something in common. It did not occur to them to report her missing, however. She often made little trips to visit relatives, and her half-friend, half-chauffeur, thirty-three-year-old Erwin Spengler, said that she had taken the train to Bremen on 11 December. He had driven her to the station in Lindau himself.

Erwin and Katharina were very good friends despite the difference in ages and financial circumstances, and she had even bought him a light-blue Mercedes Diesel in September 1987 so that he could drive her around.

Katharina was, unfortunately, a good deal overweight and she did not like walking.

Erwin was also fairly plump and he did not like walking either, but, had it not been for Katharina, he would have had to.

The fact was, Erwin was passing through a difficult period. A mason by trade, he had been unemployed for the past five years and, as he had a wife and three small children to support, his unemployment compensation of around twelve hundred marks (four hundred pounds) a month did not go far.

The Mercedes was therefore a comfort. True, it was second hand, but no one needed to know that, and it looked good, which was important. West Germany is a very materialistic society. Anyone who does not own a car is socially untouchable or forced to become an ecologist.

Finally, on 18 January 1988, which was a Monday, Erwin decided to go to the Wangen im Allgaeu police station and report Katharina missing. No one had heard or seen anything of her since her departure for Bremen and he was becoming worried, he said.

As Wangen im Algaeu has a population of under twenty-five thousand, the police force is not very large and the head of the department of criminal investigations was only a sergeant of detectives, an enormous blond sleepy-looking man named Wilhelm Baumvogel.

Having personally taken the missing-person report and having nothing better to do at the moment, he went to Auwiesen Way to investigate it himself.

The door to Mrs Kornagel's flat was locked, but the sergeant, who was more clever with his hands than might have been thought, soon got it open without breaking anything, and entered.

The first thing that caught his eye was a green slipper lying in front of the door to the living room.

The next thing was a large dark-brown patch on the floor of the entrance hall.

'Oh-oh,' said the sergeant, backing quickly out of the flat. He locked the door behind him and returned to the police station.

The assistant to the chief of police, Inspector Markus Wagner, was in his office, going thoughtfully through the week's traffic-accident reports. As in many places in Europe, the younger residents of Wangen im Allgaeu suffered from the delusion that they were highly skilled drivers and, as a result, killed and maimed themselves and others in distressing numbers.

'I think we have a murder, chief,' said the sergeant.

'Good heavens!' said the inspector. 'Are you certain?'

He was a fussy, mild-mannered man in his late fifties, with fuzzy white hair through which a good deal of pink scalp was showing. His stomach was large enough for him to prefer braces to a belt, and children loved him on sight as they thought he looked the way their grandfathers should.

The sergeant recounted the circumstances.

'We're not really equipped to take on a full-scale homicide investigation,' he said. 'I think we should call in the experts from the state criminal investigations office.'

The inspector thought this over.

'All right then,' he said finally, 'but only the technical people. For the rest, I shall take charge of the investigation personally, and the first thing we must do is determine that there has been a murder. It would be embarrassing if we got the people down here from

Stuttgart and it turned out that the old lady was taking the waters at Baden-Baden.'

The sergeant said nothing. There was nothing he could say. He had never investigated a murder and he did not think that the inspector had either.

'I shall begin,' said the inspector, getting to his feet, 'by viewing the scene of the supposed crime.'

'I only hope she is in Baden-Baden,' said the sergeant, 'but it didn't look that way to me.'

It did not look that way to the inspector either. The sergeant once again dealt with the lock, and the inspector removed his shoes and tiptoed into the flat, going further than the sergeant had and finding more indications of violence, but no trace of a body.

'Strange,' he muttered, pulling on his shoes. 'You say she was quite stout?'

'Close to fourteen stone, according to Spengler's description,' said the sergeant.

'And this Spengler?' asked the inspector. 'Is he a sort of muscle-covered giant?'

'More the fat, sloppy type,' said the sergeant. 'A little fellow.'

Most men were little fellows to the sergeant.

'Well, then he had an accomplice or he used a fork lift,' said the inspector. 'Have you ever tried lifting a corpse of that size?'

'No,' answered the sergeant. 'Not of any size. You agree that it's murder then?'

'I don't see how it could be anything else,' said the inspector. 'You see all those house plants? They're dead. A woman like that would no more go off and leave her house plants to die than she would enter a steeple-chase without a horse.'

The inspector's choice of metaphors was, perhaps, not entirely apt, but the experts from the state criminal investigations technical division were inclined to agree with him.

They came down from Stuttgart, the capital of Baden-Wuerttemberg, fifteen strong, in two cars and a minibus with a trailer full of equipment, and they went over Katharina Kornagel's flat with such thoroughness that not a hair, not a grain of dust, not a trace of foreign substance escaped them. It was what they did all the time and they were very good at it.

When they had finished, they typed up a report in duplicate, turned it in to the inspector and returned to Stuttgart.

The report was so long that the inspector needed more time to read it than the specialists had taken to go over the flat.

In part, it said:

A pot containing a quantity of sauerkraut which had gone mouldy was found standing on the kitchen stove. Fruit in a basket on the dining table was rotten. Some of the food in the refrigerator had gone bad.

In the bathroom, a toothbrush was found hanging beside the lavatory and there was a package of a product used for cleaning dental plates standing on the shelf above it.

The washing machine was partly filled with wet washing which had not been spun dry.

Six wrapped gifts suitable for children were found in the closet.

All the above items indicate an absence since Nikolaus Day or before.

'The stains on the floor and walls of the hall are human blood, type AM, RH positive. They are approximately fifty days old. From them, a drag trail of the same blood leads to the bathtub in the bathroom.

Traces of hydrochloric acid were recovered from many places in the bathroom, notably on the mirror, the tiles, the taps of the bathtub, in the trap and in the drains. The quantity employed is estimated at several gallons.

The conclusion is that a person having the above blood group suffered injuries resulting in a copious loss of blood, and was subsequently dissolved in hydrochloric acid which passed down the bathtub drain.

'Ridiculous!' exclaimed the inspector. You can't pour a fourteen-stone woman down the drain!'

But it seemed that you could. The technical squad

knew what they were talking about. Given enough hydrochloric acid and enough time, it was possible to dissolve flesh, bone and even the fillings in the teeth to a sort of jelly which would flush down the drain very well. The acid would not, however, attack the tiles, the enamel of the bathtub or the plastic drain pipes and washers.

Erwin Spengler had, of course, been arrested even before the inspector and the sergeant finished reading the report. He was a glaringly obvious suspect, penniless, unemployed, heavily in debt, and Katharina Kornagel had been, by his standards, rich.

'The question is, how did he propose to get his hands on the money?' the inspector wondered. 'He obviously knew that she didn't keep any cash in the flat because he didn't even look for it.'

'I'll see if I can find out whether his finances have shown a sudden improvement since the murder,' said the sergeant.

Erwin Spengler's finances since Nikolaus Day of 1987 had never been better. He had paid off eight thousand marks' worth of old debts, including a bill for kitchen cabinets dating from 1985. His postal savings account, normally overdrawn and blocked, showed a balance of twelve thousand marks. (A mark is worth about a third of a pound.)

'He's not very good at managing money,' reported the sergeant. 'He still has close to twenty thousand marks' worth of debts, but he traded in the Mercedes plus eight thousand marks for a BMW 520 with a custom steering wheel, fog lamps and a tachometer for another two thousand. For a man on unemployment compensation, he's doing rather well.'

Erwin, who was in the detention cells but was brought up daily to the inspector's office for questioning, said that it was all a matter of luck. He had been playing roulette at the casino in Baden-Baden and had won sixty thousand marks in a single night. Being a prudent man, he had immediately stopped playing.

Asked when this good fortune had taken place, Spengler said he could not remember exactly, but that it had been early in December.

The sergeant was sent up to Baden-Baden, where he examined the casino records. No one had won sixty thousand marks in a single evening during December.

When this was pointed out to Spengler, he said that he had not meant that he had won it all in one evening, but that it was the total of his winnings over a week or so.

'I'm not very good on details,' he said modestly.

He was very good on the details of Katharina Kornagel's departure, describing with astounding precision the clothing she had been wearing and the luggage she had been carrying when he drove her to the railway station in Lindau on 11 December.

It had been, he said, a pearl-grey dress with a deeper grey pattern, a yellow scarf with a red rose print and a brown loden coat. Specially for the trip, she had bought a new suitcase with little wheels and a handle for pulling it along.

Here, however, Spengler's memory again failed him. He could not recall where Katharina had bought the suitcase, although he admitted that he had driven her to the shop.

If his memory sometimes failed, his powers of invention did not. After the sergeant had checked with the ticket office in Lindau and learned that not one ticket to Bremen had been sold on 11 December, Spengler said that he had not actually seen Katharina buy the ticket. She had only told him that she was going to Bremen to visit her old friend Emma Fogler. There had been no place to park at the station and he had let her out in front of the main entrance.

'Maybe she went to visit relatives in East Germany or Russia,' he suggested. 'She often talked about going there.'

The inspector's response was to ask the Bremen police to contact Emma Fogler.

They reported that she had moved to Freiburg in March 1987.

'Katharina can't have known it,' said Spengler.

The inspector was becoming frustrated. Any other suspect in his experience would have long since confessed when confronted with such overwhelming evidence of his mendacity, but not Erwin Spengler. Whatever statements the inspector disproved, they were promptly replaced with others more or less credible.

'The worst part is that what he's doing is not so stupid,' said the inspector. 'We don't need the actual corpse to establish homicide, but we do need it to determine the cause of death. She could have fallen and split open her head. If he was tried for murder, he'd be acquitted. About the only charge we could sustain now would be for obtaining money under false pretences.'

But even this was not a possible charge against Erwin Spengler. Having tired of thinking up new answers to the inspector's questions, he made what was perhaps his first true statement concerning the sudden improvement in his financial situation.

Katharina, he said, had given him two signed bank transfers with the amounts left blank.

'The devil take him!' yelled the inspector. 'If it's true, he had no motive to murder her!'

It was true. The bank transfers were located and the signature on them was unquestionably that of Katharina Kornagel. The amounts, as Spengler admitted freely, had been filled in by him.

'There was nothing illegal about that,' he said. 'Katharina told me I could. We were very good friends.'

They apparently had been. Hoping for a forgery, the inspector sent the transfer slips up to Stuttgart, together with Katharina's signature cards from the bank.

Stuttgart's reply was categoric. The signatures were hers.

'I don't understand it,' said the sergeant. 'Was the woman senile? Was he threatening her? It couldn't have been a sexual relationship, could it?'

'I don't know,' mumbled the inspector, more than a little confused and embarrassed. 'I suppose older women must. . . . I never heard of such a thing. She was healthy, of course, but they were both pretty fat. The physical aspects. . . . The whole damn thing is grotesque. Maybe she was afraid of him.'

If Katharina Kornagel had been afraid of her chauffeur, there was no evidence of it. Maria and Georg Weh and another close friend and tenant of the building, forty-six-year-old Brigitte Scherer, all said that she had been very fond of Spengler and that the relationship had been that of grandmother and grandson. They had never had the impression she was afraid of him and they found the idea of a sexual relationship ludicrous.

Mrs Scherer had always looked after the house plants when Katharina went off on trips, but this time she had not been given the key to the flat. She thought it very unlikely that Katharina would have simply forgotten.

Katharina, it seemed, had not forgotten things and she was far from senile. Dr Leopold Hartrich, her doctor, stated that he had been in the habit of visiting her every fourteen days, not because there was anything wrong with her, but simply because of her age and the fact that she was a good deal overweight.

'Actually, she was sound as a dollar,' he told the sergeant, apparently unaware that the dollar was about as sound as the Nicaraguan cordoba. 'She was carrying three and a half stone more than she should, but her heart could stand it.'

'And her head?' said the sergeant.

'Better than most,' said the doctor. 'She was sound in mind and body and she was enjoying her life so much that she'd probably have lived another twenty years, particularly if she took off a little weight.'

The inspector was worried. He had long since given up any hope of extracting a confession from Erwin Spengler, and it was becoming obvious that obtaining an indictment of any kind would be difficult.

There was no doubt that Mrs Kornagel had given

Spengler the transfer slips voluntarily. Had he forced her to sign them, she could have stopped payment with a telephone call to the bank.

Sexual dependence was out of the question. Katharina's doctor had said that, in his opinion, she had not engaged in sex for twenty years.

Nor was there physical evidence of murder. The quantity of blood on the floor of the entrance hall was not so large that it could not have stemmed from a bad cut or even a severe nose bleed. Spengler's fingerprints were all over the flat, but, as he freely admitted, he had spent nearly as much time there as he had at home.

The only weak point in his defence was the hydrochloric acid. Spengler had said that he had used it to remove mineral stains from Mrs Kornagel's bathtub. He had been careless and had slopped it around a good deal. Asked if he did not realize that it was dangerous, he said no.

This statement, however, was contradicted by his wife. He had, she said, used hydrochloric acid to clean their tub too, but he had been careful to wear rubber gloves and a face mask.

The statement proved nothing other than that Spengler was, as usual, lying. It was useless anyway as, under German law, a wife could not be called upon to testify against her husband.

The inspector was left with the near certain knowledge that Erwin Spengler had murdered Katharina Kornagel, but that he was going to get away with it.

'We can't even suggest a motive,' he said glumly. 'The signed transfer slips are proof that she'd have given him anything he wanted. Killing her simply did him out of the rest of her money. He's not named in her will.'

'I can't believe he killed her deliberately,' mused the sergeant. 'She was extremely generous with him. When she bought him the Mercedes, she told the salesman, "Now, Erwin can drive me around wherever I need to go and he'll have a car for himself." It must have been an accident.'

'I don't think we'll ever know what it was,' said the inspector. 'We've all the information now that we're going to get.'

But he was mistaken.

Two days later, Maria and Georg Weh received a picture postcard from Bremen. It read, 'Having wonderful time. Wish you were here. Katharina.'

The following week, Brigitte Scherer also received a postcard signed *Katharina*. It was from Frankfurt and she asked Brigitte to scrub the building entrance hall for her. It was her turn, but she would not be back in time to do it.

Over the next few days, two more postcards were received by the occupants of the house at Auwiesen Way 3, one from as far away as the Canary Islands. All were signed *Katharina* and the recipients were addressed by their first names.

'Well, we know that it wasn't Mrs Kornagel who sent them,' said the inspector. 'The signature's not hers and the handwriting is different on every card. On the other hand, we know it wasn't Spengler. He's in the detention cells, although how much longer we can keep him there, I don't know.'

'He must have an accomplice who is travelling around and sending the postcards,' the sergeant decided, 'but how does he know their first names?'

'Maybe a former tenant,' said the inspector. 'Look into it.'

It was not a tenant at all. No one had moved out of the building for years and none of the present tenants had been absent at the time the postcards were sent.

'I even checked on his wife,' said the sergeant, 'but she couldn't afford the bus fare out of the city. Says Spengler spent every penny he got his hands on for his car. He's a real motor nut. She and the kids have only started eating since he's been in detention.'

'In detention,' repeated the inspector thoughtfully. 'Something has just occurred to me. Find out how many

Manfred and Ursula Graf with nephew (*Love among the Jewellers*)

Fernando Alonso de Celada under arrest (*Scourge of Hotel Porters*)

Kai Metzmann, heir to the family millions (*Instant Inheritance*)

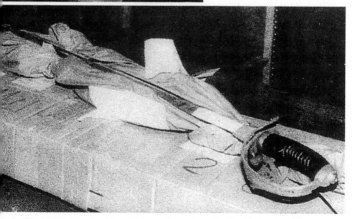

The sabre used in the Metzmann murders (*Instant Inheritance*)

Carl-Heinz and Hermine Neumann leaving court (*Extended Family*)

Alain Bara with police re-enacting the murder (*Domestic Complications*)

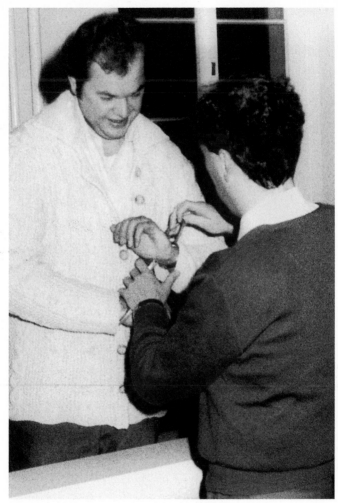

Erwin Spengler in handcuffs (*Down the Drain*)

André Bodmer and Doris Andrist, lovers who feared divine retribution (*Simulated Psychopath*)

Bernadette and Pierre Rouaux, each sentenced to 20 years' imprisonment (*Dangers of Psychology*)

people have been released from the detention cells since Spengler went in.'

The sergeant stared at him silently for a moment.

'Ah!' he said finally. 'The postcards. You're thinking of who sent the postcards.'

Seven men who had been in the detention cells with Erwin Spengler had subsequently been released. Only four of these could be traced, but one had been in Bremen and another had gone to the Canary Islands.

'Obstructing justice and providing false testimony in a criminal investigation,' said the inspector with considerable satisfaction. 'We'll bring charges against all of them and put them on the fugitive list.'

Only three of the fugitives were ever taken into custody, but two of these admitted to having sent the postcards at Spengler's request. He had given them the names and addresses, saying, 'Send a postcard when you get out. They'll have to release me then because they're not about to find any body.'

The charges against the two men were dropped in exchange for their testimony, and Spengler was confronted with the statements.

'They're lying,' he said. 'I overheard them talking about pulling off a big deal when they got out and they're trying to get me hanged so I won't testify against them.'

'Hanged?' the inspector said later. 'It'll be a wonder if he gets a fine.'

The investigation was at an end. Nothing that the police had been able to do had produced an admission of any kind from Erwin Spengler and, although the experts agreed that there was every reason to believe that a human being had been killed and dissolved in hydrochloric acid in Katharina Kornagel's flat, there was no proof that that person had been Katharina Kornagel or that it was Erwin Spengler who had killed her.

It was therefore with very little optimism that the inspector brought his suspect before the examining magistrate who would decide whether he should be tried or released.

Spengler was confident, and it came as a shock when the magistrate indicted him on suspicion of homicide and ordered him to be held for trial.

While waiting for the trial to take place, the police continued their search for further evidence, but found nothing and, when the trial began on 16 January 1989, the prosecutor could only ask for six years' imprisonment for manslaughter.

A German criminal court is not, however, bound by the demands of the prosecution and, after five days of listening to expert testimony on the dissolving of large women in acid, the jury surprised everyone, but particularly Erwin Spengler, by finding the defendant guilty of premeditated murder and sentencing him to life imprisonment.

Spengler suffered a nervous breakdown upon hearing the verdict and was carried out of the courtroom on a stretcher. He had completely destroyed the body, but he had still not got away with murder.

12

DANGEROUS NEIGHBOURS

Raked deep in the rock by the icy claws of ancient glaciers, the long narrow lakes of Maggiore, Como, Iseo and Garda form one of the most beautiful regions of northern Italy. Sheltered to the north by steep conical mountains and blessed with one of the mildest climates in Europe, they have attracted tourists since the time of the Romans and perhaps before.

It is rarely cold, rarely oppressively warm, and on many mornings soft mist lies over the lakes, blurring the outlines of the mountains to an unreal, fairy landscape that seems scarcely of this world.

There are few large cities directly on the lakes, but there is a multitude of villages, each more charming than the one before, and between them lie great villas and old hotels, their spacious grounds filled with ancient pines, palms, cypresses, oleanders, exotic trees and a profusion of flowering plants.

On a golden early-summer morning, the Italian lakes seem as close to Eden as any place on earth.

Alas! The devil once came to Eden and, on the lovely morning of 15 May 1985, he came to the tiny village of Rivoltella.

Rivoltella lies on the southern end of Lake Garda, and many of its residents work in the nearby town of Brescia. It has several shops, a volunteer fire department, two police constables and a primary school.

At approximately eight o'clock on that Wednesday morning, an eleven-year-old girl named Marzia Savio was pedalling her bicycle along a flower-bordered lane on her way to the school.

She was almost halfway there when she disappeared.

The point where this happened could be determined, for her bicycle was lying beside the path.

It was found by thirty-six-year-old Giovanni Savio, Marzia's father. When Marzia failed to appear in class, her teacher telephoned to ask if she was sick. It was the normal reaction in such a small, tightly-knit community.

The call was received by Albertina Savio, Marzia's thirty-two-year-old mother, who was frightened to the point that she called her husband at work in Brescia. Marzia was not the sort of girl to skip school and she thought that there must have been an accident.

As Giovanni knew the precise route that his daughter took to reach the school, he set out on foot to cover it and soon came upon the bicycle.

This frightened him as badly as the telephone call had frightened his wife. The bicycle was undamaged and the path was too narrow for motor vehicles. There had therefore been no accident. The conclusion was that Marzia's disappearance was the result of a deliberate act, and the first thought that occurred was of a sex crime.

It was almost a relief when the ransom call was received the following day. A man speaking in a muffled, obviously disguised voice said, 'We have Marzia. She is all right and we have left her her school things so that she will not get behind in her studies. Get the ransom money read and wait for our next call.'

The ransom demanded was the equivalent of thirty thousand pounds.

Giovanni said they would pay. Where was the money to be left?

The kidnapper said there would be further instructions later and hung up.

Savio had not been the only one listening to the kidnapper's demands. Inspector Dario Maladetti of the Brescia police department of criminal investigations, his assistant, Detective Sergeant Bruno Frascatti, and a tape recorder had been listening silently on the same line.

The Savios had reported their daughter's disappearance to the Brescia police the same evening, once a search of the village by friends, neighbours and a detachment from the local carabinieri had failed to find any trace of her.

Brescia is a city of nearly a quarter of a million inhabitants, and the criminal police carry out investigations in many of the smaller communities nearby.

The inspector, a slender, olive-skinned man with a black moustache, had immediately come out with the sergeant and listened to the details of the disappearance.

'Are you in a position to pay a ransom?' he asked.

Savio said that he was not personally, but that his father had recently sold his interest in a construction company and was comparatively well off. Marzia was his only grandchild.

'Who knows about this sale?' said the inspector.

'Everybody in Rivoltella,' said Savio, 'but no one here would kidnap a child for ransom.'

The inspector did not pursue the subject. The ransom call had not yet been received and he could only hope that the motive had been money. There were worse motives for abducting an eleven-year-old girl.

The sergeant, a large, glum young man with heavy eyebrows and a permanently morose expression, knew about the other motives, and he broached the subject once he and the inspector were alone, after the ransom call.

'The kidnapper could be trying to turn a profit on a corpse,' he suggested.

The inspector shrugged.

'The grandfather coming into a large sum of money recently is a good sign,' he said. 'Savio has more faith in the honesty of his fellow villagers than I. Somebody here may have seen a chance to make a killing.'

'I would prefer a different term,' said the sergeant.

The next day, Marzia's grandfather gave his son a

suitcase containing sixty million lire, the sum demanded, and a second identical suitcase filled with packets of paper having banknotes only on the outside. The serial numbers of all the bills were recorded.

'I assume,' said the inspector to Giovanni Savio, 'that you have had no experience in such cases so I shall explain what we are going to do.

'For the kidnapper, the moment of greatest danger is when he collects the ransom. No system has ever been devised which avoids this risk. There have been many ingenious schemes, but, in the end, the kidnapper or his accomplice must be at a certain place at a certain time to pick up the money. It is then that we catch him.

'Were it not for this, there would be a thousand kidnappings a day as it is a simple means of obtaining large sums of money and almost impossible to guard against.

'Now, you are, no doubt, prepared to pay the ransom if you get your daughter back unharmed, but Italian law forbids payment of ransom and it is therefore my duty to prevent you from making such payment.

'What we shall try to do then is lead the kidnapper to believe that the ransom is being paid, so that he will take the risk of trying to collect it, but he must not be allowed to do so. Is that clear?'

'Not at all,' said Savio. 'We don't care about the money or the law either. We want Marzia back.'

The inspector had heard this before and he knew what his reply had to be, although it pained him to make it.

'Alive, I presume,' he said coldly. 'You are not rich enough to be the target of a kidnapper. This one knew of your father's sale of the construction company, so he knows you and he may know your daughter. If he does, he cannot release her, for she can identify him.'

Mrs Savio turned pale and looked as if she were about to faint.

'What can we do?' groaned Savio, the beads of sweat popping out on his forehead.

'Don't pay out a lira without proof that your daughter

is alive,' said the inspector, 'and undertake no contact with the kidnapper without our knowledge.

The second admonition was scarcely necessary. The Savios could not contact the kidnapper without the inspector's knowledge, as he and the sergeant had moved into the Savio home and occupied the spare bedroom.

With them in the bedroom was an installation made by the police technicians which automatically recorded all telephone calls coming into or emanating from the house.

Arrangements had also been made for tracing any incoming calls, but there was little hope that this would prove to be of value. Kidnappers normally telephone from public telephone booths and, unless a police unit happens to be in the immediate vicinity, are usually gone by the time the call is traced.

The procedure is, however, routine in such cases and recording the calls is important as it provides a comparison of the voices making the calls.

They would not necessarily be from the same person. Often it occurs to people that they might be able to collect the ransom although they had nothing to do with the kidnapping.

The next two calls were, however, from the same man; his voice could be identified electronically.

Although the inspector took pains to conceal it from the Savios, he found the second and third calls puzzling and ominous.

The man offered nothing new, but merely repeated that Marzia was in good health and that he wanted the money.

Giovanni Savio replied, as he had been instructed, that the money was ready and would be paid when he was told how to pay it, and when he had proof that Marzia was all right. He could not bring himself to say, 'alive'.

The caller hung up without saying another word.

'He's trying to decide how to get the money without exposing himself,' comforted the inspector. 'He'll phone again.'

He did not want the Savios to take note that there had been no mention of proof that Marzia was alive.

'I'm afraid she isn't,' he told the sergeant privately. 'It's three weeks now and he's phoned three times. Never anything definite. If he could, he'd have tried to hand over the girl and collect by now.'

'Moreno's nearly always botched his kidnappings,' commented the sergeant.

Moreno was thirty-one-year-old Carlo Moreno, the sole potential suspect that the investigation had been able to turn up from the police files.

In some respects, he was a plausible suspect as he was a sex pervert with a long history of offences against pre-pubescent female children and he had been involved in no less than four abortive kidnappings.

He had been released three months earlier, following his last offence, and owed his liberty entirely to his incompetence. Whether kidnapping or child moles-tation, Moreno had rarely managed to carry out his intended crimes. The charges were, therefore, usually for nothing more than 'attempted' something.

In other respects, Moreno was a less likely suspect. He was not known ever to have been in Rivoltella in his life, so he would not have known of the grandfather's sale of the construction company.

He was also missing, and the last known sighting of him had been in Brescia at the beginning of May.

'But that makes him a better suspect,' said the inspec-tor. 'If he did take the Savio girl, he'd have to stay out of sight or he knows we'd tail him until he led us to her.'

'I hope it is Moreno,' commented the sergeant. 'He's never killed one of the kids yet so maybe he hasn't killed this one.'

'Work on the construction company sale angle,' said the inspector. 'If we can determine that he knew about it, we'll have confirmation of a sort.'

He and the sergeant were no longer in Rivoltella, where they had been replaced by two detectives second

158

class. Developments in the Savio case were proceeding very slowly and they had other matters to attend to.

It had been a relief for them to leave the Savios' house. The torment of the parents and grandparents of the abducted child was painful to observe.

Months had now passed and, although the kidnapper continued to telephone at ever longer intervals and insist that the child was happy and in good health, he had not provided the slightest evidence that she was even alive.

No ransom money had been paid and, on the two occasions when the kidnapper made a specific rendezvous, he had not turned up.

The case had, in the meantime, attracted great sympathy from the public and even the Pope had intervened, issuing an appeal to the kidnapper to release his little victim.

The results of the sergeant's investigations were favourable in so far as they concerned the probability of Carlo Moreno as a suspect, but portentous for the fate of the victim.

Moreno, it turned out, had actually worked briefly for the construction company in which the grandfather had had an interest and he had lived in Rivoltella, less than two streets from the Savios' home.

'The girl very probably knew him by sight, at least,' said the sergeant, 'and if he releases her, she'll be able to identify him.'

'He can't release her because she's dead,' said the inspector bluntly. 'Too much time has passed. I doubt that he's even in the area any longer. Put out a wanted-on-suspicion-of-homicide order to all police and carabiniere units nationwide. He could be in Sicily, for all we know.'

Carlo Moreno was much closer than Sicily. The day after the order was sent out, there was a response. Moreno was in jail in Verona, less than forty miles to the east of Brescia.

He had not been in jail at the time of the disappearance

of Marzia Savio, however, and the sergeant drove over to Verona to interrogate him.

He returned little wiser.

'I couldn't form an opinion,' he told the inspector. 'The man's more at home in an interrogation room than in his own house. He answers questions, but the answers don't mean anything.'

'But no alibi,' said the inspector. 'What's he in for this time?'

'Usual thing,' said the sergeant. 'Got an eight-year-old's panties off and was playing around with her and with himself when a playground guard nailed him. She wasn't injured physically. Just scared.'

'How long has he been in custody?' asked the inspector.

'Since a week ago Wednesday,' said the sergeant, 'and nobody's telephoned the Savios in that time.'

'Doesn't mean anything,' the inspector told him. 'There were no calls for weeks before that. Well, if he's responsible, this is confirmation that she's dead.'

The sergeant raised his eyebrows questioningly.

'If she was alive, he wouldn't have to pick on other little girls,' said the inspector.

Carlo Moreno remained a suspect for another two weeks, but was then exonerated by another telephone call to the family.

It was recorded and the technicians reported that the caller was the man who had made the previous calls. As always, he wanted the ransom, but was unable to suggest a way of receiving it. He refused to let Marzia's mother speak to her over the telephone.

'Good,' said the inspector grimly. 'He's not giving up. The child's dead, but he's still trying to collect the ransom. His greed will hang him.'

'Unfortunately not,' the sergeant reminded him. 'He could murder every child in Rivoltella and not serve more than thirty years for it.'

'That is not our problem,' said the inspector. 'What

we must do is adjust to the fact that Moreno is not our man. We need another suspect.'

'I don't know where we'll get one,' objected the sergeant. 'About the only people who knew about the sale of the construction company are in Rivoltella, and we've nothing against any of them.'

'Not as kidnappers for ransom,' said the inspector, 'but maybe that wasn't the primary motive. Maybe the motive was sex and the killer simply wanted to take advantage of the situation. Don't forget, from the very beginning there was never any proof that the girl was alive.'

'That doesn't alter the fact that he must have known of the sale of the construction company, which makes him a resident of Rivoltella,' argued the sergeant.

'Exactly,' said the inspector. 'So what you are going to look for is gossip in Rivoltella about men who are known to be a little too interested in little girls. The fathers may not know about it, but the kids will, and, probably, some mothers too. While you're doing that, I'll run a trace on the people Savio works with here in Brescia. He could have mentioned the sale to one of them.'

'He swears he didn't,' said the sergeant, 'and, if he wasn't from Rivoltella, the girl probably wouldn't have known him, so he wouldn't have had to murder her.'

'True,' conceded the inspector, 'but we don't know who we're dealing with. Most child molesters don't murder the victim, but for some it's part of the behaviour pattern.'

'Yes, but if he was from Brescia, that would make the motive the ransom money again,' argued the sergeant, 'and if he wasn't from Rivoltella, he wouldn't know what route the girl took to get to school or maybe even that Savio had a daughter.'

The inspector thought it over.

'You're right,' he said. 'Statistically, over eighty per cent of sexual offences against minors are committed by neighbours, friends of the family or relatives, and that's where we'll have to look, whether in Rivoltella or Brescia.'

The names of the male residents of Rivoltella had already been run through the police records section and there was no one who had been charged with an offence against a female minor. This did not, however, mean that there had been no such offences. Children frequently do not tell their parents, and parents, in cases where the child is not physically injured, often prefer not to report an incident to the police.

It was the unreported incidents which would occupy the attention of the sergeant.

'What about the people on the telephone in the Savios' house?' he asked. 'Should I pull them off?'

The inspector hesitated.

'Not yet,' he said finally. 'We'll close that operation when we close the case.'

It would turn out to be a wise decision in the end, although the next call by the kidnapper was a tantalizingly near miss for the police. The technicians had come within a few seconds of tracing the call before it was cut off.

The inspector would have been even more dismayed had it not been that the new lines of investigation were finally beginning to produce results.

One of the men working in the same company as Savio had a police record of violence against pre-pubescent children, and Sergeant Frascatti had uncovered a significant amount of gossip in Rivoltella concerning a forty-two-year-old man named Honorifio Brega.

'It may be nothing,' he told the inspector. 'Brega's an outsider and there'd be gossip about him in any case. He's not popular with the adults.'

'But with the kids,' said the inspector, nodding. 'I know the type.'

It was the type that, a generation ago, was called a bum. In a more civilized era, it was termed a person with an alternative life-style. Brega lived in an abandoned goat shed on the edge of the village, wore a huge beard, held no regular job and owned neither a car nor a television set.

'Keeps chickens and grows a few vegetables,' said the sergeant. 'Does a little begging and, probably, a little stealing too. No police record.'

'And, of course, the kids love him,' added the inspector. 'Any incidents with little girls?'

'None reported,' said the sergeant, 'but he worries the mothers and they probably have a reason for it.'

'You talked to him?' asked the inspector.

The sergeant nodded.

'He's a possibility,' he said. 'I doubt he'd kill a child deliberately, but he might if he thought she was going to report him for playing around with her. He's not as indifferent to money and comfort as people think he is. He has some nice things in that goat shed.'

'Wouldn't be the first harmless eccentric to get in a tight spot and panic,' mused the inspector. 'I don't suppose he has a telephone?'

'As a matter of fact, he does,' said the sergeant. 'God knows what he needs it for.'

'I think you had better find out,' the inspector told him.

He was less impressed by the sergeant's potential suspect than by the one who had turned up among Savio's colleagues in Brescia. No harmless eccentric, he had been charged on nine occasions with acts of violence against young children of both sexes.

Described by psychoanalysts as a case of arrested sexual development, Luciano Parisi was thought to have had an early sexual experience with a young cousin which had left such an impression that he was attracted only to young children.

However, his feelings of guilt over this attraction rendered him incapable of orgasm, and the resulting frustration found an outlet in violence against his victims.

What made Parisi interesting to the inspector was the fact that he was known to be particularly aroused by little girls riding bicycles.

Marzia Savio had been riding a bicycle the day she disappeared.

Parisi had not been working on that day and he was unable to provide an alibi for the time in question. On the other hand, a stranger in such a small village would have been noticed and no one in Rivoltella reported seeing any strangers at all on that day.

As there was insufficient evidence to hold him, the inspector ordered his release and, at the same time, telephoned the Verona police to advise them that Carlo Moreno was no longer a suspect in the Marzia Savio case.

To his consternation, he was told that Moreno had been released. The girl's parents had refused to press charges and there were no grounds on which to hold him.

'When was he released?' asked the inspector apprehensively.

It had been the day before the last telephone call to the Savios.

'More suspects all the time,' said the sergeant glumly, 'and none of them any good. I've eliminated Brega. He has an alibi for the time the girl disappeared. He's in the detention cells, if you want to talk to him.'

'What's he doing in the detention cells, if you cleared him?' demanded the inspector.

'I found out why he needed a telephone,' said the sergeant. 'He's one of the main drug suppliers for the area. The narcotics people have taken over.'

'I think we can forget about Moreno, too,' said the inspector. 'Our best bet may still be tracing one of the calls. The man's becoming more careless all the time.'

His observation turned out to be prophetic.

Two days later, there was another call to the Savios. Marzia, said the kidnapper, was in good health and pursuing her studies. He wanted to know if the ransom money was ready and said that it was to be left in a sack beside highway S11 leading to Venice. There would be another call to fix the time.

Savio had been instructed to keep the caller on the line for as long as possible, but in the past the connection had always been cut before there was time to trace the call.

This time was to be different. Pretending not to understand the instructions for leaving the ransom, Savio was able to engage the caller, who seemed to have become more confident and less wary, in a longer conversation.

Suddenly, the two detectives burst out of the spare bedroom, where they had been monitoring the call, and ran headlong off down the street.

The long wait had paid off. The call had been traced and it was not from a public telephone, but from a house only four doors away from the Savios' home.

Forty-eight-year-old Alfio Torazzina and his forty-three-year-old wife Graziella were arrested and brought to Brescia, where they were placed under intense interrogation.

Torazzina, a well-to-do butcher who owned a sausage shop and a wine merchant's, was a friend of the Savio family. He denied everything, but after eight hours of almost continuous questioning, his wife broke down and implicated him in the murder.

Confronted with her statement, Torazzina confessed.

He had known of the grandfather's sale of the construction company and thought that the family would pay a ransom without going to the police.

He had not, he insisted, intended to murder Marzia, but when pulling her off her bicycle and carrying her into his house, he held his hand so tightly over her mouth that she smothered to death.

All efforts to revive her having failed, he borrowed an axe from a neighbour and chopped the body up into small pieces, which he packed into five plastic rubbish sacks. He put the girl's clothes and school bag into another plastic sack and threw them into the long grass beside highway S11, a few miles from Brescia.

Torazzina's account of the disposal of the body was true, for the sacks with their badly decomposed contents were found that same day 10 September 1985, 111 days after the murder.

The 'accidental' version of the crime was, however, more dubious. As he was a friend of the Savio family and well known to Marzia, he could not have released her without being identified.

He was therefore indicted on charges of premeditated murder and kidnapping for ransom, while Graziella was indicted as an accessory to the fact in both instances. Torazzina had at first implicated her, saying that she had known of his plans to kidnap the girl and had set up a tent in the basement with cords for tying up the captive. Later, however, he retracted this statement and confirmed her denial of all knowledge of the crime.

As by her own admission she had been present on that day, and as it was difficult to explain how she could have failed to notice her husband chopping up a child's body in the house, the charges were retained, and on 26 September 1986 she was sentenced to ten years' imprisonment.

On the same date, her husband was found guilty of kidnapping and murder and sentenced to life imprisonment.

13

MURDER WITHOUT A MOTIVE

At seven-thirty in the morning of 26 October 1985, a French school bus turned off Route Nationale 159 at a point halfway between the towns of Alençon and Mamers and started down the narrow country road leading to the village of Le Chevrain.

It was typical autumn weather for Normandy, grey, chilly, with rising trails of mist.

Parked on the shoulder of the road was a red Renault 5 and, as bus driver Charles Ledoux slowed to manoeuvre round it, his eyes fell upon an alarming sight.

Stretched on a low bank behind the car was the body of a woman, her skirts bunched up around her waist, her legs sprawled wide apart and her blouse ripped open to expose her left breast. Even from the high driver's seat, Ledoux could see the marks of dried blood across her throat.

Immediately, Ledoux swung the bus round the car, put his foot down on the accelerator and went thundering on to Le Chevrain. He did not know whether the woman was dead or alive, but with a bus full of children he could not stop to investigate.

Le Chevrain is a very small community. It has no police department at all and the sole public official, the mayor, serves without pay.

Generally, the duties of the office are commensurate with the compensation, and Mayor Gaston Dubois, who was rather moodily dunking his bread into his breakfast bowl of coffee when the bus driver burst in upon him, had had little experience of coping with such dramatic reports.

'It must have been a car accident,' he said. 'Who goes around raping women in this weather?'

'No! No!' yelled Ledoux. 'There's no damage to the car. She's been pulled out and raped!'

'I'll go see,' said Dubois. 'You call the ambulance in Alençon.'

He hurried out to his car and drove off in the direction of the route nationale, but returned after only a few moments, looking appalled.

'She's not only been raped,' he said. 'She's been murdered. The body's completely cold.'

'What are you going to do?' Ledoux asked him.

'Call the gendarmerie post in Le Mans,' said the mayor. 'Alençon is too small to handle something like this.'

Le Mans is nearly thirty miles to the south of Le Chevrain, but it is a large town and Alençon, although much closer, has a population of under forty thousand.

Having called the gendarmerie, the mayor returned to the scene of the murder, to find the ambulance had just arrived. There was nothing that the crew could do, however, other than confirm that the woman was dead, and they returned to their base.

The mayor remained alone, waiting in his car. He did not know the correct procedure in such cases, but it seemed to him that someone had to guard the corpse until the gendarmes arrived.

It was past nine o'clock when they did, and then it was only one car with Captain Leon Descroix, Sergeant Jacques Lallois and a medical expert. The mayor's report had been received with some scepticism and their first task was to determine whether there really had been a murder.

This was quickly done by Dr Julien Laroche, a shy, unobtrusive man with regular, almost handsome features and black hair parted on the side. The woman's throat had been cut, he said, following a brief examination of the corpse, and she had been dead for five or six hours. He thought she would have been in her early thirties.

'Thirty-four,' said the mayor. 'I know her. She's Viviane Gueranger. Lives in Champfleur.'

'Is that your village?' asked the captain, a stocky man with a military bearing and a prominent jaw, whose manner was businesslike and matter-of-fact and whose remarks tended to be terse.

The mayor said that it was not, and started to explain, but Sergeant Lallois, who had been making a circuit of the body, but not approaching it as the specialists would want things disturbed as little as possible, called out, 'There are two big patches of dried blood over here!' and the captain went to look. The patches were, indeed, huge.

'Looks as if he cut her throat before he raped her,' said the sergeant.

He was a small, wiry, nervous-looking man with a white scar across his left cheek and his black stiff hair cut in a short military brush.

The inspector said nothing and went back to the car where the mayor and the doctor were waiting.

'Any idea of who might have done this?' he asked, looking at the mayor.

'None at all,' said the mayor. 'It must have been a stranger, a total madman. Viviane is popular around her. She's a highly respectable woman. Born in Champfleur and she still lives there with her father. Her mother died two years ago.'

'Not married?' said the captain.

The mayor shook his head. He had not yet managed to accept that a woman he had known all her life had been murdered and he continued to speak of her in the present tense as if she were still alive.

The sergeant went silently to the car and raised Le Mans over the radio-telephone. The advance party had determined what they had come to find out. The entire homicide squad would be needed.

As the other members of the squad had been on alert,

169

the wait was shorter this time and two gendarmerie vans soon turned into the road from the highway. They came with sirens howling and blue warning lights flashing, which annoyed the sergeant.

'You'd think they were raiding a bordello,' he muttered.

'Go over to Champfleur and bring back the father,' said the captain. 'We need a formal identification by the next of kin. We'll put a sheet over the body so that all he has to see is the face.'

'Which direction?' asked the sergeant, looking at the mayor.

The mayor pointed.

'It's less than a mile,' he said.

'That's not the direction the Renault is facing,' observed the captain.

Raymond Gueranger identified the body of his daughter and was immediately taken to the hospital in Alençon to be treated for shock and a mild heart attack. His only statement was that he had no idea of who could have murdered Viviane. He was not told that she had been raped.

The captain had not expected that he would have. The case bore all the earmarks of a crime committed by a sex psychopath, which meant that he could not be from any of the little farming communities in the area. Conservative and woefully out of tune with the modern world, they were little inclined to tolerate the dangerously deranged.

The investigation would, therefore, be long and difficult. The usual leads to the identity of the murderer would be missing. He would not be someone from her circle of friends, relatives and acquaintances. There had probably been no prior contact between him and his victim. He would not have benefited financially from the crime. And, at such a time and place, there was little hope of witnesses.

All these possibilities would have to be explored none

the less; what seemed to be a sex crime was sometimes only a simulation.

The captain did not think that this one was faked and he was surprised when the autopsy report suggested the possibility.

Following the investigations at the scene, the body had been removed to the morgue in Le Mans, where Dr Laroche had spent a good part of the night performing the postmortem.

His conclusions were presented verbally to the captain over a mug of coffee the following morning as the formal autopsy report had not yet been typed up.

'I am afraid I cannot be very precise about the time of death,' said the doctor, diffidently accepting one of the captain's cigarettes. 'It was not earlier than one-forty on Saturday morning and may have been as late as three.

'The immediate cause of death was massive loss of blood resulting from a severed carotid artery.

'The weapon was either an extremely sharp knife or a straight razor, and the cuts were shallow, less than two inches deep. There was a total of four, all across the front of the throat.

'There was manipulation of the sex organs, and something hard and angular such as a piece of wood was inserted into the vagina, causing laceration of the walls and irritation of the labia minor. No traces of semen were recovered from the body.

'There are no indications of a struggle, no defence cuts or bruises on hands or arms, and the clothing was disarranged after death.'

'Very strange,' said the captain.

He had already received the report from the laboratory, which confirmed that robbery had not been the motive of the crime.

Miss Gueranger's keys, including the keys to her car, had been found lying beside her body. The car was locked and her handbag, which was lying on the front seat, contained a substantial amount of money. A number of other objects had been recovered from the car and some of them, it appeared, had not belonged to Miss Gueranger.

The captain consequently found himself confronted with an even more difficult problem than he had thought. In the case of a sex psychopath, there was at least one lead. The crime was too violent to have been a first offence. It was therefore possible that the killer had a police record. Here, however, there was no known motive at all, neither sex nor money.

The only possibility that remained was something personal, jealousy or revenge, but Viviane Gueranger had been so well known in the area that a reconstruction of her life was not difficult and there had been no great emotional conflicts in it.

The daughter of a well-to-do farmer, she had successfully passed her baccalauréat, the difficult secondary-school examination, at the age of seventeen, and had subsequently obtained her diploma as a nurse.

She had, however, never worked as a nurse, but had taken a job as secretary-receptionist with the Edon Company in Alençon, where she had worked up until the night she was murdered.

On that Friday, she had gone after work with five of her male colleagues to the village of Essay to celebrate the departure of one of them for a better job with another company. The party went in two cars and she left her Renault 5 in the company car park.

After the celebration at the auberge in Essay, the party broke up, three of the men going home and the other two and Viviane going to dine at a popular restaurant, the Auberge de Normandie, in the hamlet of Valframbert on Route Nationale 12 leading to Paris. Viviane was a personal friend of the owners of the restaurant and had often gone on holiday with them.

At a quarter to one in the morning, after a festive evening, one of the men drove her back to the company car park in Alençon and waited long enough to see her drive off in the direction of Champfleur. It was the last time her friends had seen her alive.

'Assuming a normal speed for the road conditions at this time of year, it takes approximately twenty minutes to go from the car park in Alençon to Champfleur,' said the sergeant. 'As she left Alençon at around one o'clock, she should have arrived by one-thirty at the latest. The car was, however, heading away from Champfleur when we found it.'

'I can't believe that she would have been foolish enough to pick up a hitchhiker, unless she knew him,' commented the captain, 'but I can't think of any other explanation.'

'We've checked the men she was with,' said the sergeant. 'They're all people who've known her most of her life. They say that she had a good deal of wine, but it was with her food and she wasn't drunk. All of them were home before she was murdered.'

'And the milkman?' asked the inspector. 'Did you check on him?'

The milkman was twenty-four-year-old Jean-Pierre Pontilly, who had passed along the road leading to Le Chevrain at approximately six in the morning. He had noticed the red Renault parked beside the road, but the fog had not yet lifted at that hour and he had not seen the body. He had come voluntarily to the police immediately following the report of the murder in the newspapers.

'He's in the clear,' said the sergeant. 'His delivery schedule was too tight for him to have stopped to murder anybody.'

'The people she worked with?' suggested the captain. 'Don't forget, this wasn't really a sex crime. He just wanted us to think it was.'

'Nothing,' said the sergeant. 'She wasn't having an affair with anyone at the moment. She wasn't a threat to anybody professionally. She wasn't a lesbian or an old maid. She'd had a few lovers, none among her colleagues, but they were just casual encounters. Nobody was rejected. Nobody got angry.'

'Were any of those encounters with any of the men she was with that night?' asked the captain.

'Possibly with Jerome Mourat,' said the sergeant. 'He's the one who drove her back to the car park. The others seem to have been just friends and colleagues. She didn't have a reputation for being promiscuous.'

'Mourat married?' said the captain.

'Engaged,' the sergeant told him. 'If he and Gueranger did have an affair, it was a number of years back.'

'Someone must have been in the car with her,' mused the captain, 'but the lab says that the murder didn't take place in the car. Her throat was cut where the blood on the ground was. Why would she park the car? Why would she get out of it?'

'She must have been crazy,' said the sergeant. 'That's a lonely place at two o'clock in the morning. No houses in sight. No traffic. And the fog must have been thick.'

'We have to assume that she was rational,' said the captain. 'The only reason I can think of for stopping a car there would be to answer a call of nature. She'd drunk a good deal of wine. Maybe she didn't think she could make it home to Champfleur.'

'The car wasn't facing in the direction of Champfleur,' objected the sergeant.

'We haven't any explanation for that at all,' said the captain, 'so we'll have to skip over it. Let's say she stopped the car to relieve herself. She got out. The murderer was waiting, unseen in the fog. He cut her throat, simulated a sex crime and left.'

'Why?' said the sergeant. 'He didn't rape her. He didn't rob her. He didn't need to simulate a sex crime because there was no known motive anyway. And who locked the car door? Gueranger, when she was only going to relieve herself? Or the murderer? And if so, for what reason?'

'I don't know,' admitted the captain. 'It could only have been a homicidal maniac who killed without reason, but what he was doing out there at that time of night escapes me. One thing seems certain: he had transport. There's no public transport within miles of there and the lab found no bicycle tracks, so it must have been a car.'

'But if he was parked there waiting for her, she'd have seen the car and she wouldn't have stopped to relieve herself,' said the sergeant.

'All right. She didn't stop to relieve herself,' agreed the captain. 'She stopped because she recognized the car.'

'Meaning it was someone she knew,' said the sergeant, beginning to sound slightly more enthusiastic, 'but what was he doing sitting out there in the middle of nowhere?'

'Waiting for her,' answered the captain confidently.

'He must have known she was coming,' said the sergeant.

'Right,' said the captain. 'So all you have to do is determine who knew that she'd be passing that way late at night and then we'll start checking alibis.'

The sergeant found this a somewhat more demanding assignment than the captain had made it sound. He was already aware that Viviane Gueranger had known literally hundreds of people in the area around Alençon, and almost any of them could have learned that she was going to the farewell party for her colleague.

The road past Le Chevrain was the normal route from Alençon to Champfleur, so that merely the knowledge that she had left her car in the company car park would have been enough to permit the interception.

The operation was obviously going to be long and tedious, but the first step was to assemble a list of every male Viviane had known.

It was, of course, not certain that the murderer was male. No trace of semen had been found on or in the body, and a woman could cut a throat as well as a man. Some of the objects found in the car were, however, more suited to a man, particularly an empty wallet.

Whether the wallet, or indeed any of the objects, belonged to the murderer was another question.

The sergeant had scarcely begun on his list when he received a call from the Alençon police, who said they had in custody a man so strange that they thought he might be a suspect in the Gueranger case.

He had been arrested on Monday the twenty-eighth on a charge of attempted rape of a minor, and had turned out to have such a long and bizarre criminal record that they thought him capable of anything.

The sergeant, who had been in Champfleur at the time, drove to Alençon, where he spoke to the suspect, talked to his wife and a number of potential witnesses, collected an armload of police files and returned to Le Mans. There was so much material that it was another twenty-four hours before he was prepared to make a report to the captain.

'I don't know if he's a valid suspect or not,' he said, 'His name is Daniel Roussel. Aged thirty-nine, married, father of a three-year-old daughter. Works at a meat-processing plant in Alençon. There's no evidence that he ever met Gueranger.'

'What's his problem?' asked the captain.

'Young girls, but in a funny way,' said the sergeant. 'The case he's charged with now, the girl is sixteen. He didn't rape her. He handled her private parts and stole her handbag.'

'Weird,' commented the captain. 'He's done it before?'

'Many times,' said the sergeant. 'His record starts when he was ten years old. He was born in Epinay-sur-Seine and his parents had to put him into the reform school there because they couldn't control him.

'From reform school, he went to prison almost without a break. Been in and out ever since. Mostly morals offences, but he's never raped any of them or even tried to. He handles them in an obscene manner and sometimes he steals their handbags, but not always. Total of sixty-eight chargeable offences, almost all involving violence.

'The man has an insane temper and he can turn violent at the drop of a hat. It's a sort of miracle that he's never killed anybody before.'

'What in heaven's name is he doing in a place like Alençon?' said the captain. 'Paris would be more like it.'

What Rousell was doing in Alençon was one of the easier things to learn about him. It was apparently due to a simple error of judgement.

His twenty-two-year-old wife, Ginette, had told the sergeant all about it. She had met Roussel in 1980, shortly after he had completed one of his periodic jail sentences, in the Paris suburb of Argenteuil, where she was working in a car factory.

Because of his extensive criminal record, Roussel found it difficult to obtain work, but she managed to get him into the plant where she worked.

He did well there and, although there were one or two incidents, appeared to be settling into a normal way of life. He was even offered a promotion to foreman.

Simultaneously, however, he had an offer of a job at the meat-processing plant in Alençon and decided to take it.

They moved to Alençon in mid-1983, and it immediately became apparent that the move was a mistake. The meat plant did not pay as well and the work was harder and less interesting.

Mrs Roussel admitted that her husband was sometimes violent, although, she insisted, never to her, but he had not been in trouble with the law for over three years and he was devoted to their little daughter, because of whom they had married in November of the preceding year.

On the evening of 25 October, she said, she, Daniel and Jacques Moulineaux, her husband's best friend, went to the village of Saint-Rémy-de-Sille, where they had dinner in a restaurant called La Poule d'Or.

Daniel was nervous and irritable and became involved in such a violent quarrel with Jacques that he stormed out of the restaurant shortly before midnight.

He did not return, and Jacques drove her home at

approximately one o'clock in the morning. Daniel was not there and she went to bed alone.

'I don't know what time Daniel came in,' she said. 'My nerves are bad and I have to take very strong tablets to be able to sleep. All I know is that he was there in the morning when I woke up.'

She said, however, that Daniel could not have murdered Viviane Gueranger because their car, an old grey Citroën, was in such dire need of repairs that she did not think it could have made it to Le Chevrain and back, and, besides, the petrol tank had been nearly empty and there were no filling stations open at that hour.

Jacques Moulineaux corroborated Mrs Roussel's statement in every detail, and the owners of the restaurant confirmed that there had been a violent argument, after which Roussel had left.

'I had the car brought over to the garage,' said the sergeant, 'and the mechanic says that it's true, the clutch is practically worn out. If Roussel drove it to Le Chevrain from Saint-Rémy-de-Sille, he'd have been taking a chance.'

'He sounds a poor suspect to me,' said the captain. 'He didn't know the woman. He didn't know she'd been passing that way at that time, and she didn't know him so she wouldn't have stopped.'

The sergeant was inclined to agree, and both he and the captain were surprised when the laboratory technicians reported that they had found traces of human blood on the handbrake and in the boot of the Citroën.

Still sceptical, the captain had the Roussel's house searched, and a blood-stained shirt was found. The blood group was the same as that of Viviane Gueranger.

Roussel was formally indicated on a charge of homicide but denied all knowledge of the crime. He had, he said, come home only shortly after his wife, but she had been sleeping soundly and he had not wanted to wake her. He insisted that he had never heard the name of Viviane Gueranger until he read of the murder in the newspapers. The gendarmerie was trying him on his past record, he charged.

There was, however, some evidence that he was not telling the truth. Viviane's father had examined the objects found in his daughter's car following the murder and identified a wallet, a handkerchief, a tube of shaving cream and a folding rule as things that he had never seen in Viviane's possession.

Jacques Moulineux had been shown the same four objects and had identified the wallet and the rule as belonging to Roussel.

Mrs Roussel had not been shown the objects, as the testimony of a spouse was not admissable in a criminal case.

Inexplicably, Roussel admitted that the rule and the wallet were his, but continued to deny the murder. He had, he said, no idea how they had got into the victim's car.

The captain did not know whether to believe him or not. There were many questions which the investigation had failed to answer. The motive for the murder was not known, nor was the reason for the simulation of a sex crime. Roussel's fingerprints had not been found at the scene of the crime. Leaving his personal possessions in the car of the victim seemed an utterly senseless act and there was no explanation of how he could have known that the woman would pass that way.

The case against Daniel Roussel was far from watertight, and the captain would have been neither surprised nor dismayed by an acquittal.

The jury was, however, less troubled by the unanswered questions than the captain and, on 12 September 1986, they found Roussel guilty of wilful murder and sentenced him to life imprisonment, but with the possibility of early parole.

Roussel's only comment was that they had convicted an innocent man.

14

THE EXPLOSIVE GANGSTER

On the afternoon of Saturday, 15 August 1987, game warden Marcel Leclerc was passing through the Forest of Lisses when he saw, lying in a little clearing, an object which should have aroused his curiosity, but which did not.

The object was long, black and lumpy, and it had apparently been on fire for it was surrounded by a circle of scorched vegetation.

Setting a fire in the forest was, of course, prohibited, and the sight should have alarmed Leclerc, but he was pressed for time and the circumstance failed to register.

It did a week later on 23 August when he chanced to pass that way again. As it was a Sunday, this time he was in no hurry and he walked over to investigate.

It was a warm summer day and the object lay bathed in bright sunshine. As he drew near it, he saw that it was covered with feeding insects which, disturbed by his approach, rose in a buzzing swarm to reveal something vaguely resembling a human body.

Only vaguely, however. The sex, age and even size of the corpse were impossible to determine, for it was literally torn to shreds and Leclerc thought the wild pigs had been at it. Omnivorous, they would eat anything digestible.

As the stench of putrefying flesh was nearly unbearable even at a distance, Leclerc approached no closer, but set off at once for the gendarmerie station in nearby Corbeil-Essonnes, a town of some forty thousand, twenty miles to the southeast of Paris.

It being Sunday and Corbeil-Essonnes, stretched lazily along the banks of the Seine, being a relatively quiet community, there was only a skeleton staff on duty in the department of criminal investigations, and the members of the homicide squad had to be called in from their homes.

The afternoon was therefore well advanced by the time that Lieutenant Yves Laurent, Sergeant Jules Pichon, Dr Paul Estrelle and six specialists from the gendarmerie technical section arrived at the scene.

None of the party was pleased at being called out on a Sunday, but Sergeant Pichon was more unhappy than the others. A blond, muscular man with a very short haircut and a face that looked as if it had been chiselled out of something hard, he was a keen sportsman and had been in the middle of an amateur soccer game.

'There should be a law against game wardens running around in the woods on Sunday,' he grumbled.

'Monday would have done as well,' agreed the lieutenant. 'The body's undoubtedly been here for some time.'

'Two or three weeks,' said Dr Estrelle. 'It's a mess. I can't even tell if it's male or female.'

'Identification is going to be a problem,' observed the lieutenant. 'It looks as if it's been half eaten by something.'

'No, I don't think so,' said the doctor, a tall, slender, rather distinguished-looking man who wore a gold pince-nez and a carefully-trimmed little black moustache, 'but we'll have to get it over to the morgue before I can say anything at all. Let's see if we can get it rolled on to this plastic sheet.'

With the help of the sergeant and the specialists, the body was rolled and slid on to the square of plastic, such parts as had fallen off were added, the sheet wrapped around the whole and the bundle sealed with tape. The atmosphere improved immediately and substantially.

The lieutenant took no part in the proceedings. He was a short, somewhat pudgy man with a round head and a haircut which looked as if it had been achieved by placing a soup bowl over his skull and trimming round the edge of it.

'Well, usual procedures,' he said matter-of-factly. 'I'll be waiting for the reports in my office.'

He had come to the scene in his own car and he now got into it and drove away.

The sergeant and the specialists began staking out the area preliminary to a thorough search for potential clues, and the doctor went to the gendarmerie car to summon the ambulance over the radio-telephone.

By six o'clock, the operations at the scene had been terminated and, at seven, the specialists completed their report.

It was very short. They found nothing except a few scraps of material, presumably from the victim's clothing, but there was not enough of it to tell whether the clothing was that of a man or a woman.

'Their conclusion is that the murder, if murder it was, took place elsewhere and the body was only brought there for disposal,' said the sergeant who had brought the report to the lieutenant's office. 'There's access by car within fifty yards of where it was found.'

'Fifty yards,' mused the lieutenant. 'That could indicate that it was more than one person who brought it there. A corpse of that size is heavy. Is there any place closer to the road where they could have got rid of it?'

'Yes,' said the sergeant,' but they may have been afraid that it would be found too quickly.'

'If they took that much trouble to conceal the identity, the murderer or murderers may be closely enough associated with the victim to be obvious suspects,' said the lieutenant. 'Give Estrelle a call and see how he's getting on with the autopsy.'

The doctor was far from finished with his examination of the body, but he had already arrived at several important conclusions.

To begin with, there was clear evidence of homicide. Two of the heavy winged darts used with a twelve-gauge shotgun for shooting wild boar had been found inside the ribcage, and the doctor had sent them to the ballistics department for examination and evaluation.

The time of death was tentatively established as having taken place during the second week of August.

Finally, the physical characteristics of the victim had been determined to some extent: a man approximately five feet seven inches tall weighing between nine and a half and ten stone; between thirty and forty years of age. At some time in the past, he had suffered a severe fracture of the left ankle, which had been repaired with a small metal plate. There was nothing on the plate to indicate which hospital it came from.

For the rest the doctor was puzzled.

'I have never seen anything like this before,' he said. 'The man was blown apart by an explosion which took place inside his body.'

'You mean the corpse was cut open and a bomb placed inside it?' asked the lieutenant, frowning in an effort to comprehend the doctor's meaning.

'No,' said the doctor. 'A hand grenade or anything similar would have left fragments and there are none. The man himself was the bomb. He was filled with something explosive which blew him apart.'

'While he was alive?' exclaimed the sergeant, looking horrified.

'No, I don't think so,' said the doctor. 'The boar darts entered his upper chest and no one could have survived being shot with such heavy slugs. As there would have been no point in shooting him after he had blown up, it seems probable that he was already dead at the time.'

'And you found nothing to identify him?' asked the lieutenant. 'No rings, no wallet, no keys?'

'Not a thing,' said the doctor. 'Only the plate on his ankle.'

'Very much a professional job,' remarked the lieutenant. 'Whoever he was, the people who murdered him were underworld. Call in the informers, Jules, and see if somebody suddenly dropped out of sight around the middle of August. Better contact Paris too. This is more typical of their part of the world than here.'

'Shouldn't we canvas the area for potential witnesses?' the sergeant wondered.

'For the record,' said the lieutenant, 'I should be very surprised if we found any.'

The gendarmes did not. Although every person living or having reason to be anywhere near the scene of the discovery of the body was contacted, no one reported noticing anything out of the ordinary for the period in question.

No information was obtained from the police and gendermerie informers either. There had, of course, been disappearances in the Paris region, but the victims were either in the morgue or of the wrong size or age. There was no one unaccounted for.

'We'll solve this only if we get a break,' said the lieutenant. 'Put it on the back burner. Maybe something will turn up.'

Nothing did, but, on 28 November, a detective named Louis Lefrond, who was attached to the Corbeil-Essonnes department of criminal investigations and who had taken part in the investigation of the body found in the forest, was sent to the city of Cannes in connection with the investigation of a series of armed robberies which had taken place in widely separated parts of the country.

Cannes is on the French Riviera, six hundred and twenty-five miles south of Corbeil-Essonnes, and although the weather had turned cold and rainy in the north, in Cannes it was bright and sunny and a few brave souls were still frolicking on the beaches.

The detective was not at all unhappy about his assignment, which, however, turned out to be short as no progress in the cases concerned was made.

On Monday 30 November, the day before he was due to start back for Corbeil-Essonnes, he was sitting in a pavement café with four of the detectives from the

Cannes gendarmerie when he chanced to mention that his department was stuck with an unidentified corpse.

'And we have a corpse we can't locate,' said one of the Cannes detectives.

'How do you know it's a corpse then?' said the detective.

The Cannes gendarmes, it seemed, did not know with certainty, but they had reason to suspect that it was.

For the past two years, a gang of four had been staging a series of hold-ups, robberies and violent rapes and, although the gendarmes knew their identity, they had carried out their operations so smoothly that there was not enough evidence to even arrest them.

An unusually efficient combination of mind and muscle, the gang was masterminded by a twenty-one-year-old girl named Anna-Maria Corsaro, a former university student who had been involved in radical student activities and had converted to professional crime as a more effective means of redistributing the wealth.

Her colleague and fellow-intellectual was Martin Herisson, a thirty-five-year-old sales manager who had held responsible positions with international companies in Canada and South America.

Corsaro was an Italian national and Herisson possessed dual French and Italian citizenship.

The muscle of the gang was provided by thirty-four-year-old Thierry Lang, who came from the Paris area and whose police record went back to the age of eighteen, and Michel Berry, aged forty, who had served time in prison for everything from armed robbery to walking on the grass. As the oldest and most experienced, Berry was considered to be the head of the gang.

The Cannes gendarmes knew a great deal about this gang through their informers and these had reported that Thierry Lang had suddenly disappeared sometime during the first part of August.

'Fascinating,' said Lefrond. 'You say Lang has been in jail?'

'Repeatedly,' the Cannes gendarme confirmed. 'Do you think he might be your corpse?'

'I'm not paid enough to think,' said Lefrond, 'but the lieutenant is, and I'll mention the possibility when I get back.'

The lieutenant was intrigued.

'It could be,' he said. 'It could be. Get me this Lang's police record. I want to see if he ever broke his left ankle.'

Thierry Lang had indeed broken his left ankle, and so badly that it had been necessary to repair it with a metal plate.

'Excellent!' said the lieutenant. 'And the height, weight and age all agree. It looks to me as if we have identified our corpse.'

'And, incidentally, his murderers,' added Sergeant Pichon, 'or at least some very promising suspects.'

'We haven't found any suspects yet,' said the lieutenant, 'but we know who we're looking for and that they must have been staying somewhere around here at the time. Try the better hotels.'

'Better hotels?' queried the sergeant.

'These people are successful bank robbers,' said the lieutenant. 'They wouldn't have been staying in a flophouse.'

Indeed they had not. The sergeant's men soon found a receptionist who recognized the gang of four from their mug shots, particularly Anna-Maria, who was young, pretty and gave the impression of being not entirely unapproachable.

'They took a suite at l'Ermitage on the night of 10 August,' said the sergeant, 'and there was an incident. After they'd left the next morning, one of the hotel employees found a huge pool of half-dried blood in the car park where their car had been standing. It was a white Mercedes Diesel 190. Nobody noticed the licence number. They didn't register under their own names, of course.'

'The licence number doesn't matter,' said the lieutenant. 'The car was certainly stolen. See if the automotive division has any record of a stolen white Mercedes for about that time.'

The automotive division did. A professional violinist had reported the car stolen in Monaco on 9 June.

'Remarkable long-range planning,' said the lieutenant. 'They stole it months before they needed it. It must have been initially intended for another job.'

'And the blood in the car park?' asked the sergeant.

'Lang's,' said the lieutenant. 'They had the body in the boot. We won't find the car. It's at the bottom of the sea or a lake somewhere. Maybe we can find out where it was used, though.'

No one could be found who admitted having seen the white Mercedes from the time that it was stolen in Monaco until it was parked at l'Ermitage in Corbeil-Essonnes, but the gendarmes could guess the robbery for which it had been stolen and, presumably, used.

It was the last known raid of the Gang of Four and it had taken place on 9 August 1987, exactly one week before game warden Leclerc's first sighting of the body in the Forest of Lisses.

The scene was the cafeteria of a shopping centre in Champrosay, less than five miles from Corbeil-Essonnes. Anna-Maria Corsaro stormed into the cafeteria with a Kalashnikov machine pistol and held customers and employees at bay while Lang, Herisson and Berry rifled the cash register for a total of nearly ten thousand francs (one thousand pounds).

The operation did not pass off as smoothly as usual, for one of the customers, with more courage than common sense, flung himself on Lang and temporarily overpowered him.

Berry and Herisson hurried to the rescue, and the customer, fortunate to have escaped with his life, was knocked unconscious with a pistol butt. Lang's mask, had, however, been displaced for a few seconds.

Although the witnesses cautiously refrained from identifying him from his mug shots, the number of robbers, the fact that one had been a girl, and the manner in which the robbery had been carried out were so typical of the Gang of Four as to make their identity almost certain.

The robbers had fled in a stolen Peugeot 204, which was found abandoned a mile from the scene in open country. They had obviously switched cars at this point, in all probability to the white Mercedes.

'They must have killed Lang shortly after the robbery,' said the lieutenant, 'but the question is: Why? Did they think he was going to rat on them? Or did it have something to do with his being overpowered at the cafeteria?'

'The latter, I think,' said the sergeant. 'We have a lot of background on Lang and he wasn't a man to run to the police. More of a mad dog, actually.'

Thierry Lang's police record did indeed indicate a dangerous and unstable personality not in the least compatible with the type of criminal likely to turn informer.

He was described as nervous, short-tempered and given to sleeping with a loaded and cocked machine pistol in his arms. Garrulous and reckless when he had been drinking, he sometimes raised the hair of his fellow drinkers with descriptions of the gang's exploits, occasionally firing his pistol into the ceiling for added emphasis.

'I begin to suspect the motive,' said the lieutenant. 'He was talking so much that he was a threat to their security. It's a wonder they didn't get rid of him before. What we want now are his colleagues.'

So did many others. Putting out a wanted circular for Michel Berry, Martin Herisson and Anna-Maria Corsaro was futile. Police and gendarmerie units all over France were already looking for them.

They were not looking in the right places. Berry was in a detention cell in Paris, awaiting trial on stolen-cheque charges. As he had prudently given a false name and as the overloaded fingerprint department had not yet got around to processing his latest prints, it was not realized that he was on the wanted list.

Herisson and Anna-Maria had begun to find the French climate rather too warm for their health and had gone to ground in Italy, which turned out to be a mistake.

Following his last term in prison, Herisson had been sent to a rehabilitation centre, from which he had promptly escaped after attacking a staff member with a knife. The centre had reported the incident to the police and this report contained Herisson's last known address in Italy.

The Italian carabinieri were advised of the long list of crimes for which the couple were being sought, and Corsaro and Harisson were taken into custody. The murder of Thierry Lang was not, however, included in the list as the gendarmerie still lacked sufficient evidence to bring a charge. Both being Italian nationals, they were not returned to France, but held for eventual trial in Italy.

The iron-nerved Anna-Maria remained unmoved by her arrest, refusing to admit even to her own name, but Herisson's nervous system was more fragile and he quickly broke down and confessed to everything, including Thierry Lang's murder, of which he had not yet been accused.

He could safely do so for, according to his version of the events, he had had hardly anything to do with it.

Lang, he said, had been getting steadily more reckless with his boasting in bars over the gang's crimes and his associates were becoming concerned that one day a policeman out of uniform or an informer might be included in his audience. They therefore discussed the matter privately and came to the conclusion that there was only one way of silencing him.

Lang was not a man susceptible to persuasion and the mere suggestion that he curb his tongue would have been enough to send him into an insane rage, an undesirable state for a man armed with a machine pistol.

Kicking him out of the gang was not a practical solution. Aside from the fact that this would lead to a gun battle, Lang would undoubtedly continue his criminal career alone and, not being very bright, would soon be caught. Having been kicked out of the gang, he would have no loyalty to it and might be tempted to testify against his former associates in exchange for a reduced sentence.

It was therefore decided that Lang would be eliminated immediately following the cafeteria robbery.

The robbery went off with only the minor hitch of the customer's attack on Lang, and they did not bother to leave the area.

It was their policy, said Herisson, to come north as soon as the tourists started going south, as during the holiday season the population of the south of France more than doubled, and so did the vigilance of the gendarmerie and police.

On the evening of 9 August, they stopped at a lay-by screened by trees and bushes from the road, not far from Lyon. Anna-Maria pretended that she needed to go to the toilet and the others took the opportunity to do the same.

Lang went off into the bushes with Herisson and Anna-Maria, but Berry did not, and when Lang returned, Berry was waiting for him with a twelve-gauge pump gun loaded with boar darts.

Lang, who had left his machine pistol in the car, had just time to grasp what was happening and cry out, 'No! I'm your buddy!' when Berry fired three times, two of the slugs striking Lang in the chest and knocking him to the ground.

Rather incredibly, he had not been killed instantly and, according to Herisson, was groaning and writhing feebly when they loaded him into the boot of the car.

The groans stopped long before they arrived in Corbeil-Essonnes, where they had dinner and spent the night in l'Ermitage hotel, except Lang, who spent it in the boot of the Mercedes.

Coming out the following morning, they were disconcerted to find a large pool of blood under the back end of the Mercedes, but it was still early and no one else had, apparently, noticed it. They immediately drove away, unconcerned that the blood might be discovered later. The car was stolen and they had registered under false names, so they had no fear of being traced.

From the hotel, they went to a filling station, where they bought two ten-litre reserve cans of petrol.

Berry, who knew the area, drove to the Forest of Lisses and they unloaded the corpse from the boot. It was already quite stiff, but they prized the jaws open with a screwdriver and poured as much petrol down the dead man's throat as the body would hold. Herisson said that it had been a surprising amount and that one can of petrol had been completely used up.

The rest of the petrol was poured over the body and an improvised fuse of twisted paper inserted in the mouth.

The explosion of the petrol-filled corpse was very violent and the three gangsters were showered with clots of blood, pieces of flesh and the shredded internal organs of their late comrade.

It was necessary to go to another hotel to wash away the remains of Thierry Lang.

Although the remaining members of the gang had intended to continue their career as armed robbers, the murder depressed them more than they had expected and, after a few half-hearted and unsuccessful attempts, they separated.

Berry took the car and Herisson did not know what he had done with it. He and Anna-Maria, who was officially his mistress, but who occasionally helped out the others with their sexual problems, took the train to Italy, where they planned to open a dry-cleaning business with their part of the proceeds from the robberies. Herisson, always a businessman, had thriftily retained a large part of his and Anna-Maria's shares in a sort of retirement fund.

Anna-Maria, being only twenty-one, had given less

thought to retirement and was not very interested in financial security, regarding herself as a freedom fighter engaged in redistribution of the wealth.

Although she denied all knowledge of the murder, she eventually made a statement in which she said that the robberies were justified by the unfair economic system, and demanded the status of a prisoner of war under the terms of the Geneva convention.

Herisson she described as a traitor to the cause, and hinted that he would be dealt with at a later date. They had met while both were involved in a drive for funds in support of some left-wing cause, the precise nature of which she could no longer remember, and she now thought it significant that the sum collected had mysteriously disappeared without a trace.

Her demand for recognition as a political prisoner having been denied, she was indicted by the Italian justice department on charges of armed robbery, vehicle theft and acting as an accessory to homicide. Herisson was indicted on identical charges, and both were ordered to be held for trial without bail.

The whereabouts of Berry, however, remained unknown. Herisson said that he had had no contact with him since leaving France and that he did not know where he was. Anna-Maria said she had never heard the name of Berry.

It was only at the beginning of March that the backlog of work in the fingerprint department of the Paris police had been cleared away to the point where Berry, awaiting trial under the name of Marcel Billay, was identified and handed over to the Corbeil-Essonnes gendarmerie for charges more serious than stealing cheques.

Confronted with Herisson's confession, Berry soon gave up and admitted having been present at the murder of Thierry Lang.

He denied, however, that it was he who had pulled the trigger. The actual murderer, he said, was Herisson, who was greedy for money and had killed Lang in order to divide his share of the loot among the others.

The gendarmes were not convinced. Herrison was greedy, but he was a man with little stomach for violence, and it had been determined that he scarcely knew how to fire a gun.

Anna-Maria also grudgingly came to agree with Herisson that the actual killer had been Berry, and, faced with identical, separately taken statements by his former associates, Berry gave up and confessed to the murder. Brought to trial on 12 May 1989, he was sentenced to life imprisonment.

Herisson and Anna-Maria had already been tried in Italy on 21 April, and Herisson, in recognition of his cooperation with the police, was sentenced to twelve years.

Freedom fighter Anna-Maria, in recognition of her youth and sex, got off with seven years.

15

SICK DANCING

Running straight as stretched spaghetti southeast from Milan through Bologna to Rimini on the Adriatic, Autostrada A1 passes between the fertile plains of Lombardy to the north and the foothills of the Mountains of Emilia to the southwest.

Roughly halfway between Milan and the Adriatic lies the ancient and honourable city of Reggio nell Emilia, which, although its population numbers less than a hundred and fifty thousand, is a rather lively place.

Like many European cities, Reggio nell Emilia has a densely populated inner core of old buildings, preserved in some cases for historic reasons, in others for economic ones.

Many of these buildings have their ground-floor fronts gussied up into modern shops, cafés and bars, and such is the case with the Albergo Bar at 29 Via Montegrappa, which is further distinguished by a fine awning bearing the bar's name.

Because of the awning, the interior of the Albergo Bar is rather dark, a condition generally pleasing, however, to the patrons, of which there were, on the afternoon of 9 March 1987, two.

Barman Alcide Farri found this modest custom no cause for despair. It was Monday, and not the busiest day of the week for any bar. Many potential clients had to go to work, and those who did not were still sobering up from the weekend. Two at five in the afternoon was therefore quite acceptable.

The customers were both girls, sitting together at a

table near the door. One was black and the other was dark-skinned, although her features were not negroid. Farri had noticed little more when he served them. He was not a man who found exotic women exciting and he was preoccupied with the prospects of the Reggio soccer team in the coming year.

He had largely forgotten them and was absently polishing glasses with his back to the room, when he was torn from his thoughts by an agonized shriek.

Whirling round, he was just in time to see one of the girls race through the door. The other had disappeared entirely.

The first thought which crossed Farri's mind was that the drinks were not paid for, and he sprinted round the end of the bar and out of the door in pursuit.

The lighter-coloured girl was just rounding the corner of the street, running like a greyhound, and it was obvious that he was not going to catch her. The negress was apparently even faster. She was already out of sight.

Half angry, half inclined to laugh over what he took to be a childish trick to avoid paying for a couple of drinks, Farri returned to the bar and went to retrieve the empty glasses.

To his astonishment, they were nearly full, and as he stood staring at them in bewilderment, his eye was caught by a movement at his feet.

A narrow tongue of bright red liquid was advancing from beneath the tablecloth which hung within a few inches of the floor.

Suddenly alarmed, he caught hold of the tablecloth and whipped it back.

The second girl had not been so fast after all. She lay on her back beneath the table in the centre of a rapidly widening pool of blood, with what looked like the handle of a knife sticking out of her chest.

Farri let out his breath in a shocked whoosh. The Albergo was not the kind of bar where this sort of thing happened, and his immediate reaction was confusion and horror. Dropping to his knees, he picked up the girl's hand, but immediately dropped it again. He had had some vague thought of administering first aid, but it was obvious that the situation was too serious for that.

Leaping to his feet, he ran to the bar and telephoned the emergency ambulance. It was only some little time later that he realized that, whatever had happened, it could hardly have been an accident, and called the police.

As a result, the ambulance arrived before even the first patrol car. The crew was unable to do anything for the victim. She was dead, they said, and the matter was one for the criminal police.

The officers from the patrol car which arrived a few minutes later agreed and, at twenty-five minutes to six, the first members of the Reggio homicide squad began to arrive.

They were, however, only detectives first and second class, and they could not begin the investigation until the inspector in charge arrived. In the meantime, they sent the ambulance back to its base and the patrol car back to its beat, searched the bar, as they did not know whether Farri was telling the truth, and, having found no one, lit cigarettes and settled down at a table to wait.

It was another half-hour before Inspector Giancarlo Barcolli arrived, bringing with him his second in command, Detective Sergeant Luigi Antonelli, the police photographer, a detail from the police laboratory and the department's medical expert, Dr Paolo Oberzo.

The fact of death was quickly confirmed by Dr Oberzo, and the photographer made a series of pictures of the corpse, the table and the entire bar.

The doctor, a thin, dried-up sort of man with a knife-sharp nose and a sallow skin drawn tightly over his cheekbones, then proceeded to a more detailed examination of the corpse.

It did not take very long. The girl, he said, had been stabbed directly through the heart with what looked like a large kitchen knife and had died almost instantly. She had been dead not much over an hour. Otherwise, there was nothing he could report until after completion of the autopsy.

A woman's handbag was lying on the bench behind the table. and Sergeant Antonelli drew on a pair of rubber gloves and opened it.

It contained the usual articles carried about by a young woman: a comb, a lipstick, various other cosmetics, an unopened package of condoms, a small mirror, a purse with sixty thousand lire (thirty pounds) in small notes in it and a standard Italian identity card.

'Italian citizen,' said the sergeant. 'Naturalized, apparently. She was born in Mogadishu, Somalia, in 1964,'

'Twenty-three years old,' muttered the inspector, peering at the corpse through horn-rimmed glasses which gave him the appearance of a moderately successful dentist. 'Is it the same woman?'

'She's black,' said the sergeant, 'so I suppose it is. Her prints should be on record with the immigration office if we can't find anybody to identify her.'

"It's her,' confirmed Farri. 'She was the good-looking younger one. The other one was whiter and uglier.'

'You know them?' said the inspector. 'Are they regulars?'

'Never saw them before in my life,' replied Farri. 'It's not the kind of trade we usually get in here.'

'What do you mean by that?' said Sergeant Antonelli.

Like many northern Italians, he had light-brown hair, brown eyes and looked more like a central European than an Italian.

'I don't know her profession,' said Farri, 'but if it was evening and the place was full of men, I wouldn't let her in. Look at the way she's dressed.'

'The ID card says she's a dancer,' noted the inspector. 'She's not registered as a prostitute.'

Farri snorted. Not ten per cent of the prostitutes in Reggio nell Emilia were registered.

'Well, all right then,' said the inspector. 'Go over the area around the body and transfer her to the morgue.

Let me have the knife as soon as you can, Paolo. We may get a lead out of that.'

The area around the table was gone over carefully; but nothing was found that appeared to have any connection to the murder, and the body was taken away to the police morgue.

Inspector Barcolli returned to his office at police headquarters, but the sergeant remained behind directing a group of detectives who were canvassing the street for witnesses who might have seen the murderess leaving the scene.

None were found, which was not the same as saying that there were none. Modern city dwellers in Italy are as reluctant to become involved in criminal cases as those anywhere else.

The sergeant did a thorough job, however, and by the time that he returned to headquarters, Dr Oberzo had extracted the knife from the victim's body and it was lying in a plastic envelope on the inspector's desk.

'Any prints on it?' said the sergeant. 'We didn't turn up anything at the scene.'

'Yes,' the inspector told him. 'The victim's. If they weren't in the wrong position, it would look as if she committed suicide.'

'Funny time and place to do it,' observed the sergeant. 'Any theory of how come?'

'Paolo thinks that after she was stabbed she had an automatic reflex to pull the knife out and grabbed hold of the handle,' said the inspector. 'I expect he's right. He didn't find anything else except that she was in beautiful physical condition.'

'So she probably was a dancer despite the clothes,' said the sergeant.

The victim had been dressed in black net stockings, six-inch high heels, string panties, a see-through blouse without brassiere and a mini-skirt not much wider than a belt.

'Not classical ballet, I should think,' said the inspector dryly. 'You can nip round to her address now, and somebody there should be able to tell you where she worked.'

The address on the identity card was on the same street, nearly a quarter of a mile west of the Albergo Bar. It was not exactly a high-class building, but it was respectable. The victim, Faduma Osma, had occupied a one-roomed flat on the second floor.

There being no building superintendent and no keys having been found in the dead girl's purse, the sergeant picked the lock and entered with a team of four specialists, who went over the flat by the square inch, finding nothing of significance to the investigation.

'Unless you call the absence of any large knife in the corner kitchen significant,' said the sergeant, reporting on the results of the search to the inspector, 'but that would mean she was stabbed with her own kitchen knife, which seems unlikely.'

Unlikely or not, that was what had happened. Faduma Osman had been murdered with her own kitchen knife in a public bar a quarter of a mile from her flat.

'The dammed thing is a foot long!' exclaimed the inspector. 'How could the murderers have concealed it or, for that matter, how could she have got her hands on it in the first place?'

'Maybe the victim was carrying it,' said the sergeant. 'Self-defence or something like that.'

'The other girl would have had to get it away from her,' objected the inspector. 'There would have been a struggle and, according to Farri, there wasn't any. Anyway, Paolo couldn't find any physical indications that she even knew she was in danger.'

'Could the lab be wrong about the knife being hers?' said the sergeant.

The inspector shook his head.

'The grease and dirt on the knife handle are identical to the grease and dirt in her kitchen,' he said. 'You can't see it with the naked eye, but under the microscope . . . Of course, maybe the other woman wasn't the murderess.'

The sergeant looked startled.

'So then?' he asked.

'A third party,' said the inspector. 'A man maybe. The girl was attractive. She undoubtedly had admirers. One of them got jealous, followed the girls to the bar and stabbed her. By the time the barman turned round, he was already out of the door and away.'

'And the other girl panicked and ran,' said the sergeant slowly. 'Yes, that makes sense. It could also explain how he came to have the knife. He was probably living with her.'

'It's a theory, at least,' observed the inspector. 'We'll have to look into her recent love life, and the place to do that is the Ciao-Ciao Club.'

The Ciao-Ciao Club, a nightclub in the Via Roma which featured exotic dancers – meaning striptease artistes – was where Faduma Osman worked, according to the other tenants of the building in the Via Monte-grappa.

Contrary to the inspector's expectations, very little information resulted from the sergeant's investigations at the Ciao-Ciao Club. Faduma Osman had not worked there long, having been engaged only in May of the preceding year. She had been the star attraction and highly regarded by the nightclub owner, although not highly paid.

'We'll miss her,' said the owner. 'She wasn't quite the artiste the one before her was, but she was blacker, and that helped.'

'Her predecessor wasn't black?' said the sergeant, asking questions almost at random in the hope of hitting on something useful.

'Half,' explained the owner. 'Mother was black, but the father was Italian. Kim was the best dancer we ever had.'

'Then why did you replace her?' said the sergeant.

'Got old, stiff and ugly,' said the owner. 'We had to.'

'How old?' asked the sergeant.

'Twenty-nine,' said the owner.

'They don't last long in that business,' remarked the sergeant, reporting back to the inspector, 'but if Davoli knows what he's talking about, your theory of a jealous lover is out. He says she didn't have any boy friends. In fact, he had the impression that she was more interested in her own sex.'

Afra Davoli was the name of the owner of the Ciao-Ciao Club.

'Then why the pack of condoms in her handbag?' the inspector wondered. 'Hardly necessary for a female partner.'

'It hadn't been opened,' said the sergeant. 'Maybe it was for just-in-case. Did Paolo say she was a virgin?'

'I'd have asked for a second opinion if he had,' said the inspector. 'Of course, she may have been dual-purpose. Besides, that doesn't affect my theory. The third party could just as well have been female.'

'In that case, we have a couple of potentials,' observed the sergeant. 'Davoli says she was pretty chummy with one of the other dancers and with one of the female customers.'

'A strip joint has female customers?' said the inspector, raising his eyebrows.

'Nominally female,' conceded the sergeant.

'Black?' said the inspector.

'The dancer, yes,' said the sergeant. 'The customer, no. Her name's Angela Dorio, but she calls herself Angelo. The dancer's from Morocco and the name's Khebira Sami. Calls herself Didi professionally. Incidentally, Osman called herself Sada for the same purpose.'

' Almost more information than I can absorb,' said the inspector with mild irony. 'All right. Get some pictures of the girls and put people out in the Via Montegrappa with them. Maybe you'll have more luck finding a witness this time.'

As the sergeant did not expect any result from the operation, he was more than a little surprised when two people living in the street identified Angela Dorio as the woman they had seen running down the street near the

Albergo Bar at around five in the afternoon of Monday 9 March.

The inspector responded by ordering Angela's arrest, and she was brought to headquarters for interrogation.

As she turned out to be less tough than she looked, the interrogation did not last long.

Forty-one-year-old Angela, or Angelo, Dorio admitted that she had been in love with Faduma Osman, that she had believed her to be having an affair with Khebira Sami, that she had been jealous of her and that she had followed her to the Albergo Bar on the day of the murder.

She denied that she had murdered her and said that she had run away when a girl, whom she believed to be Khebira Sami, had come racing out of the bar and down the street, followed by a man. She had not known what had happened, but suspected that it was something tragic.

'Why something tragic?' said the inspector. 'Did you hear a cry? Did you see anyone with a knife?'

Angela had heard nothing, seen nothing.

'She was just that kind of a girl,' she said sadly. 'She was too beautiful. She attracted tragedy.'

The inspector charged her with suspicion of homicide and sent her to the detention cells.

'Tastes vary,' said the sergeant. 'Miss Osman was not my type.'

'You're not suspected of murdering her,' said the inspector. 'Bring Farri in this afternoon and we'll see if he can pick Dorio out of a line-up.'

Alcide Farri could not. Instead, he picked a woman who was younger and darker than she. He was not, he admitted, certain of his choice. He had seen the woman only briefly in the bar and had noticed that she was dark and not handsome.

'Her face was sort of swollen and puffy as if she had the flu or something,' he said. 'She wasn't young.'

The inspector dropped the charge against Angela

Dorio and ordered her release. However, she remained a suspect.

'There's not enough evidence to hold her,' he told the sergeant, 'but there's a fair chance that she's guilty. She's the only one we've found so far who has a motive.'

'Osman must have been mixed up with a third woman,' said the sergeant. 'Sami isn't puffed up or ugly. She looks younger and better than Osman did.'

'Bring her in and we'll question her,' said the inspector. 'Could be that she knows something about Osman's contacts, at least.'

Khebira Sami said that she knew nothing of Faduma's contacts, and did not believe she had had many. She admitted that she herself was not particular about the sex of her partners, but insisted Faduma had been strictly heterosexual.

'She wasn't having it off with anybody,' she said. 'She hadn't been here long and she didn't know hardly anyone. She was friendly with me and Angelo because she was lonely, but she wouldn't have sex with either of us.'

'And who else was she friendly with because she was lonely?' said the inspector.

Khebira shrugged her shoulders.

'Nobody I know of,' she said, 'but she didn't confide in me.'

The inspector sent her about her business and had Afra Davoli brought to his office.

The nightclub owner had less to offer than Khebira. He did not, he said, take a personal interest in the strippers working the Ciao-Ciao Club. If they were any good, he paid them a fair wage. If not, he let them go. He was running a business, not a social club. What the girls did in their free time and with whom was none of his affair, and the less he knew about it the better.

'Do you have an older woman with a sort of puffy, swollen face and not very good-looking working in your club?' asked the inspector.

'How long do you think I could stay in business if I

hired dogs like that?' said Davoli indignantly. 'If their looks start to go, they go.'

'No exceptions?' said the inspector.

Well, I kept Kim longer than I should have,' said Davoli. 'She'd been a big attraction and she had a following. Of course, after a while, she got beyond what you could do with make-up and she was so stiff she could hardly get out of her G-string.'

'What was the matter with her?' said the sergeant curiously.

Davoli shrugged.

'No idea,' he said. 'She was half African, and they come down with all kinds of diseases you never heard of.'

There were no further questions and Davoli left. The inspector and the sergeant remained sitting silently in the office.

'I was just thinking . . .' they began simultaneously.

'Have you ever seen this Kim?' said the inspector.

'No,' admitted the sergeant. 'She doesn't work at the club any more. She's just the girl who preceded Osman on the job.'

'Ask Davoli where she lives and bring her in,' said the inspector. I want to get a look at her.'

Lidia Elmi, professionally known as Kim, did not look good. Her face was puffy and swollen and there were strange eruptions on the skin of her face and hands. She could have easily been taken for a woman in her forties.

Questioned on the subject of Faduma Osman, she reacted violently.

'I didn't know the bitch and I didn't want to,' she snarled. 'All I know is she took my job.'

'Because you were too ill to hold it,' said the inspector. 'What's the matter with you anyway? Have you been to see a doctor?'

'Nothing's the matter with me,' said Lidia. 'I just had a cold and I was a little stiff, so that bastard fired me and hired her. She probably . . .'

She described in such graphic detail what she

imagined Faduma had done to get the job that the inspector and sergeant, both seasoned investigations officers, blushed.

'You never visited Miss Osman in her flat, then?' said the inspector. 'You did not go to the Labergo Bar with her on the afternoon of 9 March?'

'I'd sooner have tangled with a scorpion,' said Lidia.

The inspector opened the drawer of his desk and took out a large glossy photograph of a woman.

'Do you know this person?' he asked, handing her the photograph upside down.

Lidia turned it right side up, looked at it casually and returned it.

'Never saw her before in my life,' she said.

'You may go, Miss Elmi,' said the inspector. 'Don't leave town or change your address without letting us know.'

The woman left without another word.

'Why in heaven's name did you show her a picture of your wife?' said the greatly astonished sergeant. 'You didn't really think she'd know her, did you?'

'I wanted her prints,' said the inspector. 'Run this over to the fingerprint section and see whether the prints match any of those found in Osman's flat.'

The prints matched and, more important, they matched three prints taken from one of the glasses abandoned on the table in the Albergo Bar where Faduma Osman had been stabbed.

'All right,' said the inspector. 'We've got her. Elmi murdered her successor out of professional jealousy. The next thing is to prove it. We'll hold another line-up and see if Farri can pick her out.'

'Will it be enough?' asked the sergeant. 'Farri didn't witness the stabbing. All he can say is that Elmi was the girl who was in the bar with the victim and who ran away after the stabbing. She could claim that it was Dorio who did the stabbing and that she simply panicked.'

'True,' said the inspector, frowning. 'We can probably

get an indictment if Farri picks her out of the line-up, but I think a conviction would be doubtful without a confession.'

'We could wait a long time for that,' said the sergeant. 'Unless I'm greatly mistaken.'

He was not mistaken. Alcide Farri did pick Lidia Elmi out of the line-up, but the woman still refused to confess.

'I won't deny I'm glad the bitch is dead,' she said, 'but what good will that do me? Davoli isn't going to give me my job back.'

That was tragically obvious. In the short length of time since her last interview with the inspector, Lidia Elmi's condition had deteriorated shockingly.

'This woman belongs in the hospital,' said the inspector, and he sent her there.

Twenty-four hours later, he knew what was wrong with Lidia Elmi and so did she. She was infected with the active form of the AIDS virus and there was little hope that she would live out the year.

The inspector terminated the investigation. There was no point in indicting a woman who would, almost certainly, be dead before she came to trial.

Lidia, however, had different ideas. Realizing that she was doomed, she came to the conclusion that it would be wise to clear her conscience, and from her hospital bed dictated a full confession to the murder.

She had, she said, been unable to bear her replacement by another woman and had deliberately plotted to murder Faduma. Pretending to befriend the lonely Somalian girl, she visited her often in her flat and, on the day of the murder, stole the knife from the kitchen.

In the bar, she simply waited for the bartender to turn his back and then pulled the knife out of her sleeve and drove it into the unsuspecting Faduma's heart.

Although the murder was officially solved, Lidia Elmi was never indicted and, on 4 January 1988, she died in the hospital.

The Ciao-Ciao Club has since been forced to divide

star billing among three girls as no one is willing to star alone. The girls think the position unlucky.

16

HELPING OUT MOTHER

On the evening of Tuesday 27 May 1986, l'Escargot Bar closed at eleven-thirty.

This was half an hour earlier than usual, but there were no customers in the place and the owner, Claude Pierre, was anxious to get to bed so that he could make an early start the following morning.

Fifty-six-year-old Pierre was a keen gardener and the end of May was a busy time in the garden.

His companion, fifty-year-old Gisèle Brasseur, had preceded him out of the door and stood waiting patiently while he turned off the lights and prepared to lock up.

They were an old and happily unmarried couple who had just the previous week celebrated twenty years of living together.

It was a warm and lovely late spring evening, the air filled with the scent of flowers and the sleepy twittering of birds settling down for the night. There was, however, no moon and it was rather dark in the Avenue du Maréchal Foch, one of Chaumont's main streets.

Facing the door, Pierre had just pulled the key out of the lock when there was a faint popping sound and he spun half round to fall full-length on the pavement.

Gisèle, thinking that he had stumbled, knelt down beside him and, to her astonishment, saw that his face was distorted with pain and that blood was running out of his hair and on to his collar. He was struggling to speak, but only a hoarse, gasping sound issued from between his trembling lips.

Unable to comprehend how he had managed to hurt

himself so badly simply by falling, but thoroughly alarmed, Gisèle caught up the keys from the pavement where he had dropped them, let herself into the bar and called the emergency ambulance.

It arrived quickly, for the distance it had to cover was not great. Chaumont, in the north of France and roughly a hundred and fifty miles southeast of Paris, has a population of around thirty thousand and is, like many older European cities, compact.

By eleven-forty-five, the ambulance was racing through the largely deserted streets to the hospital, with Gisèle sitting in the back, holding her companion's hand. He had lost consciousness by the time the ambulance arrived and, halfway to the hospital, she felt the hand she was holding go suddenly limp and lifeless.

The paramedic sitting beside her began frantic resuscitation procedures, but his efforts were in vain. When the ambulance swung into the emergency entrance of the hospital, it was a corpse that lay on the stretcher.

Gisèle, in a state of profound shock and incapable of accepting that her companion was dead, was led, walking as stiffly as if she herself was a corpse, into the hospital, where the doctor on night duty injected her with a powerful tranquillizer and put her to bed.

Her last words as she lost consciousness were, 'But you can't kill yourself falling down!'

The doctor agreed. His examination of Pierre's corpse led to the conclusion that he had died of a bullet wound in the head, and the body was consequently returned to the ambulance for transfer to the police morgue.

Gisèle learned of the cause of death only the following morning when the tranquillizer had worn off.

'Shot?' she stammered. 'But why? He hadn't an enemy in the world! And how? I was standing right there. I didn't hear any shot.'

Later, however, she did recall hearing a faint sort of popping sound.

'It didn't sound like a gunshot to me though,' she told Inspector Jerome Pouilly, the burly, grey-haired head of the Chaumont police department of criminal investigations.

'It was only a twenty-two,' said the inspector, his broad ruddy face gravely sorrowful. 'A twenty-two long rifle.'

For him, the murder was not the impersonal criminal investigations case that it might have been in a larger community. He had known Claude Pierre well and he knew Gisèle even better.

Thirty years earlier, she had been a young waitress in the Terminus-Reine – with sixty-three rooms and a fine restaurant, Chaumont's best hotel.

She had been pretty and popular and everyone had sympathized when her lover, a waiter named Maurice, departed, leaving her pregnant and alone.

Gisèle had had to fend for herself and her little son, Michel, for nearly four years before the friendship between her and Claude Pierre, the calm, handsome owner of l'Escargot, ripened into something deeper and she and Michel moved into the little house in the rue Pierre Simon, only a few hundred yards from both l'Escargot and the Terminus-Reine.

Michel no longer lived there. He was now twenty-four years old and a successful insurance agent who regularly turned over a part of his earnings to his mother, even though she did not need the money.

Not only the inspector but a good many others were surprised at how well Michel had turned out. His mother, who called him her 'love child', had spoiled him badly and such treatment often had an unfortunate effect on a boy's character.

Michel had, however, turned out serious, hard-working and unspoiled. Although he had dropped out of school before graduation, it was only to take a job with a local garage, where he had remained for six years before becoming an insurance agent.

Inspector Pouilly sent his assistant, Detective Sergeant Louis Masson, round to take a statement from Michel the day following the murder. Although not related by blood, he was, next to Gisèle, the person who had known Claude best.

'They didn't get on all that well,' reported the sergeant, a slender, almost boyish-looking man, with a lock of honey-blond hair falling down over his forehead and large, round, deep-blue eyes. 'Everybody knows that. But there wasn't any real friction and he's as badly shaken as his mother. Says he can't imagine why anybody would kill Claude.'

'You checked his whereabouts at the time of the murder?' said the inspector. 'We can't overlook anything. This is a real mystery.'

The sergeant nodded.

'He was at the railway station with a boy named Jules Bradier. They went there to meet a friend named Didier Pirolley, who was coming in on the eleven-thirty-five from Paris.'

'Any independent confirmation of that?' said the inspector.

The Place Général-de-Gaulle, on which the railway station and the hôtel Terminus-Reine are located, was close to l'Escargot.

'Plenty,' said the sergeant. 'The station master, the ticket clerk, the baggage consignment clerk, two or three others. They all know Michel by sight and they said he was there at eleven-thirty.'

The inspector picked up his ballpoint pen and drew a firm line through the name of Michel Brasseur on the short list of potential suspects.

'Well, at least we've eliminated one possibility,' he said.

It had not been a good possibility, but neither were any of the others. Claude Pierre had been a quiet, good-natured man whose only interests were his bar, his garden and his part-time job as a swimming instructor.

L'Escargot was a comfortable sort of bar with a clientele consisting almost entirely of local regulars. Like many neighbourhood bars, it filled the function of a social club where people who knew each other well came to talk, play cards or dominoes and have a drink after work. The police had never been summoned there. It had never been necessary to throw anyone out. There was no reason for anyone to murder the owner.

The autopsy, performed by Chaumont coroner Dr Yves Saint Martin, determined that Pierre had been killed by a single twenty-two-calibre long-rifle bullet which had entered the back of the skull, passed through the brain and lodged in the bones of the upper jaw.

The bullet was recovered, and it was not too badly deformed to establish that the gun which had fired it had never been in the hands of the police.

Whether that gun had been a rifle or a pistol, the ballistics expert could not say with certainty and, as a result, Gisèle Brasseur's name for a time topped the list of suspects. As his closest associate and sole heir, she could be assumed to have the most reason to murder him.

She was eliminated immediately following the police search of the street and the buildings within range of the front door of l'Escargot.

Directly across the street from the bar was an abandoned four-storey warehouse, its windows long since smashed by the omnipresent juvenile vandals. The door to it had been padlocked, but the padlock had recently been broken.

The specialists from the small police laboratory who were searching the building found an empty, twenty-two-calibre long-rifle cartridge and half a dozen fresh cigarette ends behind a window on the first floor. The window overlooked the front door of l'Escargot.

'Perfect location for an ambush,' observed the inspector. 'It was dark inside the building. Anyone outside wouldn't have been able to see a thing. Clear line of fire and a range of about thirty yards to the front door of l'Escargot. All he had to do was wait for Claude to come out.'

'But this makes it a deliberate, carefully planned

assassination!' said the sergeant in a stupefied voice. 'And there was no motive!'

'There has to be a motive,' said the inspector. 'It wasn't a psychopath who killed just whoever happened to come along first. He wanted Claude. He knew more or less when he closed the bar and he waited for him. It wasn't an impulsive act.'

'We've almost exhausted the list of people Claude knew,' said the sergeant. 'Gisèle worked with him in the bar, so she knew everybody he knew. They were hardly ever separated. We're down to the men who delivered beer and soft drinks, and none of them had any reason to murder him either.'

The inspector could suggest nothing. He had known Pierre, and he was not a man to make enemies. The motive could not have been jealousy. He and Gisèle had been more faithful to each other than many married couples. And no one had benefited financially from his death other than Gisèle, who had inherited the bar, their modest savings, and his life insurance amounting to three hundred thousand francs (thirty thousand pounds).

'They had intended to sell the bar and buy a place in Provence,' said the sergeant. 'Gisèle's health has been poor lately and they thought a drier climate might do her good. He'd already started redecorating so that he could ask a better price.'

'Could that have anything to do with it?' muttered the inspector.

He was becoming a little desperate. Chaumont was a small place and everyone in town knew that Claude Pierre had been murdered. Everyone also knew that no arrest had been made, and a certain amount of criticism of the police was beginning to make itself heard.

As head of the department of criminal investigations, Inspector Pouilly was painfully sensitive to such criticism; but he had already assigned nearly every man in the department to the case, and most of them were standing around awaiting orders because there was nothing for them to investigate.

A re-enactment of the crime had been carried out, but had produced nothing more than what had already been surmised. Someone, a man or a woman, had been waiting at the window and chain-smoking – there were no burned matches – for Pierre to come out. He or she had shot him through the head while he was locking the door and had immediately fled.

'Good shooting, even at that close a range,' said the sergeant. 'A man's head is a small target and the light was poor.'

'Good or lucky,' said the inspector morosely. 'We've no way of knowing.'

'It had to be Gisèle,' insisted the sergeant, returning to a theme which had been broached previously. 'She didn't do it herself, but she hired somebody.'

'Why?' said the inspector. 'I knew both of them. They were happy, and they had been together for over twenty years.'

'The insurance,' said the sergeant.

'He'd had the insurance for years, so why now?' argued the inspector. 'She'd never been crazy about money and, at her age, her companion was worth more than three hundred thousand francs to her. Besides, if ever I've seen anyone sincerely grief-stricken, it's her. She's been in and out of the hospital half a dozen times since the murder and she doesn't even greet me in the street any more because we haven't solved it.'

'No one else stood to benefit,' said the sergeant stubbornly.

'All right,' conceded the inspector. 'If you're so convinced, take all the men you need and trace her movements for three months before the murder. If she hired somebody, she would have made the contact within that time.'

The sergeant did not find this as difficult an assignment as it sounded. Gisèle and Claude had been extremely well-known in Chaumont and, being the owners of a bar that was open six days a week, they had not had a great deal of free time.

'You were right,' said the sergeant, reporting on the results of the operation a week later. 'We've accounted for practically every minute of both his and her time for the past three months and there's been no opportunity for her to make contact with a killer, even assuming she knew where to find one.'

'Well, it wouldn't have been a professional anyway,' observed the inspector. 'That's one career we don't have here. Not enough demand. And, besides, a twenty-two is not a professional's weapon.'

'All right, a local amateur,' said the sergeant. 'But he would have had to be paid and with money. Gisèle is a fine woman, but she's not young so I can't see anybody doing it for love.'

'Her son could have found somebody for her,' mused the inspector. 'He gets around.'

'Possible,' said the sergeant. 'But why? Why would he or she want to kill Claude?'

'Maybe Michel hired somebody because he didn't want his mother to go off to Provence,' said the inspector. 'It's far-fetched, I admit, but . . .'

'. . . but we have nothing better,' concluded the sergeant. 'All right. I'll put everybody to work on Michel. He may not be so easy to trace.'

The sergeant's detectives found Michel's movements and activities even harder to trace than he had expected as, being an independent insurance agent, his working hours were irregular; but they did turn up one interesting fact.

Jules Bradier, the twenty-year-old youth with whom Michel had gone to the railway station to meet Didier Pirolley, had been employed briefly by Claude Pierre in the redecoration of his bar.

The association was short because Pierre had been dissatisfied with Bradier's work and had let him go.

'God knows, it's hardly a motive for murder,' said the sergeant, 'but it's the only connection that we've found at all.'

'Then concentrate on it,' said the inspector. 'What about Michel and Pirolley?'

'Pirolley's a plumber who took over the Pascha Billiard Room and Café last year and went broke nine months later,' said the sergeant. 'He moved in with Michel at 46 rue de Flemming on 2 January. They've been friends for about two years. Pirolley married in 1982 and divorced in 1985. No children. He's twenty-six years old.'

'And no criminal record,' said the inspector. 'Are you sure that he and Michel are no more than friends?'

'None of these people have a police record,' said the sergeant. 'Michel's a busy, successful insurance agent. The company is happy with him and so was the Montigny Garage, where he worked before. Snappy dresser. Likes good restaurants. Drives a small car. Moderate drinker. No steady girl friend, but he likes girls, not boys.'

All the investigation had determined was that Michel and his friends were unexceptional young men who had no more reason to murder Claude Pierre than anyone else in Chaumont.

There were a few scraps of information which, under the circumstances, had caught the sergeant's attention, but were of themselves not really significant.

Didier Pirolley had qualified as a sharpshooter during his obligatory military service, and Jules Bradier, who had not yet done his military service, was a gun enthusiast who belonged to two rifle clubs; but there were many other young men in Chaumont with similar qualifications and interests.

'A waste of time anyway,' sighed the sergeant, 'because there are dozens of witnesses who confirm that two of them were at the railway station and the third was just arriving on the train from Paris when Claude was shot.'

'It's only a couple of hundred yards,' said the inspector. 'Couldn't one of them have fired the shot and sprinted to the station?'

'No,' said the sergeant. 'Michel and Bradier were

drinking beer in the railway station café for half an hour before the train from Paris arrived. They didn't so much as go to the toilets and they walked directly to the platform from the café. As for Pirolley, he got off the train from Paris after Claude was shot.'

'Those alibis are almost too good to be real,' murmured the inspector thoughtfully. 'Normally, out of three potential suspects, at least one wouldn't be able to prove where he was at the precise time.'

As Claude and Gisèle had just been in the process of closing the bar, the time of the shooting was known within a few minutes.

'It wasn't a case of mistaken identity,' said the sergeant. 'Pirolley is well-known because he had the café. Bradier's from the other end of town and he doesn't hang out around the railway station, but the witnesses were all certain that he was the man who was with Michel.'

'He doesn't live with Michel too, does he?' asked the inspector.

'No,' said the sergeant. 'He lives with his parents. Anyway, what difference does it make? None of them could have shot Claude.'

Whereupon, there being no further potential suspects or leads, the case ended. Although not officially classified as unsolved, the investigation was suspended and the detectives assigned to other duties.

The inspector spent an uncomfortable summer. In a larger community, he might have been able to remain anonymous, but in Chaumont, everybody knew that Inspector Pouilly had personally led the investigation into the murder of Claude Pierre and had failed miserably.

However, there were also advantages in a small community, for every officer in the police knew the circumstances of the Pierre murder, and when a rather petty crime took place on the night of Sunday 12 October, the inspector was immediately pulled out of bed and called to the station.

Business in October being slow, the Hôtel Terminus-Reine had shut down for three weeks for staff holidays and redecoration, and burglars had seized the opportunity to break in and carry off a number of not very valuable items.

They were in a bar, trying to dispose of the loot, which was all clearly marked with the hotel's name, when they were arrested and brought to police headquarters.

The night desk sergeant who booked them took one look at the names and telephoned the inspector.

The three burglars were Michel Brasseur, Didier Pirolley and Jules Bradier!

The inspector and the hurriedly summoned sergeant spent the rest of the night interrogating them, but the results were not very satisfactory.

All three admitted to charges of breaking and entering and burglary, which did not interest the inspector in the least, but not to any involvement in the murder of Claude Pierre, which did.

'We've been had!' fumed the inspector. 'I knew those alibis were too good to be true. They worked some kind of a trick and now, in spite of all the background investigation, it turns out that they're crooks, and cheap ones to boot.'

'Crooks maybe,' said the sergeant, 'but not murderers. The alibis are still watertight.'

'We'll see,' said the inspector. 'Get out their statements, the witnesses' statements, everything connected with this business. We're going to go over it until we find the flaw in those alibis.'

'Even if we find one, we still don't have a motive,' objected the sergeant, rummaging in the filing cabinet.

'We can ask them the motive once we've proved they did it,' said the inspector.

That, however, was more easily said than done. No matter how many times he went over the material, the fact remained that Michel Brasseur and Jules Bradier had been in the railway station, and Didier Pirolley arriving in the train from Paris, at the time of the murder.

The sergeant's detectives repeated the entire investigation into the suspects' backgrounds, but all they turned up was evidence of Bradier's innocence.

'The boy's a gun nut and he belongs to two gun clubs,' reported the sergeant, 'but he's a rotten shot. The other people in the club say he couldn't hit the side of a barn if he was standing inside it.'

The inspector looked glum and said nothing, but the following day he went to see Giséle Brasseur as he was curious about her reaction to Michel's arrest.

She, it seemed, was tormented with feelings of guilt for having failed her son.

'If he'd only come to me!' she wailed. 'I'd have given him the money. He knew that.'

'Didn't you know that he was heavily in debt?' said the inspector, who had been told that by her son, as an excuse for the burglary.

'Of course I did,' said Gisèle. 'I'd already given him a great deal, but he was so considerate that I suppose he didn't want to ask me for more.'

The inspector returned to his office.

'This must have some connection,' he groaned, clutching his head in despair, 'but I just can't see it. The boy had expensive tastes. He got into debt and she was giving him money, but he kept on spending. She was running short . . .'

'The insurance,' said the sergeant. 'Three hundred thousand francs, and he knew she'd give him anything he asked.'

The inspector took his hands away from his head and gazed thoughtfully at his assistant.

'That's the only plausible motive that's been suggested in this case so far,' he said. 'Now, if we could just break those alibis . . .'

And three days later, as he pored over the statements for the hundredth time, he did.

'I've got it!' he bawled. 'I've got it at last!'

What the inspector had was, perhaps, no proof of murder, but it was evidence that one of the alibis at least might not be as watertight as it seemed.

The alibis of Michel Brasseur and Jules Bradier were unassailable. They had, without question, been in the railway station at the time of the murder.

Pirolley, on the other hand, had not. He had been arriving in the train from Paris.

Or had he?

In fact, the ends of the station were open. A reasonably nimble man could clamber down a small embankment, walk along beside the railway tracks to the platform and climb on to it as the train came in. To anyone in the station it would look as if he had just got off the train.

Pirolley could have done this, but was it possible to prove that he had?

To the surprise of the inspector, who had had little reason for optimism in recent months, it was.

The eleven-thirty-five from Paris had not been over-filled that evening. There had been only five passengers for Chaumont in second class and one in first.

The conductor was quite certain that none of them had been Didier Priolley, and for a good reason. They had all been women!

Confronted with the collapse of his alibi and the possibility of facing a homicide charge alone, Pirolley confessed to the murder and implicated Michel Brasseur and Jules Bradier.

The idea, he said, had been Michel's. He and Pirolley were short of money and, in discussing how they could get their hands on some, Michel remembered that Claude had a life-insurance policy of which Gisèle was the beneficiary.

As his mother would give him anything she had, this was the equivalent of being the beneficiary himself.

The only problem was, therefore, how to murder Pierre without being caught and, after much discussion and thought, they hit upon the railway station trick, which Pirolley had once played on his father when he was a boy. Bradier knew nothing of the scheme and was brought along simply to add authenticity.

The trick had worked perfectly and the crime would have been perfect had it not been for the typical procrastination of the insurance company in paying out the money. Impatient, they had decided to burgle the Terminus-Reine and had brought about their own downfall.

'I still can't believe we solved it,' the inspector told the sergeant on the afternoon of 18 September 1987 as they left the courtroom where Didier Pirolley and Michel Brasseur had just been sentenced to twenty-five years' imprisonment each.

Jules Bradier had earlier pleaded guilty to a charge of breaking and entering and had been given a six months' suspended sentence.

'You solved it,' said the sergeant diplomatically. 'Should we drop in at l'Escargot for a drink to celebrate?'

'Can't,' said the inspector. 'Gisèle wasn't speaking to me before because we hadn't solved the case. Now, she's not speaking to me because we have.'

17

NEVER CONFIDE IN YOUR CELLMATE

Sometime during the autumn of 1984, Isabel Jung fell in love.

There was nothing remarkable about this. Isabel was nineteen years old, an attractive girl and had nearly finished her teaching studies. The object of her affection was one year older and a fellow student at the University of Karlsruhe, where he was taking a degree course in construction engineering. Like Isabel, he was an only child, and his name was Bernd Klein.

From the autumn of 1984 to the winter of 1985, Isabel and Bernd revelled in the delights of young love. They went on holiday together. They went to the seaside. They went to the mountains. They wandered hand-in-hand through the picturesque cities and towns of the continent.

When not thus engaged, they attended concerts, went to the theatre, danced the night away in discotheques and dined in the best restaurants they could afford.

Bernd moved into the house at 55 Walprechtstrasse in Malsch, where Isabel lived with her grandmother, and was accepted as a son by Isabel's parents, who lived next door.

It was a cosy and practical arrangement. Malsch, a village of under thirteen thousand, was within easy commuting distance of the university, being twelve miles to the south of Karlsruhe, itself barely twelve miles from the river Rhine and border with France.

Isabel and Bernd therefore enjoyed all the advantages

of being a young married couple, but without being married, and their only child was Nina.

Nina was not a human child, but an affectionate black cat who had been a present to Isabel from Bernd and who therefore had great sentimental value.

Alas! True love was to blossom but a single season. In December 1985, Isabel met Dieter Krumholz, a twenty-four-year-old unemployed teacher with the pale, irresistible charm of the starving, unappreciated poet.

At first captivated by his exquisite, if ill-defined, suffering, an activity at which some young Germans excel, her sentiments soon evolved into affection and, eventually, into love. On or about 1 February 1986, she informed Bernd that she loved another and that all was now over between them.

Bernd did not take to the idea. A handsome, very large young man, six feet two inches tall, he wept like a child, pleaded with Isabel to reconsider, made scenes and generally conducted himself in the manner of rejected lovers the world over.

Isabel remained adamant. She no longer went out with Bernd and, on the night of 6 February 1986, it was with her eighteen-year-old cousin Ermaline Alter that she attended a Fasching ball in Karlsruhe.

Fasching is the German term for Shrove Tuesday – carnival. Although the celebrations at Karlsruhe are modest in comparison with those in Cologne or Mainz, the student balls are lively enough to cause a noticeable bump in the birth rate statistics nine months later.

Bernd was understandably concerned that his loved one was attending such a gathering with no abler chaperon than the cousin who was very pretty and far from unapproachable.

Moreover, he had every reason to suspect that the unspeakable Krumholz would also be present at the ball.

He therefore spent the evening moping miserably about the Jungs' house, wept on the shoulder of Isabel's mother Ursula, and accused her master mechanic father Klaus of permitting his daughter to behave in an immoral manner, quite forgetting that he had been sleeping with her himself for over a year.

The Jungs comforted him as best they could, but, as they pointed out, if Isabel had given her heart to another, there was little they could do about it.

At approximately three o'clock in the morning, Isabel returned home alone, Ermaline having found a better place to spend the night.

Rather incredibly, although love had flown, Isabel was still living with Bernd in the house at 55 Walprechtstrasse and, indeed, sleeping with him, as the only other bed was occupied by her aged grandmother.

Before going to bed, however, Isabel dropped in at her parents' house to telephone her new lover and, in a burst of daughterly confidence, told her mother, whom she awoke for the purpose, that she and Dieter had had sex for the first time that evening and that it had been wonderful

Her mother said she did not doubt it and went back to sleep.

Neither she nor anyone else would ever see Isabel again.

Ursula did not expect to see her daughter very early the following morning, but Isabel took her meals at the house and, when she had not yet made an appearance by four in the afternoon, she went over to look for her.

Neither Isabel nor Bernd was there and the grandmother said she had seen nothing of them since the preceding day.

Mildly concerned, Ursula returned home and telephoned Dieter Krumholz, who promptly became hysterical. She had not kept their date for lunch, but he had thought she was probably still sleeping.

Mrs Jung then telephoned Bernd's parents in Saarbruecken, a hundred miles to the northwest.

They had neither seen nor heard anything of Bernd or Isabel for several weeks.

Ursula Jung was becoming frightened and she went next door to examine the room which Isabel and Bernd shared. The bed had not only been slept in, but put to other uses as well, for the sheets were stained and the room smelled of sex. There had, it seemed, been a reconciliation.

By the time she returned to her own house, Klaus had come home from work and she told him of her unsuccessful efforts to locate their daughter and the evidence that Isabel had decided in favour of Bernd after all.

Klaus, who was rather weary of Isabel's romantic problems, reassured her that the young couple had probably simply gone off somewhere to celebrate their reunion and would undoubtedly turn up again once it was time to go to bed.

However, although he convinced his wife, he failed to convince himself and, at a little after seven that evening, he called the Karlsruhe police and reported Isabel missing.

A half hour later, a sergeant from the missing persons office arrived at the house, took a formal statement from the Jungs concerning their daughter's disappearance and collected a recent picture of her.

The Jungs, who were by now badly frightened, also provided him with a picture of Bernd Klein and went into considerable detail concerning Isabel's somewhat hectic love life.

The sergeant, a neatly dressed young man with a short haircut and a completely expressionless face, refrained from comment and asked to see the room in which Bernd and Isabel had passed the preceding night.

The Jungs complied and were startled nearly out of their wits when he brusquely ordered them out of the house and told them to take the grandmother with them.

The sergeant had found the stains on the sheets more alarming than had Ursula. They were, he thought, not only sexual secretions, but urine, excrement and, possibly, blood.

Having radioed police headquarters from his car, he remained outside, thoughtfully smoking, until a van with a detachment of technicians from the police laboratory arrived.

They promptly confirmed the sergeant's suspicions and, having sealed the doors to the house with paper tapes printed with the words 'Karlsruhe Police Department of Criminal Investigations – Do not enter', returned to headquarters, where they reported sufficient evidence of an act of violence to justify a criminal investigation.

By this, they meant possible homicide, and the rural investigations unit of the Karlsruhe homicide squad was alerted.

The sergeant from the missing persons office had returned with the technicians. Inspector Julius Schelter, the unit's officer-in-charge, listened to his account of Isabel's emotional vacillations, dispatched one team of detectives to pick up Dieter Krumholz, another to hunt for Bernd Klein, and had copies of Isabel's picture distributed to all police units in the area. Karlsruhe is a city of over three hundred thousand and the various police departments are manned around the clock.

Dieter Krumholz was easily located and, having assured the inspector that he knew nothing about Isabel's disappearance, was lodged in the detention cells for the night.

Bernd Klein was taken into custody the following morning by the Saarbruecken police when he arrived at his parents' home. He too said that he knew nothing of the disappearance and he too was sent to the detention cells.

In the meantime, the inspector's second-in-command, Detective Sergeant Peter Langbauer, a very tall, very thin man with a long, doleful face divided in two by an oblong black moustache, had telephoned the Jungs to see if, by any chance, Isabel had turned up.

She had not, and an official investigations file headed 'Suspected Homicide – Isabel Jung' was opened.

Krumholz and Klein were subjected to intense interrogation, but merely repeated their statements, according to which Krumholz had not seen her since she left his flat at approximately two-thirty in the morning of Friday and Klein had not seen her since she went off to the ball with her cousin.

Neither could establish an alibi as it was not known what time Isabel had disappeared. Asked about the stains on the bed sheets, Klein said that he had not slept in the house that night, but that some of the stains might be from him as he had slept there up until that night and the grandmother did not always change the sheets regularly.

The grandmother did not know who had slept there that night. She had been long since asleep before any of the young people came in.

The last known sighting of Isabel was, therefore, at three in the morning, when she had come to telephone her lover and tell her mother about her great sexual experience.

' Krumholz confirmed having received the call and said that Isabel had said good night and that she was looking forward to their luncheon date. He was, however, unable to explain how she had called him when he did not have a telephone.

A larger detachment from the police laboratory returned to the house and found a number of possibly significant clues. The stains on the sheets had been made by saliva, semen, female sexual secretions, urine, excrement and blood. The quantity of blood was very small and not all the stains were recent.

A down quilt in a drawer beneath the bed was missing its yellow cover, and textile fibres identical to a matching pillowcase were recovered from the frame of the door leading from the cellar to the garage.

Other identical textile fibres were found in the boot of the white Ford Fiesta belonging to Bernd Klein, and brown wool fibres, believed to be from a bedspread which was also missing, were found on a pair of gloves in the car's glove compartment.

'Seems a fairly straightforward case,' observed the

inspector, a blond, blue-eyed giant of a man with long drooping moustache. 'She left him for Krumholz and possibly told him about having sex with him. He strangled her, perhaps raped her before or after death, wrapped the body in the quilt cover and the bedspread and carried it through the cellar to his car in the garage. The only question that remains is, What did he do with it?'

'He might as well tell us,' said the sergeant. 'There's enough circumstantial evidence to indict him now and the judge has already turned down his attorney's request for bail.'

'It would make things simpler,' agreed the inspector, 'but if he doesn't, we'll have to find the body ourselves. Without it, a jury could acquit him.

Bernd Klein and his attorney were apparently aware of this for he confessed to nothing. He had not been Isabel's lover at the time she disappeared, he said. Dieter Krumholz had been. He had not liked being replaced, but he had accepted it. The last person with whom she was known to have been was Krumholz. If anything had happened to Isabel, it was Krumholz who was responsible.

The inspector, who was not even certain that the court would accept the evidence that Isabel was dead, initiated a massive search of the forests around Karlsruhe and issued appeals to the public for reports of sightings of Klein's car on the night in question.

There were no reports, and no trace of the body was found.

The Jungs, who had now accepted that Isabel was dead, were anxious to provide her with a decent burial and they repeatedly appealed to Klein to reveal what he had done with her body.

The appeals had no effect and even a visit by Nina, whom Ursula brought to the police station in a basket, failed to move him. Bernd Klein insisted that he was innocent and that he knew no more of what had happened to Isabel than did her parents.

The inspector did not believe him, but he had not been able to uncover any further evidence and was now engaged in dealing with the usual mentally disturbed people and practical jokers who were making anonymous telephone calls and sending in letters maintaining, among other things, that Isabel had been murdered because of her membership in the German Red Army Faction or the French Action Directe – both terrorist groups dedicated to the overthrow of governments in general.

As the members of these groups were often students, the reports had to be investigated, but no evidence was found that Isabel had ever engaged in political activity of any sort.

'Didn't think so,' said the inspector. 'According to her pictures, she lacks the animal, earnest look that the young world-changers generally have.'

The main suspect remained Bernd Klein and the main question remained what he had done with Isabel's body.

Assuming that it was Bernd, he had probably believed, as do many, that there could be no homicide charge without a corpus delicti, but, had he studied law rather than engineering, he would have known that the term refers to the sum of the elements connected with the supposed crime and not the corpse itself.

The essentials for an accusation of homicide are: evidence that death has occurred, that the victim was the person allegedly killed and that the death was the result of an unlawful act.

These conditions were largely fulfilled in the case against Bernd Klein. Isabel had not been suffering from any illness to make a death by natural causes probable. She had been in high spirits on the night she disappeared, which made suicide unlikely. The traces of blood mixed with saliva recovered from the bed were consistent with strangulation, and the loss of control of the bowels and bladder is a common reaction associated with violent death.

There was no other plausible suspect in the murder. Klein had had a strong motive, and her mother, the last person to see her alive, testified that Isabel had been going to join him.

Traces of the missing quilt cover and bedspread had been found in Klein's car and he had no alibi for the night in question, which he claimed to have spent driving about aimlessly in a state of despondency over his rejection by the woman he loved.

The examining magistrate, therefore, despite the lack of a corpse or concrete proof that Isabel was actually dead, found the evidence sufficient to hand down an indictment for wilful homicide and order Klein bound over for trial.

Before the trial took place, a bizarre personage suddenly appeared on the scene and made a sworn statement in which he said that he had seen Isabel in July 1986 in Paris, where she was dancing in the chorus line of a nightclub called the Chatte Moue, and that she had become a drug addict.

The man, whose name was Bruno von Eigerburg and who claimed to be an Austrian attorney-at-law, said that he did not know either Isabel or Bernd Klein and that he was merely interested in preventing an error of justice.

The inspector's first reaction was to contact the Austrian authorities, who replied that von Eigerburg had no police record in Austria and that they did not know whether he was an attorney or not. There was no record of a von Eigerburg being treated for mental illness.

These most obvious explanations of von Eigerburg's strange intervention having been eliminated, the inspector made strenuous efforts to trace a connection between him and Klein, but failed utterly. As far as could be determined, von Eigerburg had never even heard the name of Bernd Klein until he read of the case in the newspapers and hurried to Karlsruhe on what he said was his first visit.

The inspector was left with no alternative. Von Eigerburg stood to gain no advantage from his story and, improbable as it sounded, it had to be investigated.

The reluctant Sergeant Langbauer, who spoke not a

word of French although he lived within sight of the border, was therefore sent off to Paris, where, with the help of the French police, he questioned the owner of the Chatte Moue, the girls in the chorus line and as many of the customers as he could find.

The only point in von Eigerburg's statement that he could confirm was that some of the chorus girls were drug addicts. None of them could recall a dancer named Isabel Jung or recognize her picture. One girl said a German had once appeared at the nightclub, but it had been a long time ago. The owner denied that he had ever hired a German in any capacity.

The sergeant returned to Karlsruhe empty-handed, as he had expected.

'The Paris police say the statements don't mean anything,' he told the inspector. 'They say the people are drug addicts, more than half crazy, and that they lie to the police on principle. They have other sources of information though and they think that she never was there.'

'Any evidence that von Eigerburg was?' asked the inspector.

'None,' said the sergeant.

'The man's a worse liar than the chorus-line girls,' raged the inspector. 'Bring him in here and we'll grill the life out of him.'

It was a little late. Bruno von Eigerburg was no longer in Karlsruhe, and it would cost the police a great deal of time and effort before they were finally able to determine that he was not Austrian but German, that he was not an attorney but an advertising salesman and that his name was not the aristocratic von Eigerburg but the plebeian Egger. The name Bruno was the only thing about him that was genuine.

Eggar's motives in the affair were never determined, but the inspector inclined to the theory that he had been hoping to gain valuable publicity and, perhaps, write a book, but had been rendered nervous by the police investigations and had abandoned the idea.

It was not possible to ask him as his whereabouts were not known, and he could not be listed as a fugitive because he had done nothing other than make a statement to the police which could not be proved a deliberate falsehood.

Egger's diversion had considerably delayed the case and it was only in the spring of 1986 that the case finally came to trial.

The outcome was still uncertain. No body had been found and no positive proof of death. Klein had not confessed and, as there was no possibility of showing intent, the only charges which could be brought against him were manslaughter and illegal disposal of a corpse.

The defence was confident. It would be up to the prosecution to prove beyond a shadow of a doubt that Isabel was dead, that she had been killed and that Bernd Klein had killed her. A question on any of these three points could result in Klein's acquittal.

The prosecutor was, however, equally confident for he had in reserve a key witness of whom the defence knew nothing.

There were not many who knew anything about thirty-eight-year-old Holgar Lemann, who was a police under-cover agent attached to the special investigations section of the Stuttgart police, but who worked for police departments all over Germany.

The inspector had called upon his services when it became obvious that Klein was not going to confess and that no further evidence in the case was likely to become available. On the fourth day of the trial, following the testimony of close to a hundred expert witnesses, Lemann was called to the stand.

Bernd Klein, sitting in the prisoner's dock, went tense and turned pale for he knew Lemann well, although not by that name.

The witness had been his cellmate in pre-trial detention for over a month and, like many another, Klein had not been able to refrain from boasting about the perfect murder which he had committed.

In some countries, Lemann's testimony would not have been admitted as Klein had not been aware that he was talking to a police officer at the time; however, the court not only allowed his statement but even permitted the introduction of tape recordings that the police had made without Klein's knowledge.

The courtroom was bathed in total silence as a voice, easily recognizable as that of Klein, spoke from the tape recorder.

'It was some time after three in the morning when Isabel came back from telephoning her new boy friend and got into bed,' it said.

'I put my arms around her and wanted to make love, but she pushed me away. She could not be unfaithful to the man she loved, she said.

'I hit her in the face with my fist until she let me make love to her.

'She just lay there, and when it was over she laughed in my face and said I didn't know how to make love the way Dieter did.

'I squeezed the bitch's throat so hard that I got cramps in my fingers. When I let go, I thought I could hear her heart still beating, but it was my heart. I'd killed her.'

At this point, the proceedings were interrupted by Ursula Jung, who became hysterical and had to be helped from the courtroom.

The remainder of the tape recording was Klein's account of the disposal of the corpse.

Following the murder, he smoked a cigarette and tried to get the stains off the sheets with soda water. The quilt cover and the bedspread were badly marked and he put them in the boot of his car and placed the completely naked corpse on top of them.

He left the house at approximately seven in the morning and drove to Landau, where he stopped to buy petrol and an ice-cream cone and telephone his mother.

From Landau he went to the family weekend house in the Hunsrueck, a region of heavily wooded low mountains nearly a hundred miles north of Karlsruhe.

Making a fire of discarded tyres, pine branches and old motor oil, he spent the entire day burning the body until only a few small bones were left.

He crumbled them into dust with his hands, put all the ashes into a wheelbarrow and scattered them at various places in the forest.

Lemann had told Klein that he was thinking of going to Israel when he was released and Klein had asked him to send Isabel's grandmother a telegram from there. He had written out the text, which ran, 'Dear Granny, Had to clear out. Don't think so much about work. Give Nina my love. Isabel.'

Spectators and defence sat in stunned silence as Lemann left the stand and was replaced by the accused, to whom there now appeared to be no alternative but to confess, plead extenuating circumstances and throw himself on the mercy of the court.

Bernd Klein had no such intentions. He branded Lemann a liar in the pay of the police, denied that he had ever asked him to send a telegram to anyone, denied that he had ever confessed to murdering Isabel, said that the tape recording and the note for the telegram were forgeries, and charged that he was being framed by the police because of their failure to identify the real murderer.

The only result of these denials was that the charge was changed from manslaughter to murder and, on 24 April 1987, Klein was sentenced to life imprisonment.

He has never confessed to the murder and no trace of the body of Isabel Jung has ever been found.

It is said, however, that Klein speaks cautiously and only on general subjects to his cellmate.

18

SIMULATED PSYCOPATH

As André Bodmer had little else to occupy him while he lay dying in Buednerland Forest, his mind perhaps turned back nearly eighteen years to a time when he had thought himself in paradise there.

It was 22 October 1985, autumn in the forest, but then it had been high summer and he had been young . . .

Very young in every respect but one. He was only fifteen when he and Isabelle fell in love, and she was a year younger.

It was not the innocent love of childhood or even the clumsy, idealistic love of adolescence, but the hot, tormenting love of sexually mature adults. Their scandalized relatives had to pull them apart like copulating dogs.

There was such a terrible urgency in that love, such a compulsion which swept all before it that, in the end, they had to run away to the Buednerland Forest, where they slept under the stars, warmed only by each other's arms, dined on wild berries and the potatoes they stole from the farmers' gardens and roasted, and slaked their raging thirst for each other's bodies.

Eventually, of course, they were found and brought back to Schwyz, but by that time Isabella was already a month pregnant and their incredulous parents' opposition to marriage ceased. There was no alternative. André's mother was an extremely devout Catholic.

Accepting the inevitable was not, however, the same as approval. No help was given, financial or otherwise.

Two children, barely adolescent and besotted with love, they were left to fend for themselves.

'Let them stew in their own juice!' raged André's father, making unintentional use of a rather too opportune turn of phrase. 'They've made their bed. Now they can lie in it.'

Switzerland in the middle sixties was morally conservative, and sex between children who had not even achieved their full growth was an abomination.

At first, they lived in Geneva. André was born there, although the family had moved while he was still an infant to Schwyz. There was no point in remaining near families who would not even speak to them.

Later, they moved to the town of Gasel, near Berne. André was still trying to complete his apprenticeship as a butcher and Isabella was legally required to attend school, pregnant or not.

It was a hard time, a desperate time. Often, there was not even shelter other than a doorway, and going to bed with an empty stomach was routine.

In a fairy tale, their love for each other would have sustained them, but this was the real world and gradually, under the grinding weight of poverty, the magic went out of their marriage. Although desire remained, love had flown and they became increasingly preoccupied with money.

The solution was obvious, of course. Isabella was a beautiful young girl, now barely sixteen, with long curling blonde hair and cornflower-blue eyes. Her commercial value was impressive, if she chose to exploit it.

She did so choose, with a little encouragement from André, and, after that, there were no further financial problems.

The business had to be handled discreetly, of course. Isabella was still too young to prostitute herself legally. Standing beside the highway or accosting potential customers in the street would have quickly got her shut up in a home for delinquent girls, even if she was married and a mother.

There were other ways, however: discreet advertisements in certain publications, word-of-mouth recommendations, a little cautious pimping by her husband.

When clients appeared, he retired to the kitchen or, if the weather was clement, went for a walk.

They had agreed when it first began that it was only a temporary measure. Isabella would continue supporting the family until such a time as André could complete his butcher's training and find a suitable job.

But somehow it continued even after André was fully qualified as a butcher and could have found work. They had drifted into a lazy, lucrative way of life which neither had the will or inclination to change.

The change, when it came, was due to circumstances beyond their control. Although all trace of sentiment had long since vanished, they still found each other's bodies desirable and Isabella, once again, became pregnant.

Obviously, this represented a temporary suspension of business, but, even after she had regained her physical capacity, Isabella proved reluctant to resume her professional activities. She did not mind the work, she said. It was not demanding and it brought her into contact with many interesting people, but, with two children to look after, she did not see how she was going to manage.

André rose nobly to the occasion. He was a qualified journeyman butcher and he easily found employment with the Denner Wholesale Meat Products Company in Zuerich, where he was soon promoted to manager of the Zuerich branch.

A suitable house was found in Dielsdorf, three miles to the northwest of Zuerich, and the Bodmer family settled down to stodgy domesticity, with André commuting daily to his job and Isabella looking after the house and the children.

There was a reconciliation with the families and it appeared that all had turned out for the best after all. It had merely been a somewhat too early start.

It could have – should have – been a happy ending,

but there was, alas! a fatal flaw in the relationship. The Bodmers no longer loved each other emotionally or, by now, even physically, and they were still young – André twenty-nine and Isabella twenty-eight.

And whereas Isabella's professional activities had, perhaps, taken a bit of the edge off her sexual appetite, André had not been similarly engaged. His life had become virtually celibate.

On 20 December 1984, there was a fateful encounter. Arriving at the car park after work, André found himself in the presence of a damsel in distress. Doris Andrist, a sales girl in the sausage department, was unable to start her car and had no way of getting home to Dielsdorf, where she lived.

André was also going to Dielsdorf. He offered the lady a lift. It was the beginning of a rougher ride than either of them could have suspected.

Doris was, in contrast to Isabella, brunette and as lush and juicy as a ripe plum. She was twenty-six years old and, as yet, single, although she had a boy friend with whom the question of marriage had been tentatively broached on one or two occasions.

Three days after receiving her free lift from André, she bid the boy friend farewell. 'Our love is not to be,' she sighed sadly. 'I have found another . . .'

The other was André, who not only reciprocated her feelings but took advantage of them. On the evening of the twenty-third, they rented a room in a small and not too respectable hotel under the name of Mr and Mrs Dupont, the Swiss equivalent of Mr and Mrs Smith.

They could remain no more than an hour and a half as André would have to explain to Isabella that he had had to work late, but in that short length of time they devastated each other.

What there was about André which so appealed to Doris was not entirely clear, but for André, if Isabella had been the atomic bomb, Doris was nuclear fusion. A bond was formed between the two young wholesale meat products company employees which only death could sever.

The question was, Whose death?

For Doris, the answer was clear. Isabella stood in the way of their love. She had to go, one way or another. A jealous, possessive woman, she endured agonies every night when André went home to his wife, although he swore to her on his mother's devout head that he had not laid a hand on Isabella for years.

The obvious solution of a divorce was ruled out by a curious nicety on the part of André, who had, with advancing age and rising income, become increasingly conservative in his views.

'I don't want any more trouble with the family,' he told Doris as they lay naked and locked like mating boa constrictors on the none-too-comfortable hotel bed. 'Dad's just bought a restaurant in Geneva and, if I play my cards right, he'll let me manage it. He's not as religious as Mama, but, if I were to get a divorce, that would be it. I could expect to spend the rest of my life chopping up pigs.'

'Then we have to kill her,' said Doris bluntly. 'She's an obstacle to our happiness.'

André could suggest no alternative.

'But cautiously,' he said. 'Spending the rest of our lives in different prisons would be quite an obstacle to our happiness too.'

'I'll do it,' said Doris, who thought she detected a certain indecisiveness in her lover's attitude. 'You get her to come out to the woods and I'll shoot her.'

The following day, she bought a gun and an enormous supply of ammunition.

'I'll need a little target practice,' she said.

'I don't think you've ever had a gun in your hands before,' said André doubtfully. 'Do you have any idea of what you're doing?'

'No,' said Doris, 'but you'll teach me, won't you?'

André promised that he would, but, in fact, he could not. Being one of the very few Swiss never to have performed his military service, he knew no more about guns than she did.

The fiasco with the gun took place towards the end of August 1985, and by September Doris had come up with another idea.

'We'll strangle her,' she said. 'You can miss with a gun, but strangling's sure. All you have to do is get her out to the woods and I'll do the rest.'

'That's not so simple,' protested André. 'Our relations aren't such that I can invite her to go for a romantic walk in the woods. She'd think I'd gone insane.'

'Well, you'll have to think of something,' said Doris. 'I'm ready to do my part. Now, you do yours.'

It took André close to two weeks, but, in the end, he came up with a scheme so improbable that Isabella may have believed it because she thought André incapable of making up such a story.

He had entered them, he told her, in a contest for married couples called the Game of Courage. If they won, they would collect a large sum of money, and all she had to do was accompany him to an isolated place in the forest, where he would blindfold, gag and tie her to a tree. After a time, someone would come along and release her. They could then go to collect their winnings.

'Don't worry,' he reassured her. 'I shall be near. If anything goes wrong, I shall save you.'

Seen in retrospect, Isabella's acceptance of this proposal might appear grounds for admission to a mental institution, but it must be remembered that she had known André in every possible sense since the age of fourteen. She had borne him two children and, if they were no longer in love or even in lust for each other, they were still good, if superficial, friends.

Also, she did not know about Doris.

The trap was set. The quarry had taken the bait. All that remained were certain technical dispositions to be provided by Doris.

These did not include plans for concealing the corpse.

'They always find it,' said André, who was a regular

reader of the more spectacular organs of the press, 'and then they suspect the husband. They'd find out about you and me and I'd be lucky to get off with twenty years.'

'We're not going to hide the body,' said Doris. 'We'll leave it in the woods and they'll think it was a sex crime.'

'Yeah, a sex criminal,' said André. 'Nobody else would have any reason to murder her.'

He was forgetting Doris and himself.

'Okay,' said Doris. 'We'll rip off her knickers and . . .'

She stopped and snapped her fingers.

'I've got it!' she exclaimed. 'What's your blood group?'

'AB,' said André. 'Why?'

'Because the police can tell a man's blood group from his sperm,' said Doris. 'I've read that. Now, supposing the sperm in Isabella was another group. That would mean that you couldn't have done it. Right?'

'Right,' said André, 'but what sperm? I'm not going to rape her. We're just going to make it look like that.'

'It won't be your sperm, silly,' said Doris. 'That's the whole idea. It'll be somebody else's.'

'Fine,' said André a little sarcastically, 'but where are you going to get somebody else's sperm?'

'That's my business,' said Doris.

Later, several men, who testified on condition of strict anonymity, came forward to describe how Doris had gone about obtaining one of the most unusual false clues in the history of police investigation work.

There were several because locating the right one had not been all that simple. He could not have the blood group AB and he had to be prepared to put up with unexplained and intimate, if not necessarily unpleasant, treatment by a total stranger.

Doris, who was a very attractive girl, simply took up a post beside the road at the edge of town and, when a car containing a single male stopped, she got in.

The situation was, up to this point, banal. Prostitutes,

although seldom as attractive as Doris, conmmonly offer their services beside roads all over the Continent.

The sequel was, however, sufficiently bizarre for some of the potential donors promptly to put her out of the car.

Doris began by asking the man's blood group. If he said AB or did not know it, she asked to be let out, a request which left the driver with the impression that he was dealing with a seriously disturbed person.

The impression was little different if he named one of the right blood groups, for Doris's next question was whether he would like to earn a little money for a brief and painless personal service.

As the driver had picked her up in the belief that it was he who would be paying for her brief and painless personal service the sudden reversal of roles was so startling that many refused.

Persistence is the key to success, and eventually a candidate with solid nerves and the right blood group was found.

Having obtained his consent and having negotiated the level of the compensation, Doris produced a condom and, rather expertly, extracted the sample. All told, she had to go through the process three times, the first two donors being too startled or inhibited to perform satisfactorily.

Having knotted the end of the condom to preserve the precious contents, Doris dropped it into her handbag and prepared to hand over the agreed-upon payment, which was, however, gallantly refused in all three cases.

The operation completed, Doris took her leave and the bemused donor drove off. The next time he saw her would be at Zuerich police headquarters, but, as he told Inspector Anton Griess, the burly, black-moustached officer in charge of the investigation, he would never forget her. The experience was permanently fixed in his memory.

It was, perhaps, well that it was, for some little time would elapse before the second encounter.

In the meantime, Doris had stored the condom and its hard-won contents in the freezing compartment of the refrigerator, and the plan for the removal of the obstacle to true love could now proceed.

On the afternoon of Saturday 14 September 1985, a remarkably clear, sunny, early autumn day, André took the wife with whom he had shared nearly half of his life to the forest, gagged her, blindfolded her and tied her to a tree.

He withdrew to a discreet distance, then Doris emerged from the bushes where she had been hiding and choked Isabella unconscious with a scarf. As Isabella could see nothing because of the blindfold, she undoubtedly died believing that her husband was murdering her.

And, in fact, he was, for when André returned and they loosened the bonds holding her to the tree, Isabella was still alive and she began to writhe feebly, although she could not speak because of the gag. Whereupon André removed the scarf and strangled her to death with his powerful butcher's hands.

Having spent some little time with her ear pressed against Isabella's chest to make certain there was neither respiration nor heart beat, Doris tore off the dead woman's trousers and knickers, pulled up her sweater and brassiere to expose her breasts, broke two of her fingernails, gave her a few scratches on the face and belly to simulate a struggle and, with her index finger, inserted some of the contents of the condom into her sex organs and smeared the rest over her pubic hair.

As prearranged, André called the police at noon on the following day to report his wife missing. They had been having coffee in the buffet of the railway station on Saturday afternoon, he said, and had got into a quarrel because he wanted to go home and she wanted to go dancing.

She had gone dancing and he had gone home. As he had seen nothing of her since, he was becoming concerned.

The officer taking the missing-person report said that

243

steps would be taken; but none had been by two that afternoon, when Isabella's body was discovered by a young couple named Martin Thiebault and Rose Pollard who had gone to the woods for a Sunday afternoon walk.

The homicide squad, under Inspector Griess, hurried to the scene and, as Doris and André had made no effort to conceal Isabella's identity, quickly determined the name and address of the victim.

André came to the morgue and, weeping torrents, formally identified the corpse. He did not mention Doris, who had done her work so well that he was not even interrogated and remained a potential suspect only until the autopsy report was handed in.

The autopsy was performed by Dr Paul Engheim, a spare, sandy-haired man with a rather too high complexion and very pale blue eyes, and he brought it to the inspector's office personally as he found certain aspects of it disturbing.

'I find two points puzzling and perhaps suspicious,' he said after the inspector had finished skimming through the report. 'She was bound, but in a standing position, which is not ideally suited to rape, and the inner sides of the thighs are not bruised, as would be the case if she resisted penetration.'

André and Doris had, of course, removed the bonds, gag and blindfold.

'And?' said the inspector.

'It's inconsistent,' said the doctor. 'The underwear was torn off violently, but there's no indication that she was resisting him, so there was nothing to prevent penetration. Yet he may not have penetrated her at all, and ejaculation took place at the entrance to the vagina. Nothing very specific, but there's something about it . . .'

'Were you able to establish the blood group from the semen?' asked the inspector.

'It's in the report,' said the doctor. 'Blood group O.'

'That eliminates her husband then,' said the inspector.

'His blood group is AB. He showed me his medical card.'

'Maybe it was a lover,' suggested Detective Sergeant Marlon Treiber, the inspector's mild-mannered, slightly plump second-in-command, 'and he tried to make it look like rape.'

'All right. Start looking for lovers with blood group O,' said the inspector. 'It's as good a place to begin as any.'

The sergeant did not have much difficulty in determining that Isabella had had no lover. After her many years as a prostitute, she had been satisfied with the less stimulating life of a housewife and mother and had scarcely left the house other than to do her shopping.

'Then it must have been a sex psychopath after all,' said the inspector. 'See what there is in the records.'

'Any particular profile?' said the sergeant.

'Premature ejaculation, I suppose,' said the inspector. 'That's about all we know about him.'

In fact, they knew nothing about the supposed sex psychopath because he did not exist, but the records of known sex offenders at liberty in the area were examined and a squad of detectives began going through them in search of offences bearing some resemblance to the supposed rape and murder of Isabella Bodmer.

One would-be rapist with a severe problem of premature ejaculation was found. His name was Walter Krank. He was thirty-two years old and he had tried to rape upwards of forty women.

He had never succeeded because the act of exposing the woman's genitals invariably brought on his climax, after which he lost interest.

Dr Engheim was consulted and expressed the opinion that Krank was not a likely suspect in the murder of Isabella Bodmer.

'He's never achieved even partial penetration before,' he said, 'and, if he had had his orgasm, why murder her? He didn't murder any of the others.'

'True,' said the inspector, 'but I think we'll bring him

in for questioning anyway. We're a little short of suspects in this case.'

Walter Krank was arrested and, as he had an easily confirmed alibi for the time of the murder, immediately released.

In the meantime, the co-authors of a perfect murder were playing it cool. They had not rushed straight into each other's arms after the funeral and their contacts were more discreet than ever, although they continued to use their old hotel. Zuerich is a city of over half a million, so there was little chance of being recognized.

They were not, however, revelling in their new freedom. Few people in this world are capable of cold-blooded murder without later regrets. Their consciences were bothering them and, being good Catholics, they feared divine retribution.

Five weeks and three days after the murder of Isabella, on 22 October 1985, a farmer named Franz Buchenauer was passing through Buednerland Forest on his way to the village of Waldbour. At approximately four o'clock in the afternoon, he entered a small clearing and saw, lying side-by-side on the grass, a man and a woman with their hands clasped. A number of small bottles lay scattered around them.

The startled farmer hurried forward, found that both were still breathing, and ran all the way to Waldbour to summon an ambulance.

Doris and André were rushed to the nearest hospital. Their stomachs were pumped, and by that evening both were out of danger. They had absorbed massive doses of barbiturates, but Buchenauer had found them in time to save their lives.

Neither André nor Doris saw fit to discuss their motives for joint suicide and the doctors did not press them. Their job was saving lives, not determining why others chose to end them. Being human, however, there was speculation, and the conclusion was that André and Doris were lovers for whom there was an obstacle to their love.

The obstacle was, in fact, Isabella. Dead or alive, she stood between them, and now there was no way that the obstacle could ever be removed for all eternity.

Switzerland is an orderly country. The suicide attempts of André Bodmer and Doris Andrist were duly reported to the competent authorities and, suicide being illegal, the reports eventually found their way into the records of the police.

Whereupon the records section computer went 'Blip!' The Isabella Bodmer murder case was still under investigation and André Bodmer was one of the people figuring in it.

Inspector Griess was advised, and he ordered Bodmer to be taken into custody. Twenty-four hours later, the inspector learned of the existence of Doris Andrist and she was brought to join her lover, although not in the same detention cell.

Neither denied the murder, but neither would confess to it either. They were ashamed.

Their silence made matters difficult, for although the motive for the murder was now established, their guilt was not.

André's blood group had been confirmed as being AB and this caused the police to think that there had been an accomplice with blood group O.

Although André and Doris eventually confessed to the murder, they refused to discuss details, and it was nearly a year later when the donors and rejected donors of sperm saw Doris's picture in the newspapers and began reporting to the police.

Armed with this knowledge, the inspector was able to reconstruct the events leading up to and following the murder, and these were reluctantly confirmed by the murderers.

André and Doris were brought to trial on charges of premeditated murder and, although customary in such cases, did not attempt to place the responsibility on each other.

They did say that they were very sorry; and the jurors

apparently believed them, for they were granted some extenuating circumstances and, on 8 January 1988, sentenced to twenty years' imprisonment each.

19

ARRANGED SUICIDE

Had the houses been more modern, someone would surely have heard the sound of the shot. A twelve-gauge shotgun going off in an enclosed space makes a deafening noise.

This was, however, the tiny village of La Capelle-Balaguer, where there was no building less than two hundred years old nor one with walls less than two feet thick. Although Valéry and Manon Fleurette were sleeping less than twenty feet away from the quaint little house with the white shutters, they heard nothing.

They would have been very astonished if they had. La Capelle-Balaguer, buried in the heart of the French Aveyron, has one café, one shop, a church, a school and a scant dozen houses. There are no large communities within twenty miles. Nothing ever happens in La Capel-le-Balaguer.

Or, at least, nothing had ever happened there until the night of 29 to 30 July 1984, when Valéry and Manon were awakened from their sleep by the sound of someone hammering frantically on the door.

Valéry got up and put his head out of the open first-floor bedroom window. It was, as might be expected in the southwest of France, a warm, dry, summer night. In the east, a faint glow heralded the coming dawn. The hands of the clock on the night table pointed to four.

The man beating on the door below was their neighbour, twenty-nine-year-old Bernard Cazes.

'Help me!' he cried. 'Call a doctor! Myriam has shot herself!'

'Myriam' was Myriam Fraysse, a twenty-one-year-old farmer's daughter from the village of Naucelle, some fifteen miles distant. She and Cazes had moved into the little house only nine months earlier, but, the village being so small, the Fleurettes already knew them well. They were, they thought, a charming young couple, but poor, as Bernard was unemployed and their main source of income was Myriam's salary as a textile-machine operator.

Valéry immediately ran downstairs and telephoned for the emergency ambulance in Albi, ten miles to the south. Having moved in so recently, Myriam and Bernard did not yet have a telephone.

In the meantime, Manon had got into a dressing gown and followed Bernard back to the house. It was very small, with the kitchen taking up the entire ground floor and two small bedrooms above.

Myriam was in the one with a bed. She lay on her back in the middle of it, in her nightgown, the sheet pulled up to above her waist and her hands crossed on her breast in an attitude of prayer. She was unconscious and the entire right side of her head was one enormous, bleeding wound.

The appalled Manon stepped unhesitatingly forward and, as Bernard stood blubbering hysterically in the doorway, felt for a pulse.

To her surprise, there was one, faint but steady. Myriam was terribly injured, but she was still alive.

The ambulance took a little time to reach La Capelle-Balaguer. The Aveyron is a mountainous region with many small valleys and clear, fast-running streams, and the roads tend to be crooked. Myriam was, however, still breathing when it arrived.

Contrary to the expectations of the ambulance crew, she was also still breathing when the ambulance arrived at the Hospital La Chartreuse. Her injuries were found to be too serious for the hospital's facilities, and she was transferred by helicopter to the hospital in Toulouse, forty miles to the south. To the astonishment of the doctors, she was alive on arrival.

As any injuries resulting from gunshot wounds must be reported immediately to the authorities, the paramedic in charge of the ambulance crew had radioed the gendarmerie post at Villefranche-de-Rouergue and a gendarmerie team set off at once for La Capelle-Balaguer.

It was nearly six o'clock in the morning when the gendarmes passed through the handsome eighteenth-century gate leading to the house where the incident had taken place. As the crow flies, Villefranche-de-Rouergue is not far from La Capelle-Balaguer, but by road it is nearly thirty miles.

Bernard Cazes was sitting in the Fleurettes' kitchen, bawling like a calf and being comforted with liberal applications of brandy. He had, he told the gendarmes, been at a village fête the preceding night and had returned home at three in the morning to find Myriam unconscious or, as he thought at the time, dead. He had immediately run to the Fleurettes for help.

His statement was tape recorded, as were statements from the Fleurettes, and the gendarmes then went to look at the scene of the shooting.

The bed was scarcely disarranged, with only the sheet which had covered Myriam thrown back. There were a few slight traces of blood on it and, lying on the floor on the side away from the wall, was a twelve-gauge single-barrelled shotgun.

The gendarmes immediately withdrew and, while one stood guard at the door of the house, the other radioed headquarters in Villefranche-de-Rouergue for an investigations team. They did not know if Myriam had killed herself, but, even if she had not, the affair required investigation.

Myriam had not killed herself, however. Although the shotgun blast had blown away the right side of her head and face and had destroyed a part of her brain, she was alive and expected to live.

In what condition, was another matter.

'I fear that she may be almost totally paralysed,' the head physician told René and Marie-Thérèse, Myriam's parents, who had been informed of their daughter's suicide attempt and had raced to Toulouse. 'She could regain some use of her body, but even then the damage to the brain is so extensive that she might remain little more than a vegetable. We can only wait and hope. Sometimes there are miracles.'

The Fraysses were honest, hard-working farmers who had a son older than Myriam and a daughter younger. As good Catholics, they believed in miracles, but they did not believe that this had been an attempted suicide.

'Why would Myriam want to kill herself?' demanded René. 'She had no reason in the world. We'll see what she has to say when she wakes up.'

Myriam had been in a coma ever since her arrival at the hospital and, although the doctor did not say so, he was not at all certain that she ever would wake up.

In the meantime, an investigations team under Captain Jerome Plessy had arrived in La Capelle-Balaguer, to find that Bernard had left for his parents' home in Mayrazes in Myriam's much-loved Citroën BX, which she would now never drive again. Having no income other than unemployment benefit, Bernard did not own a car.

The captain, a dapper, olive-skinned man with dark, deep-set eyes and a thoughtful expression, began by dressing down the two gendarmes for allowing him to leave, and then listened to the tape recording of his statement.

While he was doing this, a team of specialists from the gendarmerie laboratory began examining the scene of the shooting in the presence, but not under the direction, of Sergeant Thierry Coutrain, a large, bland-looking man with comfortable sort of egg-shaped figure.

By the time the captain had listened to the tape recordings of the Fleurettes' statements and questioned them briefly on one or two points, the specialists had concluded their work and were able to report that they had found nothing of significance other than the blood-stained sheet and the shotgun.

It had been recently fired and the empty shell was still in the breech. As there were fingerprints on the stock, barrel and trigger guard, it had been carefully wrapped in plastic for removal to Villefranche-de-Rouergue.

'Remarkably little blood for a shotgun wound,' observed the sergeant. 'Anything unusual in the statements?'

'Not really,' said the captain slowly. 'Some discrepancy on the time. I don't know . . . If the victim hadn't survived . . . We'll have to see what she says about this.'

He did not yet know that there was little likelihood of Myriam ever saying anything again.

However, when the gendarmerie party arrived back in Villefranche-de-Rouergue, a telephone call to the hospital soon made clear that the prognosis was extremely pessimistic.

The doctor had no need for the tact he had employed in speaking to the victim's parents and he said bluntly that, in his opinion, Myriam would never move or speak again and, even if she did make noises, they would be meaningless.

'The brain centres governing rational thought and motor function are so seriously damaged that there is little prospect of even marginal improvement,' he concluded.

'Worse than death, in a way,' said the captain, putting down the telephone. 'What a pity! A young girl like that . . . She could live for years, but what a life!'

'I wonder why she did it?' mused the sergeant.

'An affair of the heart,' said the captain. 'It's almost always an affair of the heart with young girls. Her companion was threatening to leave her. He'd got mixed up with another woman. Something of that nature.'

'You want a full investigation?' asked the sergeant.

The captain nodded.

'Don't give it too much time,' he said. 'If the prints on the gun are hers, it's a clear case of attempted suicide.'

The fingerprints on the gun were Myriam's. A fingerprint expert from the Toulouse police department went to the hospital, took the still unconscious girl's fingerprints and sent them up to Villefranche-de-Rouergue, where they were found to match those taken from the shotgun.

The investigation was suspended until such time as Myriam came to, in the hope that some form of communication with her would be possible.

None was. Although Myriam eventually regained consciousness and was pronounced out of danger physically, she was, as the doctors had feared, totally paralysed, mute and incapable of rational thought.

It was not even certain that she recognized her parents, who took her home and began the round of feedings, washings and turnings to prevent bed sores which would continue for the rest of her life.

For the gendarmerie, the case was closed, although it had not been possible to discover any motive for Myriam's act. Bernard swore that he and Myriam had been on the best of terms, but that she had been rather sad and depressed of late. A superficial investigation into his movements and activities prior to the shooting had turned up no other woman.

However, the case was not closed for the Fraysses. None of them believed that Myriam had tried to kill herself. Rather, they thought that Cazes had tried to kill her and René and Marie-Thérèse went to Villefranche-de-Rouergue and filed a charge of attempted murder against X, the action necessary under French law to force an investigation that has not been initiated or has been abandoned.

This involved a great deal of bureaucratic wrangling, and it was mid-1986 before the charge was finally accepted. Even then, the affair dragged on for nearly another year and it was only in July 1987 that the investigation, under the persistent prodding of the Fraysse family, was actually resumed.

Captain Plessy and Sergeant Coutrain were still

responsible for the investigation and neither had been allowed to forget it, for the Fraysses had been patiently turning up at the gendarmerie post nearly every day of the week.

Myriam had, in the meantime, made a little progress. She could move two fingers of her right hand and, if a pencil was placed between them, she could trace letters. However, all she ever wrote was the same sentence, '*I love you.*'

The sentiment was undoubtedly addressed to her parents and her brother and sister who waited on her tirelessly. Questions on the subject of the shooting or Bernard Cazes produced no reaction.

The captain and the sergeant would have long since reopened the investigation, if for no reason other than to accommodate the Fraysse family, with whom they were now extremely well-acquainted and for whom they felt great sympathy, but the decision had been bureaucratic and not theirs to make.

They were not optimistic.

'Possibly, if we had begun immediately after the shooting,' said the captain, 'but so much time has passed now.

'We had no choice but to turn in a report of attempted suicide,' protested the sergeant. 'Her prints were on the gun and the only potential suspect had no motive.'

'True,' said the captain, 'but there were inconsistencies. I noticed them at the time. The ambulance crew said that the blood from the wound had already coagulated when they arrived, and there wouldn't have been time if the ambulance was called immediately after the shooting. The fingerprints are no proof either. He could have wiped the gun and pressed her fingers on it after she was shot.'

'There's still no reason for him to have done it,' said the sergeant. 'God knows, the man's a lazy, drunken scrounger, but why kill the girl? She was supporting him.'

The inspector and the sergeant now knew a great deal about Bernard Cazes. Although they had not been able to carry out an official investigation, they had made certain unofficial inquiries and they had been very thoroughly briefed by the Fraysses.

The Fraysses knew Bernard well for he had lived in their house for over six months and, as René said, had never held a job during that time nor looked for one. Although he pretended to go off every morning in search of work, everyone in Naucelle knew that he spent the entire day in bars, drinking up his unemployment benefit plus whatever he could bully out of Myriam.

She had met him in March 1982 while she was working as a waitress in Le Modern Café in Naucelle because, although qualified in textile-machine operation, she had been unable to find a job in her field.

Bernard came to the café with a group of other young people and, to the Fraysses' utter stupefaction, she fell hopelessly in love with him.

Less than a week later, she brought him home and he lived with the Fraysses until Myriam found work in her own field and was able to rent a flat in Albi and buy a little Simca to get her to and from work.

They remained in Albi up to the autumn of 1983, by which time Myriam had accumulated some money and was able to rent the house in La Capelle-Balaguer and trade in the Simca for the beige Citroën BX.

During all this time, Bernard behaved with admirable consistency. He was drunk, dirty, idle, rude and, occasionally, violent, not only with Myriam, but with everyone in the family.

Love had not blinded Myriam to these flaws in her lover's character. Asked by her perplexed mother not long after the move to La Capelle-Balaguer if she had it in her heart to marry Bernard, she replied, 'No. He's not a good person.'

Marie-Thérèse refrained from asking why she then continued to live with him and give him money. She was afraid that she would not understand the answer.

'When you have irrational behaviour on the part of one person, it often attracts irrational behaviour on the part of others,' said the captain. 'I'm sorry for the girl, but she acted like a fool.'

He was speaking privately to the sergeant. Such remarks could not be addressed to the members of the Fraysse family, who remained fiercely loyal to Myriam no matter how foolish her actions had been.

'You think that Cazes could have tried to murder her without a motive?' said the sergeant.

'No concrete motive,' replied the captain. 'Anger, irritation, a fit of bad temper. The man's a brute and the girl was a natural victim. The combination often leads to murder.'

'If there was no motive, we'll never be able to prove anything against Cazes,' said the sergeant. 'He's not going to confess.'

'It's not entirely hopeless,' said the captain. 'We may be able to show that Cazes was lying about the circumstances. There were time discrepancies, and we might try some tests to see if a girl that size could hold a shotgun in a position to make the wound it did and leave her fingerprints where they were on the gun.'

The initial results of the investigations were promising. It was possible for a girl of Myriam's size to shoot herself in the head with a shotgun, but not to leave the fingerprints in the position they had been found. Moreover, as the recoil would have thrown the gun out of her hands, this would have smeared the prints, and they were not smeared.

From this to an indictment for attempted murder was still a long way, and medical testimony to the effect that, on the basis of the blood coagulation observed by the ambulance crew, Myriam could not have been shot later than three o'clock was of little value, for Cazes had stated that the girl had already been shot when he arrived home. On the other hand, no one could be found who had seen him at the village fête after two o'clock.

A review of the statements made by the two gendarmes who were the first at the scene and by Manon Fleurette was more instructive.

All three statements described the girl as lying on her back with the sheet drawn up and her hands folded on her breast in an attitude of prayer.

'But,' said the captain, 'could she have pulled up the sheet and folded her hands over her chest after she had just blown away half her head?'

'The sheet could have been over her when she did it,' said the sergeant.

'Maybe so,' said the captain, 'but I doubt she could have folded her hands after shooting herself. She'd have lost consciousness instantly. Ask Dellatier to come over here, will you?'

Dr Paul Dallatier was the gendarmerie medical expert, a grey-haired, grey-moustached man who generally looked even more thoughtful than the captain.

He was not, however, very helpful concerning the captain's theory.

'It's extremely unlikely,' he said, 'but the folded hands could have been a reflex action. If she were committing suicide, she would have been under great emotional stress and it's not possible to say what reaction the impact of the charge would have caused. She could even have clasped her hands over her breast after she was unconscious.'

'I see,' said the captain disappointedly.

There was a silence of several minutes in the office.

'That's an old twelve-gauge,' said the sergeant abruptly. 'The barrel must be so badly pitted that it would kick like a mule. It seems to me that the recoil should have thrown the gun halfway across the room.'

'According to the gendarmes and Mrs Fleurette, it was lying right next to the bed,' said the captain. 'Ask the lab where it was when they picked it up.'

The sergeant reached for the telephone.

'We'll have to check with the ambulance crew as well,' said the captain.

It took a little time to locate the original ambulance crew, but the statements of all those who had been present at the scene agreed. The shotgun had been almost touching the bed.

'Is it enough?' asked the sergeant. 'Do we go for an indictment?'

'Not until the ballistics department has run tests with that gun on a bed,' said the captain. 'I don't want him to have any way out when we make the arrest.'

The tests were positive. The old shotgun kicked savagely, and time after time the recoil threw it five, six and more feet from the bed. Even a very strong gendarme, firing it while lying on his back on the bed, could not hold it closer than a yard.

'Excellent!' said the captain. 'Now, I want to talk to Dallatier about blood.'

Actually, what he wanted to talk to the doctor about was the absence of blood. It had occurred to him that the charge of shot fired at close range into Myriam's head should have spattered blood all over the room; but the specialists had found blood only on the sheet, and not much there.

The doctor agreed.

'I wasn't present at the scene,' he said, 'but if there was no blood on the floor or the walls, it can only mean that she was shot somewhere else and put in the bed after the blood had begun to coagulate.'

'What I thought,' said the captain. 'I hope it's not too late. Everything depends on whether anybody else has been living in the house all this time.'

No one had! The owner of the little house in La Capelle-Balaguer had been unable to find a tenant since Myriam Fraysse was carried out of it. The people of the region were superstitious and they believed that a house in which a suicide had taken place was unlucky.

Although nearly three years had passed, the laboratory technicians had no difficulty in recovering traces of human blood from the walls and floor and even the ceiling of the kitchen.

'Not attempted suicide, attempted murder,' said the captain with considerable satisfaction. 'Cazes shot her in the kitchen and only after she'd stopped bleeding carried her into the bedroom and set up his fake suicide. He must have thought she was dead or he'd have finished her off.'

'The defence is going to say that somebody else shot her in the kitchen and faked the suicide,' warned the sergeant.

'We have the evidence that he was lying about the time,' said the captain.

'There's still no motive,' the sergeant reminded him.

'Then you are going to have to find one,' said the captain.

Considering the length of time that the investigation had been going on and the lack of evidence to date, the sergeant thought this a tall order.

He had reckoned without the Fraysse family, who had never ceased their efforts to have Bernard Cazes not only investigated but condemned for the crime. The Fraysses had a great many allies.

Bernard was not popular in the district except with those for whom he bought drinks. Myriam, however, had been, and there was hardly anyone who did not believe that he had shot her.

Ever since the reopening of the investigation, people had been passing on information to the family. Although much of this was hearsay and worthless, some included hard facts – such as statements by people willing to swear that when the investigation was suspended, Cazes had bragged of committing a perfect crime.

The most important testimony came from a Mrs Solange Desproux, who telephoned Captain Plessy's office to say that she had something to report which she thought might have a bearing on the Myriam Fraysse case.

'At the time Myriam was still in the hospital,' she said, 'my son was in the next ward recovering from a motorbike accident. He could see her bed from where he was and he told me that he saw Cazes sneak in and shake her violently. I think he wanted to see whether she was ever going to recover enough to incriminate him.'

Cazes was immediately arrested and repeated his original statement verbatim. He had been at the village fête. He had come home and found Myriam in bed, with a wound in her head and the gun lying on the floor beside the bed. He had immediately run to seek help from the neighbours.

His interrogation continued and, twenty-four hours after the arrest, one of his drinking buddies came forward and said Cazes had told him that he had shot Myriam following an argument over his late nights and heavy drinking. She had been concerned for his health. He had been afraid to denounce him before, but now that he was in jail . . .

Three years, two months and two weeks after the shotgun blast which had turned a vivacious, high spirited young woman into a helpless, mindless vegetable, Bernard Cazes was brought to trial on a charge of attempted murder. He had still not confessed, but he became so enraged by the questions of the prosecution that he incriminated himself in court.

On 27 May, 1988, he was sentenced to twenty years' imprisonment.

The Fraysse family was vindicated in their search for justice, but one member will never know it.

Her mind can no longer deal with such concepts, and all she can do is scrawl over and over again, '*I love you, I love you, I love you.*'

20

DANGERS OF PSYCHOLOGY

In the late afternoon of 5 November 1983, Dr Michel Delescaille, a thirty-three-year-old general practitioner and psychiatrist, received a telephone call at his home.

'I have to go out,' he called to Jacqueline, his wife. 'Somebody on a walk sprained an ankle. Be back in an hour at most.'

Jacqueline made a sound indicating comprehension. As a doctor's wife, she was accustomed to her husband being called away on Saturdays or any other day.

She was not, however, accustomed to him remaining away longer than expected without contacting her, and when there was still no sign of him by nine o'clock, she went looking for him. Assesse, a village ten miles from the city of Namur, numbers only a little over five thousand inhabitants. There were not a lot of places he could be.

Jacqueline looked in all of them, but Michel was not there and she could find no one who had even seen him that afternoon. At nearly three in the morning, she returned home completely exhausted and frightened nearly out of her wits. Michel must have left the village altogether, for his grey Opel Kadett was missing, and she was in mortal terror that he had had an accident.

There was no point in calling the Assesse village constable's office. There would be no one there at this hour anyway and, besides, she had already searched the village herself. What she wanted to know was whether any traffic accidents had been reported in the region and whether any young bearded men had been admitted to a hospital. Her mind shied nervously away from the word 'morgue'.

She therefore called police headquarters in Namur, explained the circumstances and asked that a check of the hospitals be made. She did not know which direction her husband had gone or how far, so it could be a hospital anywhere in the region.

The night duty sergeant knew a simpler way of checking on traffic accidents and he called back after a short time to say that the traffic department reported no accidents involving a grey Opel Kadett within the last twenty-four hours.

Jacqueline thereupon filed a formal missing-person report and went to bed, but although she was very tired, she could not sleep. Something had happened to Michel and the most terrible visions kept flitting through her mind.

The truth was no less terrible than Jacqueline's visions, and it was to be revealed at ten o'clock the following morning by a twenty-year-old girl named Marie Angares.

Marie, who was otherwise a nice girl and a pleasant person, was given to jogging, and she had set off as usual that Sunday morning in a light rain for a run in the woods near the village of Louvin-la-Neuve, where she lived with her parents. Belgium is a wet country and the choice was often between jogging in the rain or not jogging at all.

She had not got very far, however, when she came upon a grey Opel Kadett parked in the middle of one of the trails leading through the forest. The door on the driver's side was standing open and there was no one in the car.

Puzzled and a little frightened, although she could not have explained why, Marie circled the car and came upon the body of a man lying slumped, face down, at the base of a large rock approximately ten yards away.

Even at that distance, she could see that he had suffered frightful injuries to his head. The skull was shattered like a split melon and the grey and white brain matter, washed clean of blood by the rain, had oozed out.

Marie was promptly and violently ill, but as soon as she had regained control of her stomach, she turned and ran back to Louvin-la-Neuve as fast as she could go. A man had fallen off a rock and split his head wide open, she gasped out to the startled village constable.

The constable went to look for himself and returned very quickly. Unlike Marie, he did not think that the man's injuries were the result of a fall and he immediately telephoned the department of criminal investigations in Namur.

The matter clearly required looking into and Namur, an ancient, historic city of over a hundred thousand, located at the junction of the Sambre and Meuse rivers and dominated by the great fortress of the Citidel, is the administrative centre for all of the little communities surrounding it.

The Namur department of criminal investigations was partly staffed, even on a Sunday morning, and a sergeant of detectives named Paul Soubry was dispatched to the scene, together with an ambulance. There was always the possibility that the local constable was mistaken and the man was not dead. If he was, it would be up to the sergeant, a tall, thin man with a long, nervous sort of nose and very little hair on his head, to determine the circumstances, if possible.

This the sergeant was unable to do. It did not appear probable that the man could have suffered such injuries from a fall, even had he been able to scale the nearly perpendicular rock face, and the ambulance crew thought he had been struck over the head with something heavy.

He was, however, unquestionably dead, and the sergeant sent the ambulance back to its base and radioed his office in Namur.

'It appears to be homicide,' he reported. 'The full squad will have to come out.'

This meant Inspector Yves Martin, a small, cheerful man with no more hair than the sergeant – but with a smaller nose – a short, deft and enigmatically smiling medical expert named Thierry Malmain, and some twenty technicians and specialists.

Louvin-la-Neuve being no further from Namur than Assesse, although in a different direction, they arrived in less than half an hour and the doctor, having carried out a brief but thorough examination of the corpse, confirmed the sergeant's suspicions.

'Multiple fractures of the skull resulting from repeated blows with a hard, angular object,' reported the doctor. 'The case is homicide.'

'The time?' said the inspector.

'Yesterday afternoon,' said the doctor. 'I'll have something exact for you when I've completed the autopsy.'

'Have you checked the pockets for papers?' asked the inspector, looking at the sergeant.

'I haven't touched him,' said the sergeant.

The police photographer was taking shots of the corpse, the car and the rock, holding his hand over the lens of the camera to protect it from the rain.

'Here are the car's papers,' said one of the technicians, coming over to where the inspector was standing and holding out an imitation-leather folder.

Inside the folder were the car registration, the insurance form, some repair bills, a picture of a bearded man, a pretty woman and two small children – one only a baby – and a driving licence.

'Turn him over on his back,' said the inspector, holding up the photograph. 'I want to see the face.'

The technicians complied.

'One man with a beard looks like another man with a beard,' said the inspector, 'but I'd say it was him. Go through the pockets, Paul. There may be an ID card.'

There was an ID card and it corresponded to the name and address on the driving licence.

'A doctor,' mused the inspector. 'Dr Michel Delescaille. Who murders a doctor?'

'It wasn't robbery,' said the sergeant. 'There's quite a sum in his wallet and it hasn't been touched. Love affair maybe. Could have been a homosexual. Some of them wear beards as a cover-up.'

'I doubt a homosexual,' remarked the inspector. 'The photograph looks to be his wife and children. Granted, some homosexuals do . . .'

'We have the murder weapons,' called the technician in charge of the specialists from a point some five yards beyond the car.

'Weapons?' said the inspector, hurrying over to look.

There were two heavy hammers lying in the mud. Despite the rain, there was still blood and hair sticking to them.

'Why two?' asked the sergeant in a puzzled voice.

'Two murderers, obviously,' said the technician.

The inspector looked startled.

'This was an uncommonly unpopular doctor,' he said.

The specialists from the homicide squad remained at the scene for the best part of the day, determining that the murder had taken place at the point where the body was found, but that the murderers had left no clues to their identity. Whether they had worn gloves or whether they had wiped the handles of the hammers before discarding them, there were no fingerprints.

On the basis of the marks in the mud, Delescaille appeared to have been knocked down as he got out of the car and then crawled, with the murderers raining blows on his head and shoulders, as far as the rock before collapsing.

Tyre marks, largely washed out by the rain, indicated that another car had been parked a short distance from Delescaille's, but there was no evidence that it had belonged to the murderers.

The question of what Delescaille had been doing in such an isolated place was answered when the inspector called on Jacqueline Delescaille to inform her of the death of her husband.

'There was a telephone call that afternoon,' she

sobbed. 'Somebody with a sprained ankle. He didn't say who it was or where he was going. He just said he'd be back in an hour.'

The inspector had other questions, but he refrained from posing them at the moment and returned to his office.

'It was a deliberate ambush,' he told the sergeant. 'The people lured him out into the woods to kill him. We're going to have to take a hard look at his and her romantic entanglements. The motive was definitely personal.'

'Couldn't it have been drugs?' suggested the sergeant. 'Some doctors do peddle the stuff.'

'I think the wife would have suspected,' said the inspector. 'She said she'd known him since he was six years old and that he didn't have an enemy in the world.'

'He had at least two,' said the sergeant. 'I'll see what I can do on the backgrounds.'

The investigations into the backgrounds of Michel and Jacqueline Delescaille did not last long. Like many doctors, Delescaille had had little free time to himself and he had definitely not spent it with a mistress. Nor was he a homosexual or a drug pusher. The prescriptions he had issued were on record and they included no abnormal amount of narcotics. As far as could be determined, Jacqueline was right: he had not had an enemy in the world.

Not even his wife. As the mother of a five-year-old girl and a nine-month-old baby, Jacqueline would have been hard pressed to find time for a lover.

'It must have been mistaken identity,' said the sergeant. 'They mixed him up with some other doctor with a beard.'

'More likely a disgruntled patient,' commented the inspector. 'Hey! Wait a minute! The man was also a psychiatrist. He must have had patients who were mentally deranged.'

'Two of them joining in a murder scheme?' said the

sergeant. 'If the murderers are mentally deranged, they're sharper than we are. We haven't found a clue.'

'Being mentally deranged doesn't exclude being clever,' observed the inspector. 'I want you to get a list of all of Delescaille's mental patients. There could be a couple of homicidal maniacs among them.'

The sergeant spent the next eighteen months reviewing the medical records of Dr Delescaille's patients, whether they had been treated for mental illness or stomach disorders, and interviewed every one of them. In cases where there was the slightest question, he attempted to establish an alibi for the relevant time, which the autopsy had fixed at four-thirty on Saturday afternoon, with a margin of error of fifteen minutes in either direction.

The results were unsatisfactory.

'None of his patients was that nutty,' reported the sergeant. 'Mostly depressives with family problems. Don't forget, he hadn't been practising long. The only really serious case he was treating, the patient committed suicide.'

'Before the murder or after?' said the inspector.

'Before,' the sergeant told him. 'On 6 December '82. Twenty-two-year-old philosophy student named Philippe Rouaux. He was found dead in his car, which was parked across the street from his girl friend's parents' home. Her name is Pascale Iserbiet. Twenty years old at the time. They'd been engaged, but she'd broken it off the week before. Inspector Lebeau investigated. There's a file on it, if you want to see it.'

'I don't see what connection there could be,' said the inspector. 'The boy's hardly a suspect if he was already dead at the time of the murder. I'll look at it though. I'm ready to look at anything.'

According to the record of the investigation, Rouaux had been killed by a single twenty-two calibre long-rifle bullet fired into his head at extremely close range. The carbine from which it had been fired lay across his knees and the fingerprint of his right index finger was on the trigger. The death had been pronounced suicide and the motive was assumed to have been Miss Iserbiet's termination of the engagement.

Rouaux had, however, been receiving treatment from Dr Delescaille for some time prior to his death. Diagnosed as a manic-depressive, his mental problems were possibly inherited, for no less than three members of his mother's family had committed suicide by hanging themselves, and he himself had made an unsuccessful suicide attempt two years earlier, following rejection by another girl.

The case was therefore closed, despite a number of strange and unexplained circumstances. No empty cartridge case had been found in the car and, although one round was missing from the magazine of the carbine, there was no empty shell in the chamber. As the doors and windows of the car were closed, it was difficult to account for what had happened to the cartridge that had been fired.

The official explanation was that there had been a slip-up by the specialists who examined the car or that the shell had gone astray before it arrived at the police garage.

Browsing slowly through the report, the inspector came upon a surprising number of other discrepancies. Rouaux had been left-handed, but the print on the trigger was from his right index finger. He had been found wrapped in a sleeping bag which displayed only a very few blood stains, although the bullet had severed a vein in his head and he had bled copiously.

'Lebeau thought this was a strange case,' said the inspector, handing the file to the sergeant, 'and I do too, but apparently the examining magistrate found his history of mental illness and the statement by Pelletier enough to declare it suicide.'

Bruno Pelletier, one of Philippe's fellow students at the university and his closest friend, had testified that Philippe had told him he was going to kill himself because he hated his father and wanted to make him feel guilty. Pelletier had urged him to talk the matter over with his psychiatrist.

Rouaux did not appear to have had any particular grounds for hating his father, but many of the residents of Assesse did. Fifty-five-year-old Pierre Rouaux, a coal and fuel merchant, was a stubborn and contentious man, and he had taken it into his head to install an enormous underground fuel tank within twenty feet of the village school.

This had generated such violent opposition, particularly among the parents of school-age children, that nearly everyone in the village had stopped talking to Rouaux and his fifty-four-year-old wife Bernadette. Even the village priest had been drawn into the fray, with the result that Bernadette had resigned from the church choir, where she had sung for over twenty-five years. Both the Rouauxes were natives of Assesse, having been born in neighbouring houses there.

Philippe, however, had not been involved in the quarrel. He had not been living in Assesse, but in a studio in Namur near the university. He had been an only child and, according to some, badly spoiled.

'I have a sort of feeling that there's some connection between Rouaux's death and Delescaille's murder,' said the inspector pensively, 'but I'll be dammed if I can put my finger on it.'

'I'm beginning to doubt that we'll ever know the truth in either case,' said the sergeant. 'The Rouaux affair is closed and we're making no progress with Delescaille. I'm afraid it's going to end up unsolved.'

The sergeant was only half wrong, for the Delescaille murder would eventually be solved. The Rouaux suicide never would be, although the case was soon to be reopened as the result of an anonymous letter received at police headquarters in which Pascale Iserbiet and her current fiancé, twenty-four-year-old Georges Landry, were accused of having murdered Philippe.

'A crank?' said the sergeant, handing the letter back to the inspector.

'Not after all this time,' disagreed the inspector. 'There are always nuts who write in when there's a murder or a suicide in the newspapers, but this case has had no publicity for close to three years.'

'There really were a lot of unexplained things about the case,' said the sergeant, frowning, 'but I fail to see the motive. If Rouaux had pinched Landry's girl . . . but it was the other way around.'

'I don't think Iserbiet and Landry had anything to do with it,' the inspector told him. 'I think somebody is trying to get them into trouble.'

'After three years?' said the sergeant.

'After three years,' repeated the inspector, 'and that means somebody still hates the girl. Landry's probably included only because he's her boy friend.'

'Sounds like a psychopath with a fixation,' ventured the sergeant.

'Exactly,' said the inspector, 'and there's something psychopathic in both cases. Delescaille was a psychiatrist and Rouaux was his patient. Rouaux had a record of one suicide attempt and three suicides in the family. Both died under unexplained circumstances. There's got to be a connection.'

'Are we going to tell Iserbiet and Landry about the letter?' asked the sergeant.

'We're legally required to,' said the inspector. 'They have a right to know if someone is making anonymous accusations against them, and while you're at it, you can look into the question of whether they even knew each other in 1982.'

Pascale and Georges had not known each other at the time of Philippe's death and Landy, who did not come from the area, had not even been in Namur. Both expressed amazement and indignation at the accusation.

Their statements were taken and they were neither detained nor charged. The unexplained factors in the Rouaux suicide could not, however, be ignored any longer and the case was reopened.

Practically speaking, this meant trying to trace the

identity of the author of the anonymous letter, and the inspector, who had assumed the investigation of the Rouaux case, spared no efforts.

The letter was sent to the crime laboratory in Brussels, where it was examined by graphologists and other experts. They came to the conclusion that the writer was a man not younger than forty who had worked a good deal with his hands, but was better educated than a common labourer. He was left-handed and had had experience addressing envelopes. The paper was cheap foolscap, untraceable because of its availability in many places, and the envelope was of a type sold in packages at almost any stationery store. There were very faint traces of fuel oil on both letter and envelope. Fingerprints on the envelope were presumed to be those of post office employees. There were no prints on the letter itself.

'It may be enough to trace the author,' said the inspector. 'It was mailed in Assesse, and that's a small post office. Could be that someone in the post office remembers it. There couldn't be too many letters addressed to the Namur Criminal Police, and he'd have had to read the address to sort it.'

One of the postmen in Assesse did remember the letter. However, as it had not been mailed at the post office but dropped into one of the letter boxes, he had no way of knowing who had posted it.

'He says the handwriting strikes him as familiar,' said the sergeant. 'He's sure he's seen it before, so it was probably somebody from the village. Could we collect handwriting samples from everybody in Assesse?'

'Adult males only?' pondered the inspector. 'That would be around two thousand. It would be a big operation and we couldn't force people to cooperate.'

'Adult males over forty, according to Brussels,' said the sergeant. 'That would cut the number down some more.'

'I have a better idea,' said the inspector. 'The postman thinks he's seen the writing before and Brussels says the man has experience in addressing envelopes. Maybe he's still addressing them and, if we give the postal employees copies of the envelope, they'll recognize any more letters that come through.'

'How would that help us?' objected the sergeant. 'We still wouldn't know who mailed them.'

'He presumably doesn't send all his mail anonymously,' said the inspector. 'There could be a return address, but even if there wasn't, we'd have the name and address of the person to whom it was sent and he or she would know who had sent it.'

Three days later, the post office in Assesse called to say that not only one letter with the same handwriting had been posted, but a whole stack. The envelopes not only had a printed business address on them, but the author had turned them in at the post office himself.

'Pierre Rouaux,' said the sergeant. 'They're the bills to his fuel-oil customers.'

'I rather thought so when Brussels mentioned fuel oil,' said the inspector. 'Bring him in. We'll begin by charging him with providing false information to the police in the investigation of a felony.'

Pierre Rouaux made no attempt to deny that he was the author of the anonymous letter, but insisted that the information it contained was true.

'The girl anyway,' he said. 'I don't know about her lover. She killed Philippe when she broke off their engagement.'

'Indirectly, perhaps,' agreed the inspector, 'but you can't hold her responsible for your son's mental problems. He had them before he met her.'

'I know who was responsible,' said Rouaux menacingly. 'And I knew what to do about it.'

As the charge against Rouaux was minor, he was released on his own recognizance and the inspector settled down to think over what he had said.

'I doubt that he knows anything about his son's death,' he told the sergeant. 'In fact, I think he believes it was suicide. What bothers me is what he said about knowing who was responsible and what to do about it. He wasn't talking about the girl.'

'He couldn't mean Pelletier,' said the sergeant. 'What about Delescaille? He was the boy's doctor.'

The inspector stared at him in amazement.

'Paul,' he said. 'You've just solved our murder case.'

And he had. Rouaux and his wife were brought back to police headquarters, where it took less than four hours of interrogation to extract a confession to the murder of Dr Michel Delescaille out of them. The Rouauxes had come to the conclusion that Philippe had committed suicide as the result of negligence on the part of his psychiatrist and had deliberately set out to avenge him.

'We're Philippe's parents,' said Rouaux. 'It was our sacred duty.'

'But why did you send us the anonymous letter?' asked the inspector. 'You'd got away with it. Nobody suspected you.'

'I knew that Philippe had killed himself,' said Rouaux. 'It's in his mother's family, but Bernadette didn't believe it. She wanted the investigation reopened.'

The trial, which began on 29 March 1988, was mainly characterized by a duel between defence psychologists, who testified that the Rouauxes were legally insane and not responsible for their act, and prosecution psychologists, who maintained the contrary.

As far as the jury was concerned, the prosecution won and, although the Rouauxes were granted some extenuating circumstances, they were found guilty of murder and sentenced to twenty years' imprisonment each.

The investigation into the death of Philippe Rouaux was eventually terminated for lack of evidence and the finding of suicide revoked. Ironically, had it been declared murder in the first place, his parents would never have killed Dr Delescaille.

STRANGE DEATHS
A chilling collection of terrifying true murders.

Fifteen true stories of the most shocking and unusual murders of this century, each one retold in frighteningly accurate detail by an outstanding historian of crime. Stories that are guaranteed to send shivers of terror down your spine.

MURDEROUS WOMEN
Where the female is deadlier than the male.

A chilling collection of horrific crimes where women play a deadly role.

The gruesome details of these eighteen true stories – dramatically reconstructed by an outstanding crime historian from the newspaper files of three continents – prove that the female can sometimes be as deadly, if not deadlier, than the male.